☆ *THE MINDLEBERG PAPERS* ☆

☆ BY JACOB HAY ☆

The Bomb in the Attic

The Mindleberg Papers

THE
Mindleberg Papers

☞   ☞   ☞   *A Novel*

by JACOB HAY ☜   ☜

WILDSIDE PRESS

☆ FOR JOY ☆

IT is not, I trust, too much to hope that by the time this sees print, partisan passions will have cooled to a certain extent, and it will be possible to discuss the Textilia Affair without heat and small arms. Colonel Marius Mindleberg belongs to history now, and whether his tenebrous career was a triumph or a disaster is a question the answer to which must depend on your view of the late War for Southern Independence. Me, I wash my hands of him. But . . . well, he was, in a sense, my discovery, and I feel a certain amount of responsibility for what happened; a certain duty to explain and clarify the fiasco.

The whole wretched business may properly be said to have begun with the decision of Pierre G. T. Mindleberg, chairman of the board and president of Mindleberg Mills, to make some manner of contribution to the observance of the centennial of the Civil War, as planned by the city of Textilia, North Carolina, seat of the far-flung Mindleberg textile empire. Such a contribution, he further decided, might best take the form of a brief history of the firm's activities during that conflict, to be compiled and published at the firm's expense. It was my peculiar fortune to be at loose ends during the period shortly after this latter decision was reached and communicated to the many-fabled Bannastre Masters Associates, the public relations practitioners who handled the Mindleberg account, and by them in turn to my agent, Sam Brewer, who knew the state of my finances to the last cent.

Sam is a realist. "Frankly, I think it's a good offer and I think you ought to take it," he told me earnestly while I gnawed my knuckles in furious doubt. "The thing ought to damn near write itself, and you should be able to wrap it up inside a couple of months. It's money for jam, Nick."

"Nicholas Saltire, demon boy hack," I muttered morosely. On the other hand, the lease for my tiny rustic slum in Connecticut was due for renewal in a month, assuming I were mad enough to sign on for another year of damp ceilings, dry rot and a chimney that smoked like a dump. Which meant that I'd have to be looking around for another relatively cheap place to rent. And there was the problem—looming no larger than a man's hand at the moment, but capable, I felt, of blooming abruptly and dangerously—of Mrs. Patricia Thirsby, the all-too-richly-vibrant wife of the owner of the estate of which my rented guesthouse formed one of the amenities. Pat, as she insisted I call her, "did an occasional piece" for the *Farmer's Advocate*, our local weekly, and she was wont to drop by my cottage to seek out my advice more frequently than was, perhaps, strictly necessary. Of late, she had taken to discussing the significance of D. H. Lawrence. Moreover, her husband, Lonsdale Thirsby, was a large, beef-faced man, once well-known in sailing circles before he had been forced to resign from his yacht club after ramming and sinking, in a fit of pique and off Shelter Island, a fellow contender for the club's Commodore's Bowl.

"Well, what's it going to be?" Sam asked firmly.

"I suppose I could rent me a hotel room here in town and let the Mindleberg P.R. people feed me whatever they've got."

Sam was shaking his head. "No go, Nick. You'll have to work out of their main offices, down in Textilia. It's part of the deal."

"Now wait just a goddamn minute!" I protested hotly, but he wasn't listening. He'd picked up his telephone and was talking into it: "—that's right, Gregory; Walter Gregory at Bannastre Masters Associates. Thank you, Joan." Sam cupped his palm over the mouthpiece and addressed himself to me: "Gregory's the account executive in charge of the Mindleberg program; tipped me off on this thing. Just want to let him know he's off the hook."

☆ 2 ☆

There was a rapid succession of tiny voices, clicks and buzzings, indicative of the call's progress, and then Sam uncupped the mouthpiece: "Walter? Sam Brewer this end. I think I've got some good news for you. That's right. Sitting here in my office right now. Nicholas Saltire. Saltire. S-A-L-T-I-R-E. That's right. He's very interested in the Mindleberg history—" I sneered quietly. "Oh, yes indeed, Walter; he's in hard covers, of course. He's the one I've been telling you about, you remember? Fine, fine. What's that? I'm not sure; better let me check." Sam looked at me: "You tied for lunch?" I shook my head and he returned to Gregory: "We're free as the birds. Say twenty minutes; that okay? Fine. Look forward to it." He hung up.

"To get back to this working in Textilia bit?" I resumed.

"Gregory will explain it better than I can."

"Yes, and how about this Gregory? Is he going to be breathing down my neck?"

Sam stood up behind his desk and stretched luxuriously, pulling his forearms up close to his expanded chest. "Relax," he grunted, exhaling. "He won't worry you. All he's doing is lining things up, and once you start work, you probably won't bump into him again until he throws a nice fat cocktail party on publication day."

It was such a spectacular autumn day that we decided to walk across town from Sam's office to the restaurant in the East Fifties where we were to meet Gregory. In the crystal sunlight, New York looked as good as New York can look, and while I'm not in love with the place, as Sam is, the thought of leaving it for the Heart of Dixie was a sobering one.

Someone must have at one time or another told Walter Gregory that he was not unlike the actor, Walter Pidgeon, and Gregory had apparently liked the idea just fine. He looked every inch the British Brigadier from Central Casting, lacking only the brittle accent, but, in all fairness, I must say that he seemed like a very decent guy, giving us a hearty welcome when the captain led us past the cattle in the restaurant's outer dining room and to his table in the inner chamber reserved for the anointed. We exchanged the usual introductions and pleasantries while our waiter fetched drinks, and then Gregory got down to brass tacks.

"I'm not sure how far Sam, here, has been able to fill you in on Mindleberg Mills," he began, "but maybe the best way I could put it would be to say they're pretty much the General Motors of the textile industry. I mention that only so you'll know that you won't be expected to cut any corners. Not only that, but this history thing is one of Pierre Mindleberg's pet projects.

"Now the thing is, the Mindlebergs *built* Textilia. Before old Solomon Mindleberg arrived there and built his first cotton mill, there was nothing but a crossroads store, surrounded by cotton fields. As the mills grew, the town grew, and the Mindlebergs have been behind it all. So when, a couple of years back, people started talking up the Civil War Centennial, and then Textilia itself got interested in the idea, Pierre thought up this idea of having someone write a history, the point being that since the mills and the town were so closely tied together, the story of one couldn't help but be the story of the other."

"Which explains why the job has to be done in Textilia," Sam Brewer put in helpfully.

"There's this tremendous *loyalty*, see?" Gregory resumed intensely. "One of those things you don't often see these days. I mean, put it this way: the Mindlebergs feel that if *they* made Textilia, why Textilia also made *them*. Here's old Solly Mindleberg arriving with nothing more than the peddler's pack on his back and a dream—don't take the cotton to the mill, bring the mill to the cotton—and here, just over a hundred years later, here is Pierre Mindleberg, heading up the largest single textile firm in the world. It's one hell of a story, by God!"

So it was. I was beginning to feel that this could turn into an interesting job. Gregory signaled for a second round of drinks, and got back to the subject.

☆ *4* ☆

"Sorry if I got sidetracked, Saltire. But maybe it'll help clear up why Mr. Mindleberg feels so strongly that whoever writes this thing should work in Textilia."

"I think I've got the picture," I told him as the drinks arrived. "It makes sense." Gregory looked relieved.

"What about the time element, Walter?" Sam asked.

"Ah. That's another point. Mr. Mindleberg would like to see the book published by next June, which is going to be pushing things pretty hard. But that will be the centennial of the first shipment of Mindleberg cloth to the Confederate Army, and Textilia is planning some sort of civic wingding around it—you know the type of thing; high school pageants and so on."

"Think you can do it, Nick?" Sam inquired. How the hell would I know without having the foggiest idea of how much research I'd have to do through God only knew how much material? And also, how come Sam hadn't mentioned this tight deadline beforehand? Probably because he figured I might turn the deal down.

"Before you answer that one, Nick," Gregory put in smoothly, "I think I ought to tell you that, assuming you would have no objections, we're prepared to assign one of our own staff research people to work with you on a full-time basis for as long as you need it."

"Mind you, I'm not committing myself. All I'm saying is that I think it could be done. Provided, that is, I don't have this Mindleberg character hanging over my shoulder checking the commas." It was an arrogant speech, but I was feeling a little miffed. Gregory took it neatly in stride.

"You can ease your mind on that score," he declared, and then put me tactfully in my place. "He usually spends a couple of months in Europe around this time of year, so you may not even meet him. The man you'll probably be working closest with is Syd Cheek, who is Mr. Mindleberg's personal assistant and a very nice Joe. Of course, you'll have your own office space and any secretarial help you may need, and Syd will look after finding living quarters for you, so that's one worry you won't have when you get there. Meantime, I'll send you a file of our releases on the company, so you'll have some idea of its scope and so on."

"Sounds good," I said, and so it did. It was clear that when Pierre Mindleberg got a bee in his bonnet, things happened, and I was beginning to feel that he might be interesting to meet. "About this research assistant? Where do I get together with him?" Gregory looked momentarily blank and then pleased with himself.

"It's a her, not a him. Girl named Brooke Hastings; very intelligent and a hard worker; been with us, oh, say three, four years now. Whenever you're ready to go, give her a call, and she can have the office line up your tickets and reservations."

"I'd say you've got yourself a good deal, Nick," Sam Brewer observed.

"And I've got a feeling that the sooner I get on down to Textilia, the better. Barring disasters and assuming I can get some storage outfit to pick up my stuff, I should be able to make it within the next two weeks. Would that suit your Miss Hastings?"

"When you move, she does. As simple as that."

"Gentlemen, I don't know about you two, but I'm getting hungry," Sam said firmly.

So there it was, all tied up in a neat little ball. I wasn't going to get rich on the deal, certainly, and I didn't see the history of the Mindleberg Mills's contributions to the fortunes of the late Confederacy zooming to the top of any best-seller lists, but it was still far and away a better deal than any regular job I could think of.

After lunch, I stopped by a bookstore and picked up Fletcher Pratt's short history of the Civil War, a conflict in which I had never taken too much interest, with the object of learning something of the period. But my clerk looked baffled when I asked if he knew of a good, concise study of the textile industry, so I told him to forget it, feeling reasonably certain that a town like Textilia was bound to have a public library chock-full of learned texts on the subject. Then I grabbed a train home, feeling fairly blithe and bonny. The more fool I.

☞ *2* *TWO* Sunday afternoons later, had you chanced to be passing through the echoing vastness of Pennsylvania Station, you might have observed a thoroughly disgruntled Nicholas Saltire stomping grimly along in the wake of an elderly redcap pushing a handcart piled high with luggage, and accompanied by a small, handsome wench who bore a striking resemblance to Miss Leslie Caron in one of her more determined moods. This was Miss Brooke Hastings.

Ahead of us lay, hissing softly behind the Tuscan red Pennsy locomotive that would haul it as far as Washington, the Rebel Raider, all-Pullman pride of the Potomac, Richmond & Jacksonville Railway. And somewhere on down the line, blissfully unaware of what the future held in store, lay Textilia, North Carolina, the final repository of the small, black tin trunk containing the astounding record of Colonel Marius Mindleberg, the Ashenden of the Confederate States of America.

As anticipated, there had been no difficulty over the non-renewal of my lease, Lonsdale Thirsby having become positively cordial when I announced my intention of vacating his guest-house during an interview I had carefully arranged to take place while his wife was on one of her regular shopping visits to the metropolis. My meager stock of furniture and books had been picked up by the merry men of the Fogle-Security Storage Company and swept off to their mothproof warehouses, and an unsuspecting college youth had purchased my six-year-old Morgan in the mistaken belief that its Cheyne-Stokes breathing represented a song of power.

☆ 8 ☆

With my name safely signed to a contract, Walter Gregory had showered me with blessings, including several credit cards and a guest membership in something called the Mindleberg Hills Country Club. Additionally, a courteous letter from J. Sydney Cheek advised that an efficiency apartment, fully furnished, had been reserved in the Mindleberg Arms Apartments for my occupancy. Another letter, from a Miss Lydia Younghusband Bowers, secretary of the Dancey County Historical Society, assured me of her fullest cooperation, and yet another, over the signature of a man who called himself John R. ("Rebel Jack") Ploughman, apprised me of my nomination to honorary membership in the Textilia Civil War Round Table.

Then, my affairs in order, I had telephoned to the offices of Bannastre Masters Associates to notify Miss Hastings of my readiness to put the show on the road, and, having got through to her, suggested that we could fly down of a Sunday evening so as to be ready to begin work on the Monday morning, full of beans and vinegar. It was then that she told me that since the Associates included among their clients the Atlantic Coast Railway Management Association, travel by B.M.A. personnel within the continental limits of the United States was restricted to the rails except in situations of direst emergency. Of course, she said, if I wished to fly down she could have her office make the necessary arrangements, but she herself would be required to travel by train. I assured her that I had no major objections to this mode of conveyance, and we arranged to meet just outside the Savarin Restaurant.

Miss Hastings' voice sounded low and pleasant, and I looked forward to meeting its owner. Too, the long trip South would give us a splendid opportunity to become acquainted and to discuss the work upon which we were embarked.

Thus it was that we came to be headed for the Rebel Raider that Sunday afternoon. As I have mentioned, a certain amount of disgruntlement clouded my normally sunny temperament, and there was little prospect that the next twenty-four hours should find me gruntled. The principal reason for this somber outlook was the fact that the accommodations which the Bannastre Masters office had secured for Miss Hastings and myself were something less than desirable, thanks to the assembly of the 35th Annual Conclave of the Eastern Sheikdom of the Ancient and Mystic Order of Saracen Knights in Jacksonville, Florida, Tuesday morning. Only a cad and a bounder would have suffered Miss Hastings to occupy the upper berth which was the lesser of the two spaces still available aboard the Raider, and it was at my firm insistence that she had consented to occupy the bedroom canceled at the last minute by some unfortunate Knight. Which left me with the previously cited dismal prospect of spending a sleepless night aloft in a car full of howling drunks.

Miss Hastings, on the other hand, had proved to be an eminently attractive young woman, petite and well-formed and with, as I say, a notable resemblance to Leslie Caron and an air of brisk efficiency. I therefore did my best to conceal from her my forebodings.

My spirits were not greatly lightened as our redcap led us down the platform past the gleaming, stainless-steel lengths of the John Singleton Mosby, the Nathan Bedford Forrest, the Turner Ashby, the John Hunt Morgan, the Jeb Stuart and the Wade Hampton Club toward the towering, old-fashioned standard Pullmans which had been added to the train's normal consist to handle the knightly overflow. My grimmest anticipations were confirmed as we passed a gaggle of gaudily uniformed buffoons, briefly freed from cashier's cage and funeral parlor, to the accompaniment of a chorus of wolf whistles and tongue-clucking.

"The bar car will be hell on wheels," Miss Hastings observed knowledgeably. "We may as well stick to my compartment if you'd like a quiet drink." And then the redcap was handing her baggage to the porter of the Tintagel Castle and, seconds later, leading me along the platform to the car in which my pitiful lodging for the night was situated. Happily, it was the next car forward, and within minutes I was more or less installed aboard the Wappingers Falls, already loud with song and good-fellowship, and brilliant with golden-tasseled orange fezzes.

"What stronghold, Sir Knight?" boomed the portly Saracen who would, I gathered, fill the berth below my aerial couch that night. He was holding an open fifth of Old Granddad, much depleted, and wearing an expression of great geniality beneath his fez, upon which I perceived to be embroidered in silver thread the title, "Past Grand Senior Castellan."

"I beg pardon?"

"Sorry, friend. Thought you were one of us. Quetschler's the name; Harold R. Quetschler, Moorish Citadel Number Thirty-four, Harrisburg, P.A." Sir Harold extended a plump, pink pandy and we were, presumably, sworn to eternal friendship, infidel dog though I might be. "Care for a belt, friend? Gonna be a long night and a hard morning."

Muttering hasty but, I trust, courteous excuses, I declined this hospitable proffer and made my way aft toward the Tintagel Castle, a feat rendered temporarily impossible by the sudden eruption from one of the bedrooms adjacent to the berth section of six men, garbed as for the siege of Malta and all bearing scimitars. They shuffled self-consciously into line along the aisle.

"All right now, goddammit men, let's get together on this thing," an angry-looking Knight who was, it must be supposed, the leader of this pantalooned band, begged hoarsely. "Pre-ZAANT HAHMZ!" Six gleaming weapons were thrust raggedly upward, and there was an explosive tinkle of fractured glass as one smashed the lighting fixture directly above its owner's fez, occasioning a great burst of merriment from one and all. And as if this had been a musical cue, there now arose from yet another of the bedrooms an unearthly clangor of cymbals, the rumble of tabors and a cacophony of high, reedy noise in what sounded like an Arabic rendition of the "Skye Boat Song."

☆ *11* ☆

"Let's really hear those tambourines," a voice off bawled as I finally made my way from the Wappingers Falls, the drill team of Oasis Stronghold No. 62, Syracuse, N.Y., and the Supreme Pasha's Oriental Marching Band of Levantine Stronghold No. 207, of Hartford, Conn., as their headgear proclaimed them.

Tintagel Castle, an all-compartment car, was in somewhat better shape, the general thunder being to a slight extent muted by the partitions, but sieged it doubtless was. From nearly every compartment door, standing companionably open, surged eddies of blue cigar smoke and the commingled fragrance of shaving lotions and neat whiskey, and, as I proceeded along the passageway in search of the porter who could tell me the location of Miss Hastings's quarters, I received several jovial invitations to come on in and strike a blow for the common people. Located at last, the porter told me that my research assistant was to be found in Bedroom Number Four. He was already looking badly harassed, and it seemed likely that we would not be able to depend on him much past Philadelphia.

Entering her compartment upon an acquiescent reply to my knock, I discovered Miss Hastings comfortably ensconced upon the berth which stretched across one end of the room, her feet up, her shoes off, a plastic cup in one hand and a cigarette in the other. On the carpeted floor, convenient to hand, stood no mere Thermos bottle but one of those picnic jugs, complete with spout and capable of supplying the entire Bobbsey family. I had not observed this commodious vessel among her luggage, and its appearance came as a decidedly pleasant surprise, further buttressing my already generally favorable estimate of her. The picnic jug showed foresight and the ability to plan ahead, both admirable qualities.

"Forewarned is forearmed," she observed, waving her cigarette at the jug. "Pour yourself something, please."

I did as bid, and eased the frame into one of the two sturdy armchairs with which the bedroom was provided, and it was only then that I found time to inspect our surroundings. They were of Edwardian, albeit faded elegance, all deep green plush and solid walnut and honest incandescent bulbs glowing cheerily yellow beneath their opalescent glass shades, tulip-shaped at the end of brass tubular brackets that curled gracefully from the walls. Clearly, the Tintagel Castle had been hauled out of some elephant's graveyard of a sleeping-car pool and pressed into service to meet the needs of the Saracen Knights, and I was strongly reminded of my Aunt Elizabeth's upstairs parlor in her home in Overbrook, just outside Philadelphia. All that was lacking was a Wallace Nutting photograph and a steel engraving of "When Did You Last See Your Father?"

"And how is Mrs. Lincoln surviving the journey?" I asked as I sampled the contents of the Thermos and instantly regretted this flippancy as the palate informed the higher thought centers that it had just checked in a martini utterly beyond cavil. Our accommodations were not, after all, to be blamed on Miss Hastings. She smiled amiably, and I was about to make some less cutting remark by way of amends when the Rebel Raider gave a titanic lurch as its skillful engineer artfully set his monarch of the rails in motion. The contents of her plastic cup promptly sloshed out, just missing her skirt, and like a shot I was on my feet and groping for a towel from the rack over the washbasin. This secured, I was extending it to her when our daredevil locomotive driver, seemingly eager to be away to Florida's sunny shore, gave his steed another goose and there, by God, I sprawled, safe in the comfortable arms of Miss Brooke Hastings.

Blushing like a schoolboy at my clumsiness, I managed to regain my chair and refill her cup as we trundled beneath the Hudson to begin the long run southward.

"Is this your first trip South?" I inquired, and as she reached for her cup I was able to note that she wore no engagement ring.

"I was born in North Carolina," she said. "What about yourself?"

"You mean, is it my first trip South, or where was I born?"

"Both."

"A few trips to New Orleans. And the answer to the second question is Pennsylvania. Little place called Dexter; I doubt if you would have heard of it."

"And now you're free-lancing." Her eyes sparkled. "That must be a wonderful way to live—no hours, live where you please, write when you want to and how you want to. I'm green with envy."

"You make it sound much better than it really is. This deal we're on, for example; when you come right down to it, it's pretty much of a hack job; so many thousand words, so many bucks."

"That's true in a way, I suppose. But you've written other things, too."

"I don't think John Steinbeck is losing any sleep over my competition," I told her honestly. "Couple of novels that got remaindered, some magazine stuff, some editing. Nicholas Saltire, journeyman writer, about wraps it up. What about you, if I may inquire, Miss H.?"

"I wish you'd call me Brooke, and I'll call you—what do they call you, anyhow? Nick? Nicky? Or what?"

"Nick, mostly. Sounds like a Greek gambler, but 'Nicky' sounds even worse. Like a poodle. Actually, my friends call me 'Bent,' after my middle name, which is Bentley, and that sounds like one of those Hollywood inventions—Bent Saltire, Rock Ribbed, Dull Thud."

" 'Bent' sounds fine."

"You haven't answered my question."

"About me? Nothing to tell, really. I just sort of drifted into this job after I got my divorce, and that's about all there is to it. It keeps the wolf from the door."

A certain finality in the tone of her voice indicated that her former marriage was not a subject upon which she desired to expatiate, and I did not, therefore, pursue the question, much as

I would have liked to have done. In the brief silence that followed, I perceived her cup to be empty again, as was my own, and poured us another sampling of the contents of that splendid jug. We were bucketing across the Jersey Meadows, and it struck me that I might have been mistaken in my initial displeasure at our means of transport. We were snug as bugs in a rug, Miss Hastings and I in our little steel cocoon, and safely insulated from the Saracen Knights. From time to time, to be sure, heavy thumpings along the corridor wall signaled the passage of convivial fraternalists toward the bar car astern, and we heard occasional snatches of knightly glee, but all was at a satisfactory remove.

"Being from North Carolina," I deftly changed the subject, "have you ever heard tell of these Mindlebergs?" Brooke shot me a look of gratitude, and nodded.

"They're a pretty fantastic bunch," she replied, accepting her newly filled cup. "There are two branches; the cotton Mindlebergs and the tobacco Mindlebergs, and there's a lot of rivalry between them. The family came to North Carolina a few years before the war—the Civil War, that is—"

"Natch. Go on, please."

Brooke shrugged. "They're all crazy rich, and they do good works and they annoy the daylights out of the hard-shell Baptists."

"I'm not with you. How annoy, I mean?"

"In the Bible Belt the old-time religion, which is strictly Fundamentalist, is built on good, solid, old-fashioned hate, and the Mindlebergs are hard to hate. Simple?"

It figured. We chatted on, past Princeton Junction into Trenton and all the way to Philadelphia, occasionally pausing to restore the fabric by judicious application to the picnic jug as we exchanged bits and pieces of information about ourselves. By the time we eased out of Philadelphia, we'd learned a fair amount concerning each other, and the germ of an idea had begun to develop, the essence of which was, to be blunt, that it might not be utterly beyond the realm of conjecture to consider the possibility of spending the night here in this warm and cozy bedroom with this warm and cozy girl. She had, after all, experienced the pleasures of the flesh and might logically, in view of her status as a divorcee, be expected to take a worldly and tolerant attitude toward the idea, well aware that there need be no emotional involvement.

First, as I envisioned it, a leisurely dinner after the Knights had sated themselves, accompanied by a bottle of whatever suitable wine was available, this to be followed by a brandy or two and a return to our rolling love-nest for a few postprandial highballs, assuming our porter were still functioning, as I suavely guided the conversation toward the problem of the individual's need for communication, of his loneliness amid the madding crowd. Perhaps, too, a light but informative comment on the Tintagel Castle, noting its association with the Arthurian legend and the plight of Guinevere, trapped as she was by a morality equally as sinister as the very sins it sought vainly to prevent. And so on.

In retrospect, of course, I have no choice but to describe my intentions as unspeakably knavish, but, in all fairness, I would have it remembered that I was a young bachelor, with all the healthy animal instincts operating at full steam, the old glands bubbling away like a beer vat in bock time. Further, I was encloseted with an eminently well-developed young woman with full lips and a superbly rounded bosom that seemed to cry out, as it were, for some lonely head to cradle, and who, to iterate, was not unacquainted with the concept that sex can be fun. The defense rests.

BALTIMORE brought a gradual diminu-
☞ *3* tion of the thumpings along the corridor
wall, informing us that the majority of the
Saracen chivalry had got their evening ration aboard, so we
made our way forward to the dining car and the unhurried enjoyment of whatever rich dainties the Dining Car Department
of the Potomac, Richmond & Jacksonville might have seen fit to
provide its patrons. We found it still fairly full of fezzes, but the
steward managed to find us a table and to take my order for a
couple of martinis wherewith I hoped to maintain the roseate
glow our session with the picnic jug had induced before it ran
dry just west of the broad Susquehanna. So far, all had gone
well, and Brooke and I had achieved something of a meeting of
minds on a number of subjects, ranging from the excellence of
T. H. White to the best recipe for spaghetti sauce Bolognese.

In the fullness of time, our waiter appeared, and, having in
mind the general caliber of dining car cuisine, I suggested that
we play it safe and order steaks. When I communicated this aim
to our dusky servitor, however, he permitted himself a broad
smile and advised that the lodge gentlemen had already eaten
all the steaks and roast beef. "Ain' nothin' lef' but turkey hash 'n'
cream sauce, hahvuhd beet an' boil carrot," he concluded happily.

It was not the sort of dinner I would normally have selected
as the proper prelude to a full-dress seduction. Much would now
have to depend on the brandy and, later, the highballs.

Our ghastly repast concluded, we were sampling our brandy as
we rumbled into the Union Station in Washington, and shortly

after we halted there came a succession of heavy jars as yet more sleepers were coupled to the rear of the train, presumably bearing Saracens from Pittsburgh and points west. Anticipating the new arrivals, our steward began hovering impatiently, and I took the hint.

Then, as I led the way from the dining car and we passed into the clamorous length of the John Hunt Morgan, there occurred one of those regrettable episodes so often to be encountered, alas, when good fellows get together. A large, fairly young and monumentally sloshed Saracen Knight, leaning in the door of a compartment, placed his arm as a barrier across the corridor, blocking our further progress. He leered at me, blearily pugnacious.

"Thissis toll road, buddy-boy," he croaked. "Don' 'low no pretty girls ge' by 'less they pay th' toll, w'ish means one eash kish." He turned and spoke to his compartment companions: "Ain' tha' right, fellas?" There came a loud chorus of assent: "Ya goddamn right tha's right, Chuck ol' buddy-boy."

"Couldn't we just knock it off, friend?" I suggested quietly, while Brooke stood, uncertain, behind me.

"Hey, now! How 'bout that jazz. Lady's boy frien' says le's knock it off, for Chrissake!" Our roadblock returned his attention from his chums to me, and I saw with sinking heart that my remark had only served to arouse further that latent resentment of one's fellow creatures so frequently a concomitant of neat whiskey taken indiscreetly. "You gonna try 'n' make me, bud?"

In a confrontation of this nature, philosophical reasoning is of little value, and harsh experience during my career with the military during the Korean conflict had taught that in immediate and, if possible, decisive action lies the only solution. Therefore, and with the perhaps unfair advantage of somewhat greater sobriety, I hit him as hard as I could in the tummy. He had clearly been expecting our conversation to continue for at least a few seconds more, and my blow came as a distinct surprise, driving him backward into his compartment where he sat heavily down amid a great smashing of glasses and cries of astonishment and wrath.

"Get ahead of me," I ordered Brooke, standing aside to let her slip on past, and we moved hastily down the corridor. I was fully expecting a strong rearguard action, but it must be presumed that the sudden and unexpected violence of my attack had confused the Saracen horde, for no pursuit manifested itself. To tell the truth, I was a little confused myself; as a general rule, I don't go around belting people, and now that the deed was done I found myself a trifle shaken and breathing rapidly. We kept going at a fast pace until we were once more within the walls of the Tintagel Castle.

"I'm impressed," Brooke declared simply as we arrived before the door of her compartment. "I'm also wondering whether that big ox will decide to hunt you down, once he gets his breath back." Her expression was one of girlish concern.

"I doubt it. His friends will pour him another jolt and he'll forget all about it. I'm just sorry it had to happen."

"Girls get used to it."

Nonetheless, I felt almost certain the incident had cast a slight pall, reminding her, as it must have done, of the bestiality of men and their chronic ruttishness, and a girl who has just been reminded of these subjects is not usually, it may be argued without much fear of contradiction, in a receptive mood for more of the same, however subtly advanced. In the light of this thinking, I decided that it would be well to postpone until a more propitious moment my still vague designs upon her virtue and to remain Bent the Gent.

I reckoned, however, without taking into account the almost total illogicality of the feminine thought processes. If the sloshed Saracen had repelled, the Chevalier sans peur had warmed, so that when I made to bid Brooke a courteous good evening she laid a hand gently on my arm and gazed up at me with softly glowing eyes.

"If you're in with me, he won't be able to find you. So why don't you give me a few minutes to get comfortable and then come on back for a nightcap? It's hopeless to think about getting any sleep until this bunch of drunks quiets down, anyhow. And besides, until they do, I'd sort of like to have somebody handy. Just in case. Would you mind terribly?"

"Of course not," I replied, so heartily that it came out much louder than intended. "You know better than that, Brooke," I added with considerably less volume.

"See you, then."

With all things once more possible, it was with lightsome heart that I withdrew to the gentlemen's smoking room of the Wappingers Falls, there to smoke two cigarettes with savage restraint as I stared out of the filthy window at the smoking room's insubstantial reflection scudding over the dark Virginia countryside through which we were now gathering speed. When my watch showed that fifteen minutes had elapsed, I returned again to the Tintagel Castle and the door of Brooke's bedroom. In response to my knock there came the sound of a lock snicking open, and I entered to find that my all-American girl had, in very truth, changed into something comfy.

Nothing immodest, mind you; nothing vulgarly suggestive in sheerest black nylon, cunningly draped artfully to expose. Nothing like that, but on the other hand not precisely the sort of thing suitable for a Senior Girl Scout. Actually, she wore a full-length housecoat of some kind of greeny gold, very fine velvet, closely fitted topside and flaring gracefully at the hips, with a deep V neckline that gave onto a limited vista of feminine cleavage so fully and perfectly symmetrical as to cause the beholder to salivate freely. I swallowed before finding voice.

"Well, sir," I hoarsed. "Well, sir." Brooke gave a grin of the sort customarily described as gamine. She had resumed the position in which I had found her earlier, gracefully disposed along her berth which, during our turkey hash debauch, had been made up for the night.

"Hope you don't object," she said, and waved a hand at two miniature bottles, a pitcher of ice and two glasses on the small round table which stood between the room's two armchairs. "Would you do the honors, Bent?"

"There is," I observed casually after we had sampled my skill as a barman, "a rather interesting legend connected with the name of this car. King Arthur's birthplace, as a matter of fact, on the north coast of Cornwall. You remember King Arthur, of course?"

"And Guinevere and Launcelot. A touching story. . . . Bent?"

"Yes." Clearly, the Tintagel gambit wasn't going anywhere.

"How come you've never married?"

"I nearly did, once." And so I told her about Ardyth, of whom perhaps the less said the better. Heaven knows I'm no prude, but Ardyth had shaken my composure badly. "Poor Bent," Brooke murmured sympathetically when I had concluded my less than edifying tale. "It must have come as a hell of a jolt. Still, better then than later. That's when I found out about Paul."

"Paul? You mean, your husband?" I stared at Brooke. "You mean he also liked boys?"

She shrugged. "Girls, boys, it was all the same and the more the merrier. A little shattering for a simple country girl whose mama told her never to marry an actor. Although, in all honesty, Paul's a good actor. You may have seen him; he does quite a lot of TV—Paul Kenyon." I shook my head; the name meant nothing to me.

"I'd say he was a damned fool," I told her.

"I could say the same thing for your Ardyth."

It was a wildly improbable bond with which to forge a friendship, but certainly it was better than none at all. "Mind you,"

I said firmly, "I'm not Victorian about sex. In fact, I stand four-square for it, in the time-honored sense, that is."

"Bravo, and hear, hear."

"In other words, I'm not a-Freud, not even a little bit."

Which sally Brooke rewarded with a merry laugh as I saw that it was time to ring for the porter to fetch us another couple of bourbons; this was no time to stop the flow of either stimulant or conversation. Brooke stopped me as I reached toward the porter's buzzer: "It won't do any good unless you want to switch to light wine or beer. I'd forgotten all about Virginia law, but our porter was sweet and sneaked these two in to me after I crossed my heart and promised I wouldn't tell. He said he wouldn't dare bring any more, though."

"You must be kidding," I protested, but Brooke shook her head. "Bible Belt, remember?" she reminded me.

Now this was ridiculous. Beer, despite its many nutritive quali-ties, was not the accompaniment for the sort of occasion I had in mind, and it seemed unlikely that the limited stock of wines carried aboard the dining car would include champagne. The Saltire brain, already keyed to concert pitch by the prospect be-fore it, rose nobly to the challenge. "In which case," I said blithely, "it behooves me to take corrective measures. Leave it to Bent, in sum."

"Don't tell me you thought to pack a bottle of bourbon in your bags."

"I claim no such foresight, but I'm willing to bet that one of our pals among the Knights has a bottle he'd spare."

"It would be worth trying," Brooke conceded, extracting a cigarette from its box and placing it between her lips.

"And it won't take longer than a few minutes to find out," I assured her as I leaped to offer my lighter. She inhaled and then looked up at me calmly and appraisingly, almost brazenly.

"Don't be too long, Bent," she said softly as she exhaled. I left her, her image seductively hazed about by the swirling, blue-gray smoke of her cigarette. Unless I were hideously mistaken, she had reached some manner of decision about us, and from all appearances it was one eminently favorable to my intentions. We had at last got onto Topic A, and Brooke seemed disposed to explore the problem in considerably more detail, possibly even to the extent of passing from theory to practice. In such a mood, time was of the essence.

The Rebel Raider was slowing ponderously as I hastened on winged feet from Tintagel Castle to Wappingers Falls, the interior of which now bore an eerie resemblance to an old steel engraving I had once seen in the window of a Third Avenue print dealer, entitled "Mutiny of the Turkish Garrison at Dubrovnik," and produced by Thomas Megg, of London, in 1831. It was, consequently, not without some difficulty that I made my way to my berth in the hope of spotting my sworn chum, Sir Harold Quetschler, the Past Grand Senior Castellan. Nor was I disappointed. The Knights were by now well settled down to serious poker and drinking, and it came as no surprise to find our berths still unmade and our section occupied by no less than eight souls in the midst of a no-quarter game of stud, the stakes of which formed an imposing pile of bills on the folding table between the seats. The air was a semisolid compound of cigar smoke and whiskey fumes.

Sir Harold greeted me as greets the father the prodigal son and bade me join in the sport. Upon my declining, on the grounds that I had no wish to crowd the group, he urged me, at the very least, to have just one little drink. By this stage of the evening he was not to be denied, and, indeed, it was possible to suspect that a refusal, however tactfully phrased, might have brought out in his nature a streak of belligerency which would have dismayed his mother, confirming her direst suspicions. Since it was in my interest to maintain his amiable disposition, I accepted with thanks a murderous jolt of Old Granddad. I then explained the purpose of my visit, leering, I confess, horridly in the hope of arousing masculine sympathy for my plight . . . needs must when the devil drives

"Y'say ya've got this babe all lined up for a lay, huh?" one of Sir Harold's companions inquired, matching me leer for leer. "Jeezkrice." He turned to his mates: "Be a goddamn shame 'fwe couldn' do an ol' frien' a favor, now, wouldn' it? I mean, Jeezkrice!"

" 'Specially the way he don't mind our settin' 'n' playin' cards 'n' keepin' him outta his berth," spoke up another, his voice choked with emotion at the thought of my sacrifice. "Any you guys gotta spare bottle, for Chrissakes? 'S'lease we can do."

"Even a pint would help," I added in the thoughtful silence that followed. "I'd be glad to pay double."

"Hey! Ol' Herve Bonesteel's gotta whole goddamn case in his room," cried a third of this hospitable band. "Ol' Herve's Sh'preme High Sheriff of the Provinch of New Zhersy," he explained for my benefit. "Real prinsh of a guy. Le's us go see ol' Herve, fella."

At this capital suggestion, the poker game rose as one Knight and then sat down abruptly as the Rebel Raider came to a groaning halt and began squeaking and hissing in relief. On the second try, they made it, and off we traipsed in the direction of good ol' Herve's quarters, looking for all the world like a Middle Eastern government going into a fast exile. Our destination, it developed, lay two cars farther forward, and, impatient as I was to return to Tintagel Castle, I seemed to have little choice but to go through with my audience before the High Sheriff. Our progress was rendered somewhat erratic, not only by the amount of bourbon previously absorbed by my brilliantly caparisoned escort but as well by a series of very heavy jolts and jerks that shivered the length of the train.

"Mus' be Charlo'ssville," Sir Harold Quetschler declared knowledgeably. "Use'ta travel this territory. Pro'lly changin' engines up ahead." A porter, wearing the panic-stricken expression of one near to nervous collapse, suddenly appeared in the corridor ahead and Sir Harold besought of him confirmation of this surmise: "Hey, George! Wha'ssup, huh? They changin' engines or what?"

"Nossuh. Moh likeleh taken' on moh cahs. This heah's Jahvus Sprengs—junction with the Chesapeake 'n Oh-hiuh. We pro'lly pickin' up the Lou'ville cahs 'long 'bout now, Lou'ville 'n Cincinnateh."

Finally we arrived at the Supreme High Sheriff's keep, a double bedroom in which His Supremacy was holding court for his pals. "Ya mind waitin' ou'side here for a secon'," one of my escort muttered, his tone embarrassed. "I mean, now don' take no offense, but you not bein' a Saracen, might be jus' a li'l easier get ol' Herve give us a bottle like it was just for ourselves. Y'understand?"

"By all means," I replied promptly, much relieved at being spared the humiliating necessity of repeating my sordid plea before yet another group. I was left alone in the corridor, peering through the paleolithic grime on the windows at what appeared to be a railroad yard of some size, floodlit and spangled with those mysteriously flashing lights and varicolored signal lamps by means of which they keep the trains sorted out. The Rebel Raider continued to be buffeted by more ominous jolts. From the High Sheriff's chambers came a muffled roar of laughter. My boys seemed to be taking one hell of a time conning good ol' Herve into the sacrifice, and it struck me that in their present condition they might forget all about me.

I had just concluded to take my search elsewhere when Sir Harold eased his bulk out of the door in conspiratorial fashion and produced from beneath his coat a fifth of Old Overholt. "Hope you don't mind rye, fella," he stage-whispered, glancing furtively behind him. "Di'n wan' ol' Herve see me slip this outta his room." He sighed and looked at me enviously. "Lottsa luck, pal."

"What do I owe you, please?" I asked, masking my impatience to be away. God knew how long I had already been absent.

☆ 25 ☆

"I wouldn't take a nickel, pal, not a goddamn nickel. You go have yourself a ball." Sir Harold beamed at me, and I was much moved by his wholehearted generosity.

Uttering my sincere thanks, I took off once more back in the direction of Tintagel Castle and Bedroom Number Four, marveling at the spontaneous kindness of these stranger Knights. Perhaps, I thought, as I made my way past what sounded like yet another Oriental marching band in impromptu rehearsal, I had been unduly harsh in my previous judgment of these great-hearted men who were, when you stopped to analyze it, merely seeking release in conviviality from the drabness of their business and professional worlds. As I marched along, the Rebel Raider jerked convulsively and heaved itself into reluctant motion.

Entering Wappingers Falls I thought briefly of pausing by my berth and securing from my suitcase a dressing gown, but a moment's reflection decided me against any such forward move, and I pressed on. Rounding the sharp corner past the smoking room, I flung open the heavy door to the vestibule and stopped dead, my way barred by one of those waist-high folding steel gates hooked across the exterior door. This door's window was dark, and in one shattering instant I sensed what had happened.

"No, by God!" It was a cry from the heart.

"You wasn't up in the nex' cah behind, was you?" asked a deeply worried voice from behind my shoulder, and in the darkened mirror of the door window I saw the reflection of the brown, concerned face of Mr. Lucius Holloway, my friendly porter on duty, according to the small blue card I had earlier observed hanging just inside the vestibule. " 'Cause tha's gon' on ahead with Numbeh One Section. We runnin' ten minutes behin' it."

☆ *26* ☆

TEXTILIA, "The Spindle City," the Tarheel State's fastest-growing, most prosperous and progressive industrial and financial community, is more than a great commercial complex—it is a fine place to live and raise a family. Here, in the bracing climate of the North Carolina Piedmont, culture marches hand in hand with business. The city's splendid public school system is nationally known, as are Dancey College for Women (founded 1880), and the Haynie Mechanical & Agricultural Institute for Negroes (founded 1907). Here more than 40 churches of many denominations serve the religious needs of the city's 77,800 residents (1940). The Textilia Symphony, formed in 1947, is one of the State's outstanding musical organizations, annually presenting a series of four public concerts under a professional director. The Mindleberg Museum houses many works of art by regional artists, as well as the nation's largest library of books pertaining to the textile industry. The world-famed Mindleberg Mills are the largest on the face of the globe devoted to the spinning of cotton and man-made fibers. On permanent display in the lobby of the general offices of the King Cotton Life Insurance Corporation, one of the South's largest, is a comprehensive exhibit of furniture manufactured locally by the city's second major industry.

    Yes, Textilia is a great place to live! Come and join us!

        —Spindle City Saga, *published by the Development Committee, Textilia Association of Commerce. Copyright 1955.*

I had my first glimpse of Textilia filtered through the dismal murk of a truly lethal hangover, the blackened fruit of the remainder of my nightmare journey aboard the Rebel Raider. When all is said and done, what can you do with a bottle of bonded rye, borrowed for a tryst which fails to materialize, but murder thought? I should, of course, have attempted to return it to Sir Harold Quetschler, but considerations of decency and conduct becoming a gentleman were overborne by pride: I simply could not bring myself to face Sir Hal and friends after what had happened, feeling certain that one jovial smirk, one genial jibe at my shattered hopes would fetch out in me a streak of pure nastiness *my* mother would have been distressed to see. Thus, with no end of nervous dodging in and out of smoking rooms and toilet compartments to avoid encountering my benefactors, I made my tortured way all the inhuman distance forward and spent the night wretchedly in the gents' room of the first car, working morosely on the rye that should have been shared with Brooke Hastings. To cap my misery, thought resolutely refused to be murdered, and the mind, adamantly sober, continued to function with a terrible lucidity, conjuring up precise visions of my lost lady, until sheer exhaustion brought the surcease of sleep.

But the hangover was all boy, kicking and screaming inside Daddy's head, which now seemed constructed of Gruyère cheese, now of sounding brass. Despite the best efforts of the finest brains on the Pepsodent research staff, I could distinctly taste whale, while my eyes seemed to have receded far into the skull. I had the uneasy feeling that unless I exercised the sternest control they would roll slowly upward, never to be seen more.

Happily, Sir Harold was still out cold in his berth when I returned to Wappingers Falls to gather my possessions shortly after dawn and take them to the lavatory where I performed the matutinal ablutions between great sea-swells of nausea occasioned by the aroma, which defied coherent description even had I dared to permit myself to dwell on the subject. Breakfast, thereafter, was out of the question.

Brooke, looking fresh as the first daffodil, was waiting on the brilliantly sunlit platform of the Textilia station when I tottered, wincing, down from Wappingers Falls, her expression a rich mixture of amusement and sympathy. "Oh, Bent, I *am* so sorry for you. The porter explained what happened. Did you get any sleep at all?" At which point she failed to suppress a giggle. "You look simply awful."

"Nothing a little embalming fluid won't clear up in a jiffy," I advised her stiffly. "And heaven's curse upon the Potomac, Richmond & Jacksonville Railway."

Approaching us now at a brisk pace was a small, portly chap wearing a tiny black moustache, rimless octagonal spectacles, a worried expression and the dark garb of a man prepared to take me up on the embalming fluid proposition. Behind him strode a tall, distinguished-looking Negro in gray chauffeur's uniform.

"Mr. Saltire? Miss Hastings?" the little fellow asked. "I bid you welcome to Textilia. I am Sydney Cheek, Mr. Mindleberg's assistant. All your baggage off the train all right? Fine. I know you'd both probably like to freshen up a bit after the trip, so why don't we drive straight out to the Arms, and then a little later on this morning you can come downtown and see your office." Mr. Cheek turned to the tall Negro. "Will you see to the bags, Johnston, please? Thanks."

"Immediately, sir," replied the Negro in an Oxford accent, and sloped off to pick up our luggage.

"Jamaican," Mr. Cheek explained, smiling a trifle bleakly at the flash of astonishment which crossed Brooke's face, and led us off through the depot to an enormous black Rolls-Royce limousine parked just outside.

"This is Elm Street, our main shopping district," Cheek told us from his perch on one of the jump seats amidships as we purred smoothly through the city. "Miss Hastings, you might like Montefiore's, just over there on your left; one of our best ladies' shops, my wife tells me. That's the First Dancey Trust just next door, with the Piedmont Guaranty across the street. The tall white building is the King Cotton Life, and there on the opposite corner is the Mindleberg Tower. Tallest building between Richmond and Atlanta; that's where you'll have your office." Mr. Cheek was a veritable Baedeker, and I confess that I was pleasantly impressed by Textilia's broad streets and prosperous air.

We oozed past the Dancey County Courthouse (limestone), the United States Post Office and Federal Court (granite), the Textilia City Hall (marble), and so on into what was definitely a high-income residential area, slowing at last as we drew nigh a sprawling Tudor manor house, all russet brick, yellow stucco, half-timbering (fake) and stone-framed, diamond-paned leaded windows. The Rolls swung sedately in through a stone-arched gateway set into the center of the facade, and we ended up in an honest-to-God cobbled courtyard before a massive oaken door.

"The Mindleberg Arms," Mr. Cheek announced proudly. "Supposed to be an exact reproduction of a place called Mockbeggars Hall, in England. The cobbles were all imported."

Within minutes, Brooke and I were installed in the efficiency apartments which had been reserved for our use. And while the purist might conceivably cavil at a Tudor mansion set down in Piedmont North Carolina, he could not fault the amenities provided the tenants. My furnishings were beyond reproach.

A broad and deep, dark green leather sofa fronted on a working fireplace, and at the touch of a concealed button it collapsed in various directions to become a double bed. Another button, set into the wall, caused a large slice of oak paneling to slide aside to disclose a gleaming kitchenette; yet another sliding panel gave access to the bath. These were surroundings in which Nicholas Bentley Saltire, Gent., might feel at home. There was even a nicely framed print of "Mr. Throppe's Hounds in Full Cry on Muckle Down" hanging over the hearth. In short, the sort of place in which a nobleman of the county might have invented Worcestershire sauce.

J. Sydney Cheek had remained with me while Brooke unpacked her bags in her apartment. With a merry smile, he opened the door of the kitchenette's compact refrigerator. A fresh case of beer constituted its contents. "Thought you might appreciate something like this," he said, his spectacles sparkling with honest pleasure. "Care for a cold one before we pick up Miss Hastings?"

I could have whimpered with gratitude.

Too, I had the definite impression that J. Sydney had something on his mind which he desired to discuss. Probably, I thought, he wished to brief me on the character of Pierre Mindleberg before introducing me to the great man. It would be, I felt, sound policy on my part to get on well with J. Sydney, since he would undoubtedly be my principal liaison officer with the master of the Mindleberg millions. Initially, I will admit, the prospect had not pleased; as a general rule, if you show me a small, portly man who goes in for little moustaches and rimless, octagonal glasses, I will show you a pill. Consequently I felt a measure of relief in the fact that Cheek had suggested a cold beer during working hours and before noon: a man who will do that can't be all bad.

"Cheers." I raised my beer can to Cheek, and sat down on, or rather in my magnificent sofa while my guest lowered himself into one of the pair of club chairs flanking it. "Luck," he responded, shoving his glasses up on his forehead and thus making himself look considerably younger and less pillish.

"I'm looking forward to getting down to work on this book of yours," I said after a deep swallow of the foaming, feeling at last the thrill of life along my keel.

"Hmmm," murmured Cheek, and drank deeply. "That brings up what I wanted to have a little talk with you about." He shot me a curious glance. "Walter Gregory tells us you have a great reputation for journalistic integrity, Mr. Saltire."

The instincts sprang alert: now what the hell?

"I've never been sued for libel, if that's what you mean."

"You would not conceal the facts, even if they hurt, then? Or even if someone were to, ah, shall we say make it worth your while to—how shall I put it?—make certain discreet changes?" J. Sydney appeared to be on the verge of breaking into a light sweat, and I wasn't liking the turn our chat was taking.

"Look," I said. "I'm afraid I'm not with you. I signed on to do a straight, factual book on the Mindleberg operation during the Civil War, period. On the other hand, the firm is subsidizing the project, and if there are some skeletons in the corporate closet the Mindlebergs would rather not have stressed, naturally I'm prepared to go along with them. But if you mean will I write that black is white and vice versa, the answer is no, and as a matter of fact, I resent the suggestion. What the hell is this all about anyhow?"

"Colonel Marius Mindleberg," Cheek replied heavily, and took another hefty swig from his can of beer. "The black sheep of the family, and Pierre Mindleberg's granduncle. Believe me, Saltire, I intended no offense, but I'm afraid Marius is going to be a problem. Theodore Roosevelt would stoop to anything to keep him buried, and—"

"Theodore Roosevelt? What in God's name has he—"

"I beg your pardon, I was forgetting. I should have said Theodore Roosevelt Mindleberg, Pierre's cousin. He's the tobacco Mindleberg from Greensboro. Unfortunately—" Cheek paused. "Unfortunately," he said again and paused again. "Look, would you mind terribly if I opened another can of beer?"

"By all means, do," I replied quickly, observing a certain agitation in the man's manner. "You may as well crack two, while you're at it. I have a feeling we're going to need them."

"As I was saying," J. Sydney resumed once his second beer was opened, "unfortunately, Theodore Roosevelt Mindleberg is a horse's ass. Everything, in fact, that Pierre is not. I've been Pierre's confidential assistant for the past twenty years, and in my considered opinion he's one of the most brilliant men I've ever known, but . . ." And yet once more did J. Sydney hesitate. I hung upon his lips. He furrowed his brow in search of a word.

"An oddball?" I suggested when the silence threatened to start echoing.

"I think it would be more accurate to say that he eschews the orthodox, or perhaps it might be better to . . ." And suddenly the mask dropped as J. Sydney turned the other Cheek and became just a plump little guy with a problem. "Oh, hell, Saltire, who am I trying to kid? You're right about the Old Man. You met Johnston, the chauffeur; well, all the household staff are Jamaicans, and you know why? Because the Old Man gets a quiet bang out of watching his guests' reactions, especially the Southerners'. They're expecting Old Black Joe and out comes Charles Laughton. Does that put you into the picture?" He stared at me beseechingly, and his glasses slipped down from his forehead onto his nose. "The truth is, my friend, that Pierre is having this whole goddamn book written as a kind of giant needle to slip into his cousin Teddy, the fat-assed son of a bitch."

I simply wasn't taking any of this in. The thought flickered briefly through the gray cells that J. Sydney had slipped his cable under the frightening pressures and responsibilities associated with his sensitive position within the Mindleberg empire, but my eyes proclaimed that, while much distressed, the man was still in possession of his faculties: no flecks of froth about the lips; not too much white showing in the eyeballs; no involuntary spasms of the facial musculature. What was clear was that here sat a man racked by strong emotions.

It was at this juncture that, her unpacking presumably accomplished and her makeup suitably refreshed, Brooke arrived on the scene looking cool and calm. I bade her be seated and started opening three fresh beers.

"But I don't want a beer at this hour," she protested.

"Take it," I told her firmly. "You'll need the strength." She looked uncomprehending, but not for long as, with considerably more detail than need burden this narrative of A Yankee Lad's Voyage Through Darkest Hell, J. Sydney put us, to employ his phrase, into the picture. It was a canvas in which Hieronymus Bosch might have taken a good deal of quiet pride.

I'll skip all that bit about the arrival of young Solomon Mindleberg, fresh from Leipzig by way of Baltimore, at the straggling village of Funderburk's Store, later to become Textilia, in the spring of 1849, staggering under his great peddler's pack; his decision to settle there, and his inception, a year or so later over a glass of Old Man Funderburk's Special Monongahela, of the idea of bringing the mill to the cotton rather than vice versa, and the subsequent vast success of this concept.

The Great Schism cracked open in 1913, when Solomon's younger grandson, Nathan, who had been placed in charge of the family's extensive corduroy works in Greensboro, finally bowed to his young wife's constant niggling and joined the Protestant Episcopal Church of St. Cyprian Martyr in that city. What, to the Textilia branch of the family, was almost as reprehensible was his decision to leave the business, having concluded, mistakenly as it turned out, that corduroy was a dead end, textilewise. He had then invested his savings in the purchase of the property and goodwill of the Tar Heel Chewing Tobacco & Snuff Company, which some years before had added a small sideline in cigarettes. Under his astute management, it had grown into the giant Carolina Cigarette Corporation and when, in 1936, he turned over its direction to his son, Theodore Roosevelt, Congressional, the Cigarette of Statesmen, was one of the top half-dozen brands in the nation. And between the two branches of the family had grown a rivalry no less intense for all that it was amicable. Happily for Textilia and Greensboro, it was expressed largely in philanthropy. When Theodore Roosevelt built Greensboro a library, Pierre had countered with a museum; when T. R. had endowed the Nathan Mindleberg Memorial Chair of History at the Women's College of the University of North Carolina,

Pierre had riposted with the Isaac Mindleberg Memorial Hospital in Textilia. And so it had gone.

"The thing is, T. R. is a stuffed shirt," J. Sydney Cheek concluded morosely, "and Pierre cannot abide stuffed shirts."

"I'm afraid I don't see what all this has to do with Bent's— I mean Mr. Saltire's book," Brooke said, as bemused as I was.

"It's simple. T. R. doesn't want the book written."

"But why not, for Pete's sake?" I asked.

"Because it will remind people of Colonel Marius Mindleberg."

"Will somebody please explain what this is all about?" Brooke said desperately. "Who is this Colonel Marius and what's he done?"

"God knows he had a lot of competition," J. Sydney Cheek spoke gravely, "but there is a sizable body of thought which holds that he was, if you'll excuse the expression, Miss Hastings, the greatest sonofabitch produced by the late Confederate States of America."

☞ *5* "WAR PROFITEER, cotton speculator, blockade-runner—that was Marius," J. Sydney took up the tale again. "Nobody's sure how he got the colonelcy—God knows he didn't get it fighting; probably another one of his deals. He was old Solomon's eldest son, and brilliant as they come; graduated from Harvard when he was only seventeen—they took 'em young in those days—and in less than a year he was practically running the old man's operations.

"Then the war came along. Marius was in his early twenties, and while this section of North Carolina wasn't wildly secessionist, it didn't sit too well when he went around saying the whole thing was sheer stupidity. It sat even worse when he flatly refused to join the army, and, according to family legend, he once got no fewer than six white feathers in one day's mail from various young ladies. After that, he started going to hell in a bucket; there were rumors of all sorts; he was trading with the enemy, he was selling shoddy cloth to the government, he was making a killing on cotton. Then he took to disappearing for weeks or months at a time. Some said he was up North, some said he was abroad, buying blockade-runners. Finally, old Solomon had to give in to public opinion. He announced that he was turning over the management of his mills to his younger son, Octavius—seems the old boy had a passion for Roman names—and that, so far as he was concerned, he never wanted to see his older boy again. He never did, and Marius never came back to Textilia. He went abroad and stayed there, living it up like a Russian grand duke on his ill-gotten gains until he died in the arms of his mistress, a prima ballerina of the Paris Opéra, in his villa at Nice, after a surfeit of oysters and champagne, at the ripe old age of forty-one."

"How marvelous!" Brooke breathed, her eyes aglow. "I can see Laurence Olivier in the part."

"The point is that you can't write a book about the Mindleberg Mills in the Civil War without hauling Marius in—that's what's bothering this Theodore Roosevelt Mindleberg?" I asked. Cheek nodded solemnly.

"You know," he said thoughtfully, "it's a funny thing, but in a lot of ways Pierre is something like Marius. Or so it seems to me. I must confess I've got a sneaking liking for the old bast— I beg your pardon, scoundrel. For instance, Pierre thinks this whole Civil War Centennial business is a lot of nonsense; what's the point of celebrating a war that never should have happened? But when T. R. announced that Carolina Cigarette was going to sponsor Greensboro's Civil War Centennial and make it the biggest and best in the state, Pierre wasn't about to sit still for it. That's when he got the idea for this book you're doing—a perfectly legitimate and worthy contribution to the centennial, and also a wonderful way to needle the living bejaysus out of Cousin Teddy."

It was at that precise moment I decided that this book was going to be fun, and that Pierre Mindleberg must be a kindred soul. Maybe my artistic sensibilities should have been offended, and perhaps I should have resented the use of my so-called creative abilities for no nobler purpose than the satisfaction of a textile tycoon's whim, but I don't think along those lines.

An odd, snuffling noise obtruded itself upon my musings, and I glanced up sharply to ascertain the source of this suppressed gurgling. It was Brooke Hastings. Giggling like a mad creature. Then J. Sydney Cheek's shoulders began to quiver and his small, pink face turned an alarming shade of crimson as he, too, succumbed to the contagion, making little chugging noises as his eyes filled and tears of joy trickled down the sides of his neat little nose.

"I've had some weird jobs in my day," I started to say, lost control, and lay back, honking like a hysterical duck.

Curiously enough, when I finally winded myself and sat alternately hooting and gasping for breath, I discovered that my hangover had vanished quite away.

I could not be aware of it, of course, but that was the last completely carefree laughter I was to enjoy for many a long month: the following day I discovered what have since come to be known as the Mindleberg Papers, the ciphered diaries containing the improbable record of Marius Mindleberg's peculiar contribution to the War of the Rebellion.

☞ *6* *JOKER* or no, Pierre Mindleberg hadn't spared the horses when it came to setting us up. Brooke and I were assigned a private office suite which would have rejoiced a senior vice-president in charge of denim, high up on the nineteenth floor of the Mindleberg Tower, the outer door to which bore the imposing legend, "Historical Project—Mr. N. B. Saltire." Additionally, J. Sydney Cheek had turned over to us the keys to one of the company's fleet of Ford sedans, and we were in business.

"I'll say this for the textile industry: they know how to live," Brooke exulted as she sampled the comfy leather armchair behind her desk in the only slightly smaller office adjoining mine. From the outer office which guarded our privacy came the bustling sounds made by a Miss Jermyn, a gray-haired, motherly type who had been temporarily assigned to us as secretary. She was, she told us proudly, the third generation of her family to work for the Mindlebergs, and was as well a member of the Golden Quarter Club by virtue of her twenty-five years of service to the corporation.

From my office window I could look down on Textilia's hub, Dancey Square, in the center of which and atop a granite and marble base a bronze Colonel Micah Dancey bestrode a bronze horse in an attitude which suggested almost total resignation to what the pigeons were doing to his three-cornered hat and epaulets: it was difficult to believe that this man had commanded the center against the British regulars at the Battle of Cowpens. Facing one another across the square stood Textilia's principal hotels, the Micah Dancey and the Cotton Queen. At a farther remove, out on the southern edge of the city, I could descry the sprawling complex of the Mindleberg Mills themselves, surrounded by what would have been called a mill village, I guess, except that in this instance it looked more like a model housing development. Beyond lay the rolling countryside.

Until we managed to get things sorted out, Brooke and I agreed that she should concentrate her initial efforts on the corporate files while I ascertained what materials were available to us from the archives of the Dancey County Historical Society. This decision achieved over a cup of coffee fetched by the admirable Miss Jermyn, we figured we had done enough for our first day on duty and decided to spend the rest of the afternoon exploring Textilia in our company Ford. "Get the feel of the place, that's what we'll be doing," I told Brooke.

The rest of the city confirmed my first impression of prosperity and general newness and cleanliness, and I confess to a certain degree of astonishment at the lack of what is usually termed Suth'n chawm.

"This is the New South," Brooke observed when I commented on the absence of pillared mansions and suchlike. "And bear in mind that there never was anything like a plantation aristocracy in this part of the state. They were all small farmers, Scotch-Irish mostly, and some Pennsylvania Dutchmen drifting South. Not po'h white trash, but not rich, by a long shot. Result, not enough slaves around to let the young gentlemen get lazy and foul-tempered and uppity. That's why this section never was terribly strong for the idea of secession."

"I didn't know you went in for sociology," I said. Brooke shrugged her handsome shoulders and grinned.

"You know how it is with us research people. Love them hard facts. You ever tried barbecue, Bent?"

"Not knowingly. Why?"

"Part of your education. That looks like a fairly decent place over there on the right. Pull on in and I'll introduce you to the stuff."

Following her bidding, I steered the car onto a large, macadam-surfaced parking lot, in the center of which stood an enormous jukebox fitted with a massive brick chimney, across the broad beam of which was painted "Fat John's Real Hickory-Smoked Southern Barbecue—A Treat To Eat That Can't Be Beat—Thick Shakes." From the flanks of this monstrosity sprang two soaring wings, beneath which, it must be supposed, customers could park their automobiles during inclement weather. As we drew to a stop, a blonde young woman garbed as a drum majorette detached herself from a similarly costumed companion at the long counter which ran along the front of the jukebox and strolled toward us dreamily. Her walk, clearly patterned after that affected by Miss Marilyn Monroe, can only be described as sensuous, and upon her near approach it was possible to suspect that her uniform would never have got past the mother's majorette committee of anybody's Parent-Teacher Association. At least its top half wouldn't, for, when she bent by my window to inquire our wants, I was seized by a momentary and fascinating fear that her exuberantly endowed bosom might burst from her bodice. And it occurred to me that she wouldn't have minded in the least had this untoward event taken place.

"Hut'chall lak?" she inquired, giving me a bold, knowing smile as I succeeded in ripping my gaze from her bulging mammaries.

"Two ribs and a couple of dopes," Brooke spoke up crisply in the native vernacular.

"Two riyubs enna coupla dopes? Raht. Gotcha." Our blonde bombshell turned away, took a few steps and then returned, her expression vaguely troubled. "Gahdamn," she said, bending to give me another blasting view of ripely swelling flesh, "Ah keep fuhgettin' t'ast. Y'all lak a li'l dip on yoh riyubs?" I stared, baffled by this query, but Brooke appeared to comprehend.

"Please," she said.

"Raht, honeh," our carhop replied, gave me another brazen grin and swayed back toward the service counter, rolling her generous buttocks in time with another drum.

"Wow," said I.

"Linthead," Brooke said succinctly, her lip curling.

"I beg pardon?"

"Linthead," Brooke repeated. "From one of the mill families. Figures anything is better than going into the mills, and I'm willing to bet she makes more after hours than she does working here."

"Why, Miss Hastings, I do declare," I feigned amazement. "Such a thing to say about a young lady like that, really!"

"I'll bet you money," Brooke replied stubbornly. "The way she waggled her bosom at you—and you leering like a goat."

"I was not either leering. And what was that bit about a little dip on our ribs?"

"Barbecue sauce," Brooke explained. "They call it dip. Some people don't care for it with spare ribs—too messy—so they always ask if you'd like a little dip on your ribs. Simple?"

"I wouldn't mind putting a little dip on her ribs," I said lewdly. Brooke snorted.

In an astonishingly short time our blonde returned, bearing a tray upon which were set out two cardboard plates and two Coca-Cola bottles, straws emerging from their necks. This she affixed dexterously to the window frame on my side, affording me yet another leisurely vision of the depths, and then returned once more to her post by the service counter.

Handing across Brooke's plate, I gazed without enthusiasm at the contents of my own. They looked like part of a nasty accident, surrounded by coleslaw and surmounted by two small brown cannonballs.

"You eat the ribs with your fingers, and there should be a couple of wooden forks or spoons on the tray for the slaw." There were. "These things on top are hush puppies," Brooke went on with my tutorial. She picked one up and unhesitatingly bit into it. "Ummm. Scrumptious," she said crumbily. "They can be as heavy as lead. But these are delicious."

Well, I'd eaten snails in France and we Saltires are nothing if not men of courage What the hell? And besides, the natives appeared to thrive on the stuff. I dived into the mess in my cardboard trough, and, do you know, it was absolutely marvelous. You can say what you like about the Southland, but when it comes to barbecue, those people know what they're doing, by God! And another thing: until that moment, I'd always considered myself a solid knife-and-fork man, on the theory that they work well and raise us a step above the beasts, but getting my fingers onto my sauce-slobbered spare ribs gave me a kind of primitive satisfaction. Within ten minutes, I too looked like an accident victim, such was the ebullience with which I attacked my food. And Coke, the *vin du pays* of Dixie, seemed the ideal beverage to accompany the orgy.

"Wonderful," I told Brooke. "In fact, terrific. Why don't they export the stuff?"

"It doesn't travel well. You mean to say you've never really eaten barbecue before this? Even the awful gook they serve up North?"

"Never."

"And you enjoyed it, really and truly?"

"Scout's honor, hope to die."

"I'm glad. For liking barbecue, I'll even forgive you for ogling our carhop's bustline."

To this I was strongly tempted to reply that I would much prefer to ogle her own, but dismissed the idea as less than tasteful in view of the beautiful meeting of minds we seem to have achieved.

"Next time, I'll introduce you to Brunswick stew," Brooke said after I'd paid the bill (keeping my eyes strictly to myself), heard Miss Embonpoint tell us y'all come on back, now, yuh heah, and we were driving back toward the Mindleberg Arms. "The South's answer to chile con carne."

I suggested that we get together for dinner that evening, but, to my disappointment, Brooke demurred, saying that she intended to get a good night's rest after our hectic journey aboard the Rebel Raider. She planned to be in bed by nine o'clock, come hell or high water.

"But first I'm going to try out my kitchenette," she said firmly. "And if I don't blow the place up, maybe I'll ask you to come by for a steak some evening."

"I'll bring the champagne."

"Of course, you could ask me out for tomorrow evening."

"Consider yourself asked."

"Consider yourself accepted."

It was just as well that we didn't go out that evening, since I spent most of it fighting down a really spectacular case of heartburn, the consequence of my frenzied encounter with Fat John and his dipped ribs. The discomfort, however, failed to diminish my admiration for its cause: you don't get something for nothing, as my mother was fond of telling me. Garlic gives me heartburn, too, but you don't give up spaghetti just because of a little heartburn, do you?

When I finally managed to extinguish the four-alarmer in my stomach and get to sleep, the carhop of the afternoon came and joined me, minus her uniform, and I was amazed and delighted by the extent and depravity of her imagination. Oddly enough, she had somehow succeeded in learning to talk with the voice and inflection of Sophia Loren—a phenomenon we had no time to explore during our wanton revels, which ended only when J. Sydney Cheek appeared to say that some men were on their way to lynch me, and that he knew of an escape route through the swamps. It took me the rest of the night to get through that damned swamp, or so it seemed. I don't know what became of the carhop.

7 ☞ THE HEADQUARTERS of the Dancey County Historical Society occupied one of the older buildings in Textilia, a Victorian monster which had been deeded to the society by its desperate owner sometime during the Great Depression, and tucked away in what had been the butler's pantry was the office of the society's secretary, Miss Lydia Younghusband Bowers. This I reached the following morning after a leisurely inspection of the society's collection of historic knickknackery, which was housed in the former parlor, library and dining room. In glass-fronted cabinets reposed a stiffly stuffed horde of birds and beasts native to the region, all staring furiously. Here was the walnut desk, presented by Mrs. Heber Faulconer in memory of her husband, upon which Jefferson Davis, passing through Textilia on his way to Richmond, had written a brief speech addressed to the citizens of the town. There, the uniform, much faded, worn by Captain Jonas Frey, commanding a company of the 19th North Carolina Volunteer Infantry, C.S.A. Under glass, too, was the original manuscript of "Southrons, Rise!" which, according to the card attached to it, had once been favorably considered as the North Carolina State Anthem. It was the work, I read, of Miss Amelia Stokes Davis, "The Poetess of the Piedmont, 1861–1923." Sated, I followed a directional sign toward the office of the secretary, and there discovered Miss Bowers, a wispy woman with the mad, lost look of a Tennessee Williams mother.

"Now where on earth did I put that bloody file?" she was asking feverishly of an even wispier, but younger, woman who was, I deduced expertly, her assistant, as I appeared at the door, gaping slightly at the unexpectedly coarse nature of her language.

"Are you looking for the Abraham Bloody or the Levi Bloody file, Miss Bowers?" the younger woman inquired anxiously. "We sent Abraham Bloody over to Raleigh last week, you remember."

"No, it's Levi I need. We have this letter from this woman in California and— Oh! Can I help you, please?" Miss Bowers asked, catching sight of me. "I'm afraid our genealogical files are in a state," she added apologetically. "Why the Bloodys settled here at least thirty years before the Revolution."

I made haste to introduce myself and to explain the purpose of my visit, and Miss Liddie ("Evrehboddeh heah en Textahlyah calls me Miss Liddie" is as much of her accent as I am going to trouble you with now or ever, for both our sakes) was immediately and almost overwhelmingly helpful. In a trice she had installed me in the society's reading room before the two giant, buckram-bound volumes of the Reverend Ian MacIndoe's definitive *History of Dancey County, North Carolina, With Gazetteer and Notes on Place Names,* published under the society's auspices and copyrighted in 1913. Piled by the side of these two tomes were other, lesser works, including, I noted, a monograph by John R. Ploughman entitled *A Survey of Positions Occupied by Battery C, 24th North Carolina Volunteer Artillery, C.S.A., During the Movement from Petersburg to Appomattox Court House."* That would be a big help.

"And here is my own little effort," Miss Liddie said archly, handing me a slim volume entitled, incomprehensibly, *The Saga of the Dorcas Flag.* "It's the history of the battle flag sewed by the Dorcas Ladies' Bible Circle of the First Presbyterian Church and presented to the Dancey County Light Infantry Guard, which later became part of the 19th North Carolina," she explained. "Why, Mr. Saltire, that flag was carried through every day of the war, every blessed one, and after the surrender it was saved, somehow, and brought back here to Textilia. It hangs today in our board room upstairs."

☆ *46* ☆

"I'll look forward to reading its story," I lied heartily.

"And now I'll just leave you alone to your work," Miss Liddie said, giving me one of her mad-eyed smiles as she lurched toward the door. I opened *The Saga of the Dorcas Flag* and read: "And so they brought that tattered banner home once more, home to their ravaged land, stained with the blood of Christian heroes, torn by the shell of the Northern foe . . ." and quickly shut it again. I got the picture.

The Reverend Mr. MacIndoe was something else again. No sparrow fell without old MacIndoe latching on to the fact and putting it down on paper, complete with the sparrow's vital statistics. "He must needs be beyond the persuasive powers of logic who would argue in contradiction of the statement that rarely has generous nature so bounteously and abundantly displayed her wares as she has in the tasty vista which is the valley of the Hixahattamoy River as it passes through the rolling farmlands of Dancey County to pursue its peaceful course eastward towards the rolling deeps of the mighty Atlantic" gives you some idea of the MacIndoe prose style. Clearly, the old boy had been paid so much a line, and damned if I didn't find myself becoming fascinated by his sheer, stunning verbosity. A man who can spin a sentence out to a dozen lines and say only that the first train into Textilia from anywhere arrived at 9:15 A.M. on July 10, 1855, has my unbounded admiration, speaking professionally.

I skipped all the chapters which took Dancey County out of the Ice Age and through the Revolution, and began reading in some earnest at the chapter headed, *"The Tocsin Sounds at Sumter and Dancey's Sons Spring to Arms: Organization of the Light Infantry Guard; Election of Captain Funderburk; Incident at Mr. Hugh's Farm & Arrest of Mr. Cargill; Swearing-in Ceremonies at County Court House & Speech by Col. Jennings."* I would, I decided, have to arrange to borrow MacIndoe's two volumes, otherwise I'd be spending the next ten years in the historical society's reading room. Indeed, it would be sound policy to borrow all of the books Miss Liddie had piled onto the desk before me. I headed once again for her office.

"Jesus Christ!" she was saying as I put in my second appearance at her door. "Where on earth will we find room to hang a picture of Jesus Christ?"

"Reverend Emspacher says the children of his Daily Vacation Bible School painted it all by hand," the wispy assistant said, holding her hand over the mouthpiece of her telephone. "He says it was their class project and they all voted to give it to us."

"Oh, dear. Well, tell him thanks very much and we'll be glad to have it," Miss Liddie commanded as I wondered when and how she would find herself fitting one or another of the four-letter Anglo-Saxon words into her conversation. She spied me in the doorway: "Why, Mr. Saltire, don't tell me you've finished all your reading already! My, my, but you certainly are a fast reader, and isn't that a fact?"

I told her of my wish to borrow MacIndoe & Co. for study at home, and she assented at once, asking whether I wished her to have Thomas, the janitor, deliver the books to my office. I said that I would be delighted to have Thomas perform this service and then, casually, inquired whether the society's files might possibly include some information about Colonel Marius Mindleberg. Miss Liddie stiffened, and the atmosphere chilled slightly.

"May I ask why you ask?"

To which I replied that my request was made at the behest of Mr. Pierre Mindleberg himself. "We-ll," Miss Liddie said doubtfully, "I suppose if Mr. Pierre said it was all right, it must be. As a matter of fact, we do have quite a collection of Mindleberg papers of one sort or another we keep stored in the attic. We simply haven't had the chance to catalog them, and, mind you, I'm not certain we have anything concerning Marius—" the Bowers lip curled in fair imitation of Brooke Hastings as she pronounced the name— "but you're more than welcome to look around. I suppose you've heard something about Colonel Mindleberg, as he called himself?"

"A little," I conceded. "He sounds like quite a character."

Miss Liddie sniffed. "That's as may be. Here in Textilia, he's not much thought of. Or talked about. Out of *loyalty* to the family, to speak truth. I'm surprised, I really am surprised that Mr. Pierre would want him dug up." In reply, I could only shrug by way of dismissing the responsibility for this grave robbery from my shoulders. "I'll call Thomas and have him show you the way to the attic," Miss Liddie added.

Summoned from the basement, Thomas shuffled slowly into view as the telephone rang again on the wispy assistant's desk, and, as I departed in Thomas's molasses-like wake, my soul leaped up and my heart rejoiced to hear Miss Bowers say that the society would be absolutely delighted to receive a piece of ash taken from the framework of the Wright brothers' second aeroplane.

The attic was every bit as hot and uncomfortable as I had expected it would be, and it was obvious that Thomas did not consider that his janitorial duties included the custody of this preserve of the glorious past, judging from the rich accumulation of dust which covered all. To add to my problems, a lonely wasp, living beyond his time, was loose somewhere up there under the beams and in a nasty frame of mind, if angry buzzings were to be deemed a reliable index of his feelings.

"Awlla deh Min'nulbuhg papehs oveh heah innuh cohnuh," Thomas advised, waving an arm sadly toward the darkest section of the attic. "Ain' much light, eithuh."

"That's perfectly all right," I declared, and as Thomas shambled off downstairs I made my way into the shadows where reposed a number of quite large wooden boxes, some smaller cardboard cartons and several stacks of those thick, reddish-brown fiberboard folders people use to store wills and deeds. I pawed aimlessly among these, feeling faintly as though I were rummaging through somebody's bedroom, reading the labels which had been stuck on them: "Papers Relating to the Purchase of the Hixahattamoy Knitting Co., 1914," "Newspaper Clippings Describing the Marriage of P. G. T. Mindleberg to Miss Elaine Judith Behrenstein, 1935," "Obituary Notices of Mrs. P. G. T. Mindleberg, 1950," and so on. I examined one of the wooden boxes, labeled "Business Papers of Octavius Mindleberg." Still no Marius. It was at this point that, moving swiftly to avoid a low-level attack by my fellow attic-dweller, the wasp, I knocked a pile of folders to the floor. They had been resting, I perceived, on a small, black tin trunk, to the lid of which was glued a square of yellowed paper. I bent to read it, but the light was too poor and the writing on the paper too faded for me to read. The cloud of dust raised by the collapse of the stack of folders having to some extent subsided, I succeeded in heaving the trunk to a more advantageous position beneath one of the oval dormer windows set into the mansard roof, through whose grimy pane a certain amount of light managed to filter. And there I was able to read the yellowed label: "Personal Papers of Col. Marius Mindleberg, Relating to His Service in the War of 1860–65."

I was struck by that "War of 1860–65." Not "The War for Southern Independence," not even "The Civil War." It could have been anybody's war. In any event, I'd discovered what I'd come to search for, for whatever it might be worth.

The trunk's lid was secured by a couple of simple clips, and, these dealt with, I opened it to discover that it was packed with bundles of letters, all neatly tied in lawyers' red tape. Opening one of the topmost layer of bundles, I saw that all the letters were addressed to Solomon Mindleberg, Esq. I tried a second bundle. Again, every letter in it was addressed to Solomon Mindleberg, and it struck me that whatever else he may have been, Marius was certainly a dutiful son. Presumably this correspondence would contain a great deal of information concerning the colonel's activities. Idly, I extracted one of the letters from its fragile envelope.

It was dated December 10, 1860, at Washington, D.C., and began conventionally enough with "My Dear Father." But after that, it was all gobbledygook, some sort of code or another. Which figured: I'd read somewhere that coded letters dealing with business affairs were fairly common practice during the Civil War period, and if Marius had been wheeling and dealing in the crinoline version of the black market, it was hardly surprising that he should have elected to describe his shenanigans in cipher. I sampled a few more letters from other bundles—all coded, and utterly meaningless to me.

And I realized that I was miserably hot and filthy with dust and that spending any more time poring over coded letters in that grubby attic was idiotic. It was probable that the code in which these letters were cast was in regular use by the Mindle-bergs for their private business correspondence, and it was equally probable, therefore, that a copy of the code, containing the key or whatever it was, would be available in the company's archives. J. Sydney Cheek could clear that problem up for me. No, the sensible thing to do would be to arrange with Miss Liddie to have the trunk delivered to my office, where I could work on its contents in comfort. Or, come to think of it, why should I saddle myself with the drudgery? Given the key, our Miss Jermyn could have at the letters and I could be going on with more important matters.

I was about to replace the letters and close the trunk when I spotted, partially concealed by a packet I hadn't removed, a large envelope, separate from the neatly tied bundles. On the off chance that this might contain the code and thus spare us a search of the company files, I pulled it out. Across the front was scrawled in large letters, "Private and Confidential." The flap was sealed shut by a blob of red sealing wax bearing the impression of what

I suppose must have been a signet ring. This, with the feeling of in for a penny, in for a Pound, I broke. It was, after all, in the line of duty.

A thin packet of letters fell out. I glanced at the first.

It was addressed to Col. Marius Mindleberg, C.S.A., in care of Spotswood's Hotel, Richmond, Virginia. I opened the envelope and read its contents:

Headquarters
Army of Northern Virginia
March 3, 1865

Dear Colonel Mindleberg:

The Commanding General has directed me to extend to you his warmest thanks and appreciation for the singular services rendered him by you during the course of the past several years, and to express his sincere regret that these services cannot, by their nature, receive the proper recognition and commendation they so richly merit. Suffice it to say that the Commanding General regards himself deeply indebted to you for your continuing efforts in his behalf. I have the honor to remain, sir,

Your obedient Servant
Chas. Marshall
Colonel, Adjutant.
C.S.A.

Now what the hell was all this about? The Commanding General, Army of Northern Virginia? That could only be Marse Robert, and, besides, hadn't I read somewhere that Lee's adjutant had been a chap named Marshall? And what were these "singular services"? I reread the letter with a growing sense of excitement. "Deeply indebted," eh? Was it possible that I had stumbled across an ancient scandal? Would the Mindleberg papers disclose that good old Robert E. had clay feet?

Hoo-eey, as they say in North Carolina.

Suppose it turned out that Robert E. had been playing the

cotton market on the side, or speculating in tobacco shares between campaigns. Brother! And it occurred to me that the man who uncovered the fact that R. E. Lee was really a secret war profiteer stood a very good chance of getting himself lynched by a screaming mob of Daughters of the Confederacy.

I opened a second letter, this one addressed to Col. M. Mindleberg, in care of Monkton's Hotel, Charleston, South Carolina:

> *Office of the Secretary of State*
> *Richmond, Virginia*
> *December 27, 1864*
>
> *My Dear Marius,*
> *It would be less than honorable in me to fail to tell you, in this necessarily unofficial and informal fashion, how greatly the many peculiar services you have performed at my behest have been appreciated. Never for a moment free of the hazard of exposure and disgrace, you nevertheless continued your operations in circumstances which would surely have appalled and dismayed one less coolly courageous and skilled than yourself. Would that it were possible to say these things to you openly, but we are both aware of the conditions which make this not only unwise but, in truth, potentially suicidal, should disaster befall us. Pray present my compliments to your esteemed father.*
> *Faithfully yours*
> *Judah P. Benjamin*

So-ho! Benjamin was in on the racket, too, was he? Using his inside knowledge and employing the nefarious Marius as his agent, no doubt, as he grew rich while the Confederacy bled to death. Small wonder old Judah had said it would be suicidal to disclose his true relations with Marius Mindleberg.

All that was lacking now was a guarded note from Jeff Davis. That turned up in the third envelope I opened.

☞ *8*　　"WHAT in God's name . . . ?" Brooke gargled as I heaved myself and my black tin trunk into my office, plonked the trunk onto my desk and collapsed, puffing powerfully, into my chair, where I began to shudder as the air conditioning bit like an arctic gale through my perspiration-soaked jacket and shirt. I hadn't seen myself in a mirror, but I could well understand the Hastings reaction; I must have looked pretty dreadful, my face smeared with dust and sweat, my collar wilted and filthy, my tie askew. I'd decided that my find was too important to entrust to the historical society's Thomas, and had determined to take it along with me. Considering that it contained nothing but paper, it seemed as heavy as lead, and while autumn may be crisp as a fresh apple in other parts of the country, in North Carolina it was doing a damned fine imitation of midsummer. Additionally, that bloody wasp had apparently decided that he had suffered all he could stand of the sight of me and, when both of my hands were engaged in holding the trunk, acted accordingly. I dropped the trunk, naturally, but by then it was too late to do anything but scream. In consequence, the back of my neck now felt as if it had been dealt with by a clumsy headsman. I hadn't been stung by a wasp since I was at summer camp in my thirteenth year, and I'd forgotten how savage the pain is. My agonized yelp had fetched Miss Liddie to the foot of the attic stairs, and it was only by dint of great firmness that I was able to persuade her not to dash out into the garden alongside the building to procure some nice fresh mud wherewith to make a poultice highly regarded by the local practitioners of folk medicine. What I wanted was a good, stiff drink and an ice pack.

Briefly, between spasmodic bursts of pain as the wasp sting got in its licks, I told Brooke of what I had found and what I had reason to suspect.

"Holy cow," she murmured, awed, as the possible ramifications and repercussions of the Mindleberg papers revealed themselves to her. "There's bound to be some other explanation, Bent."

"Granted we won't know anything definite until we can figure out the code, and even then we may not learn much—maybe Marius didn't tell his daddy everything. Or maybe there's nothing to it at all, but you've got to admit that it sounds slightly fishy." I hauled myself to my feet. "Look, would you give Syd Cheek a call and find out if he's ever heard of or knows anything at all about a private Mindleberg business code. I'm going to the gents' room and get some cold water on my neck."

"You could use some on your face, too," Brooke called as I left. Miss Jermyn clucked sympathetically as I passed through the outer office.

Only slightly refreshed and cleansed by my hasty ablutions, I returned to learn that Sydney Cheek had never heard tell of a private family code and, what was more, was disinclined to believe that one had ever existed. Old Solomon Mindleberg, he'd told Brooke, had been a fanatic about doing business openly and aboveboard, in line with his severely orthodox Jewish upbringing, and a code, with its implications of secret dealings, would have been entirely out of character for the old boy, Cheek explained.

"Nevertheless, he's going to check into it, just in case," Brooke told me. "He says he'll ask Pierre Mindleberg, too."

"The great man is in town, then?"

"Must be."

"Did you tell Cheek why you were asking about a code?"

"Why, yes. Shouldn't I?"

"No reason. But I'm wondering whether Pierre's going to be so enthusiastic about getting his Uncle Marius into print if it develops that the old boy corrupted most of the Confederate pantheon."

"Of course, you wouldn't have to decode those letters. Assuming you can, that is," Brooke said thoughtfully. "Just let sleeping profiteers lie, so to speak."

"You have a thought there. But what about my integrity, pray tell? How could I face myself in my shaving mirror if I compromise my honor? Who steals my purse, steals trash, who steals my name, et cetera."

"You know, I think you're really looking forward to pulling poor old Robert E. Lee down off his pedestal, Bentley Saltire."

"Carpetbagger Saltire to you, if you please. And it's Black Market Bob, if you don't mind."

"Yankee dog. And by the way, are you still taking me to dinner this evening."

"Ah showleh ayem, mayum, effen Ah lives."

"Well, don't forget to pick up a bottle to take along. And I won't tell a soul if you knock off now and go home and rest your poor tired brain. I like my escorts to be full of beans, and you look half dead."

Accepting this kindly suggestion with unseemly alacrity, I left the tin trunk on my desk and made my way streetward with the object of purchasing a bottle of spirits to take along to dinner. Such is the iron determination and dogged persistence with which the virtuous enforce their will upon the sinful in North Carolina that the service of any beverage having a greater alcoholic content than beer and light wines is prohibited in public eating establishments. By a curious oversight, however, the Baptist brethren somehow failed to ram through a law which prohibits the drinking of ardent waters in same. The solution is to take your own bottle with you, and it is usually advisable to do so, as I can say with some assurance after having thoroughly sampled the standards of the cuisine in the area. (Excepting barbecue, that is.) Greece has much to answer for. Thus it was that I turned my footsteps down East Dancey Street toward the nearest municipally owned spirits dispensary, which occupied what had formerly been an automobile showroom. The interior of this place was painted a shade of men's-room green, and it was bleakly lighted by a number of fluorescent fixtures dependent from the ceiling. The walls were gay with posters denouncing alcohol: "Liquor Kills More People Every Year Than Died During The Bubonic Plague," for example. The clerical staff, civil servants to a man, went slowly and sadly about the business of killing their fellow townsmen.

"I'd like a fifth of Cutty Sark, please," I said pleasantly to the thinly disguised missionary who oozed morosely out from between the shelves to attend my needs. He gazed at me for some seconds, his great, lantern jaw crushing and recrushing what I sincerely trust was a wad of chewing gum. Then, silently, he pointed a hair-tufted forefinger at a large printed notice taped to the back of the cash register on the counter before me. "North Carolina State Law forbids the sale of intoxicating liquors to minors, the mentally ill and known alcoholics. By order of the Textilia City Council."

"I beg your pardon?" I asked. "I mean, you don't think I'm under twenty-one, by any chance?"

"Yew look pretteh rough to be buyin' whiskeh, frien'," Lantern-jaw observed equably. "Howdah Ah know yew sobeh?"

"Well, now, goddammit," I protested, outraged. "Of course I'm sober. I've been working with some old files all day and so I'm dusty. Is there any law in this town against being dusty, for God's sake?"

"Takin' the name of th' Lawd in vain ain' gonna prove enneh-thin', frien'. Jus' wannid make sure yew wasn' no alcoholic, thass'all. No offense meant. Now, what kine whiskeh yew say yew wannid?"

"Cutty Sark," I repeated, holding my temper well in hand.

"Cutteh Sahk? Whut'ud thet be, then? Thet a buhbuhn, mebbeh?"

"No. It's a Scotch. A Scotch whiskey."

"Cutteh Sahk?" Lantern-jaw absorbed this information solemnly and then turned around to face back toward the shelves. "Hey, Udell! Y'eveh heah a Scawtch whiskeh name uh Cutteh Sahk?"

"Whut name was thet?" came a hollow voice from somewhere deep among the bottles.

"Cutteh SAHK!" Lantern-jaw bawled hoarsely.

"Thet a Scawtch whiskey?"

"Thet's whut Ah jus' finish tellin' yew."

"An' it's called Cutteh Sahk, yew say."

"Tha'ss ri'."

"Neveh huhd of it."

Lantern-jaw returned his attentions to me. "Udell does the orderin'," he explained. "We ain' got enneh."

Dipping dangerously deep into my last reserves of patience and sanity, I said that in view of the situation I would be content to substitute—I was about to name another favorite of mine, Justerini & Brooks, when I realized that this way lay madness, and, catching the words at my lips, said "Teacher's," instead.

"Fi'th uh Teachuh," Lantern-jaw repeated my order and then shambled off among the shelves in search of my bottle, muttering to himself. It was at this juncture that the door of the store burst open to admit the entrance of a bearded prophet.

"Jesus saves!" he yelled, catching sight of me. His eyes blazed with maniacal fires. "Yes, Lawd, Ah axesepp the Lawd Jesus as mah puhsonal saveyuh." There seemed to be no suitable reply to this except, perhaps, "Bully for you," which, in the circumstances, seemed somehow less than appropriate.

"Sinnuh," the prophet howled, advancing upon me and producing from beneath his arm an enormous Bible in such a manner that I thought momentarily that he intended hurling it at my head, "repent! Go, an' sin no moweh! Put asahd temtayshun! Tuhn yoh back on Sayten, frien', and axesepp the Lawd Jesus befoh it's too late. Get down on yoh knees with me raht heah and now, frien', and lets us pray togetheh foh yoh salvayshun." With which the madman sank to his knees, threw back his head and began to pray in a loud, rapid fashion which, had I been in a position of heavenly authority, I would have found annoying. I gazed down at him in some confusion and embarrassment, being relatively unfamiliar with the sensation of being prayed for in public.

Just as I thought I detected flecks of foam forming on the outer fringes of the madman's moustaches, Lantern-jaw reappeared and, hearing the sound of these fundamentalist orisons, leaned over his counter to discover their source.

"Hey," he said rudely, disregarding the sacred nature of the monologue. "Hey! Brotheh Foleh! Gawddammit, how often Ah have to tell yew yew cain't come on in heah and pray oveh people?"

Brother Foley ignored the interruption; indeed, seemed to see it a challenge to his vocal powers and his Christian duty. He began to roar, and I could see that several passersby on the street outside had paused to ascertain what the hell was up.

"OH LAWD JEEZUS CHRASS HELP MUH!" Brother Foley thundered. "HELP MUH, AH PRAY. HELP MUH SAVE THIS MIZZUBLE SINNUH FROM THE TEMPTAYSHUNS UV THE FLAYUSH! HELP MUH DELIVEH HEM FUM FAWNICAYSHUN AND DRUNKENNESS AN' FUM ALL THE DEEVAHCES UV SAYTUN, AH PRAY!"

The passersby who had paused were now gathered at the door of the store, staring not at Brother Foley, whose outbursts were probably familiar to them, but at the object of his ministry, me.

"Give 'im hell, Brotheh Foleh!" shouted one.

☆ 59 ☆

"Hoo-eey!" hooted another. "Lissen 'im go, willya!"

"CAST OUT THUH SCAWLUT WOMUN!" Brother Foley hollered, gaining power as he warmed to his task.

"GAWDDAMMIT, SHUT TO HAYULL UP, FOLEH!" Lantern-jaw yelled as a man who I assume to have been Udell arrived from the rear of the store.

"GET THAT CRAZEH SON OF A BITCH OUTTA HEAH!" Udell yelled, even louder than Lantern-jaw. "CALL THE GAWDDAMN COPS!"

As suddenly as he had begun, Brother Foley quit. He arose from his knees, tucked his Bible back under his arm and stared with majestic wrath at Udell. "Yew allwes wuz a loudmouth li'l bastehd, Udell Funkle," he observed coldly, and strode out, brushing masterfully through the small but delighted throng at the door.

"Heah's yoh Teachuh's, frien'," Lantern-jaw said amiably as the crowd at the door dispersed. I accepted the bottle with trembling hands and paid him. "Ain' he sumpin', thet Foleh?" Lantern-jaw inquired proudly. "Crazy as a gawddamn bedbug, an' tha'ssa fack."

I forebore to remind Lantern-jaw of his previous injunction against the speaking of the Lord's name in vain, and fled. Halfway down the block I saw Brother Foley stomping along with the straight back of a man who has done a great day's work in the vineyard.

Shaken, I arrived back in my apartment and poured myself a belt fit for a race of giants. I needed it.

9   *SHOWERED* and considerably restored by my therapeutic noggin, I was arraying myself in fresh linens preparatory to picking Brooke up for our dinner date when my telephone rang.

"Mr. Saltire?" a baritone voice inquired courteously when I answered. "Pierre Mindleberg here. Sorry I wasn't on hand to meet you and Miss Hastings when you arrived in town. I was just wondering whether you might care to come by for cocktails in, oh, say about an hour."

Damn!

"I'd be delighted," I replied immediately and spinelessly.

"I asked Syd Cheek to see if Miss Hastings could join us, but it seems she had a previous engagement, so we'll have to bring her along another time. Now as to yourself, are you driving or shall I send a car for you."

"Thanks to you, I'll be driving."

"That's right. Slipped my mind. You know where we are?"

"I'm sure I'll be able to find it."

"Just continue on out Beauregard Road and through the brick gateposts. You can't miss it."

I'll just bet I can't, I thought. "Right, sir. In about an hour, then."

"Fine. Look forward to meeting you, Saltire."

Which put paid to my plans for an evening with Brooke, and left me with the not entirely cheery prospect of telephoning her and explaining that dinner was off. On the other hand, she would surely understand that a man in my position cannot lightly decline to be present for a command performance, and certainly

Pierre Mindleberg was entitled to know what manner of fellow he had retained to compile his history book.

Nor did Brooke let me down. Intelligent girl that she was, she understood the situation at once and without a lot of hoo-hah. "Are you going to tell him anything about the letters?" she asked.

"I don't see any reason not to. After all, he's got to find out sometime."

"Suppose he tells you to forget all about them."

"Somehow, I don't think he will. But if he does, I don't see that we have much choice. It's his money, you know."

"Where's all that journalistic integrity you were talking about, Bentley Saltire?" The Hastings tone was crisp.

"Okay, okay. Let's not rub it in. About all I can do is play it by ear, and, like I say, I have an idea that Big Daddy will tell me to go right ahead and let the chips fall where they may.

"Now look, let's not be worrying about bridges we haven't burned yet, and get to the more important matter which is, how about we make it for dinner tomorrow evening?"

"Sorry—can't make it tomorrow. Maybe later this week."

"Oh. Anybody I know?"

"I doubt it."

"I don't suppose you'd care to—"

"You'll be late for your cocktail, and I've got the bath water running. 'Bye, Bent." And so saying, my research assistant gently rang off, leaving me holding the telephone to my ear. I said "Good-bye" automatically, and hung the phone back in its cradle in a manner that can only be described as thoughtful. We'd been in Textilia barely two days and already Brooke had a date for dinner with one of the locals, which, while hardly surprising in view of the girl's piquant charm, good looks, etc., indicated the presence of an alert and aggressive competition lurking some-where about. Yet who was I to object? I had no strings on Brooke.

Still and all . . .

I mean, you would have thought that at least she . . .

☆ 62 ☆

The hell with it, I told myself firmly; this is no time to be brooding and nibbling the nails. The wits must be sharp, the repartee bright, the conversation informed during my tête-à-tête with Pierre Mindleberg. I found myself wishing to God I knew something about the textile industry so that I could speak knowledgeably of such things as import restrictions, cotton futures and the Japanese labor market. And I would do well to be on my guard, in the presence of this spinning tycoon, lest I sound too writerish: straightforward, manly and honest as the day is long, that was the ticket for N. B. Saltire.

Neatly and unobtrusively attired in my best and darkest olive-gray suit and wearing a foulard cravat of impeccable discretion, I descended to the company Ford and prepared to keep my rendezvous with the Master of Mindlebergia. Beauregard Road, I recalled from the drive Brooke and I had taken the day before, was a broad, tree-shaded boulevard that swept grandly off North Elm Street, and it was out this latter thoroughfare that I drove, past the carefully kept campus of the Dancey College for Women, with its collection of authentic Victorian and fake Georgian brick buildings, past the North Carolina State Historical Marker noting the birthplace of the Reverend Alpheus Turnbull, "composer of many of the best-known hymns of the modern Methodist Church," past the massive stone bulk of the First Baptist Church, with its even more massive educational building and gymnasium attached, and finally into the older residential section of North Elm, already showing the first signs of genteel decay in the form of one or two "Tourist Lodging" signs tucked among the shrubbery.

Beauregard Road, however, was clearly Textilia's finest residential area, and I wondered where in the city there were so many plush jobs to provide the wherewithal for so many splendid homes. Then I remembered the city's eminence as an insurance center and furniture manufactory.

Sure enough, Beauregard Road dead-ended at two large brick gateposts supporting a pair of elaborately curlicued wrought-iron gates in a permanently opened position. Appropriately enough, atop each gatepost was a stone head of Janus, the double-faced Roman god of doorways. In the right-hand gatepost was set a small marble plaque into which was carved the name "January Hill." It would be interesting, I pondered as I headed the Ford up the macadam driveway, to know how the place acquired its wintry title.

The house itself, which I reached after what seemed like a half-mile drive, came as something of a surprise. For no particular reason, I'd been expecting to find either a moonlight-and-magnolia-style Southern mansion or something vast and ultra-modern in the Miami Beach fashion. Instead, it was vast and rambling, a turn-of-the-century country house designed by an architect who had got a couple of periods and styles happily confused in his mind. There were bits of half-timbering here and there, a great many shingled gables and dormer windows and fancy-Dan chimneys, a kind of tower, and a porte cochere atop which was perched a solarium or conservatory. It looked as Southern as New England clam chowder, but it looked comfortable and relaxed in its setting of magnificent old trees.

I drove under the porte cochere and on behind the mansion into a large parking area before what had once been a two-story carriage house and was now doing duty as a garage. I parked and walked back to the door beneath the porte cochere.

As advertised by Sydney Cheek, the white-jacketed Negro houseman who answered my knock spoke with a British accent. I followed him down a broad, brick-floored, oak-beamed hallway toward the library where, the houseman had explained, Mr. Mindleberg awaited my arrival. After a few minutes we came to a pair of tall, open double doors, and my guide said, "Mr. Saltire, sir," and there I was, in the presence.

Like his house, Pierre Mindleberg, too, wasn't what I'd been expecting. I'm as susceptible to clichés as the next man, and when I think of tycoons, I think of large, paunchy types smoking expensive cigars and wearing vests with the letters, "G.O.P." printed on them. Or Bernard Baruch, say. Not Pierre Mindleberg. If I'd been a Hollywood casting director lining up characters for one of Mr. C. B. De Mille's Biblical epics, Pierre would have been a natural for the role of one of the fiercer Hebrew captains. For that matter, he could have played Cochise, chief of the Apaches. He was of medium height, tanned and very trim, with iron-gray hair cut *en brosse*, surmounting a tall forehead beneath which was the visage of a hawk, albeit a hawk inclined to the tolerant view, prone to give the odd rabbit the sporting chance. He was wearing a brown tweed jacket and gray flannel trousers, both of mature years, which pleased me for some obscure reason.

He came forward, hand outstretched, and we gave each other the firm grip requisite in such situations, after which he motioned me to one of the deep, comfortable armchairs grouped informally before a fireplace capable of roasting a steer. A silver tray bearing an assortment of bottles, a silver ice bucket, a soda siphon, various tools and several glasses reposed on the marble-topped coffee table set in the middle of the semicircle of chairs.

"What's your pleasure?" Pierre asked, to which I replied that I would enjoy a bourbon and soda. I observed that the bottle he selected from the tray bore a simple white label. Mindleberg caught my glance and grinned. "Thanks to my father's foresight, we're drinking bourbon that's almost as old as I am," he said, offering me my glass. "He laid in God knows how many barrels of the stuff when it appeared definite that Prohibition was coming in, and we draw off a few bottles every so often when company's coming. See what you think of it."

I took a sip of my drink. It was magnificent.

"I feel like a criminal, asking you to add soda to this," I said. "This should be sipped like brandy."

"Glad you like it. Mind you, I'm selfish about it. Wouldn't dream of serving it to a woman. Women don't know how to appreciate good whiskey, I'm afraid."

"What's this about women not liking good whiskey?" asked a low, female voice from behind us, and I rose and turned toward the door. The voice's owner, whoever she was, was something to behold. I mean to say, this girl was terrific, in that smoldering Semitic fashion that always reminds me of the young Elizabeth Taylor—banked fires, or something, ready to leap into an inferno, I think the simile goes. Her eyes were fantastic, although that doesn't seem to be the adjective I'm groping for; very large and black and glowing. Now I know what they mean when they say that somebody is transfixed by a gaze. Wow!

"Join us, Hetty," Pierre invited. "My cousin, Henrietta Mindleberg. This is Mr. Saltire, who's going to do our book for us, Het," he went on as the girl came into the room. "I ought to warn you, Saltire, that Henrietta has come over from Greensboro for the dubious purpose of trying to con her cousin out of his pet project. She is a woman of infinite guile, and I caution you to be on your guard at all times in her presense. Or out of it, for that matter," he added amiably.

Henrietta, who was wearing a very simple—who am I kidding? It was probably something Dior ran up for her—afternoon dress, offered me a small, cool hand and then eased herself into an adjoining armchair with all the silky grace of a contented cat and gazed at me with frank, and disturbing, interest. She would be, I reasoned, the daughter of Theodore Roosevelt Mindleberg, the tobacco magnate.

"It looks like my Cousin Pierre is con-proof," she said, smiling.

"One hundred percent," Pierre agreed. "What will you have?"

"You could salve my disappointment with some of that antique bourbon of yours."

"It's against my better judgment, but for you I just might make an exception." Pierre mixed her a highball and handed it across the coffee table to her. Then he addressed himself to me. "Well, now, how does the project look to you after your first couple of days down here?"

"Extremely interesting, as a matter of fact. It's not impossible that we might have a book of more than purely local interest on our hands," I said, taking the bull firmly by the horns. Pierre looked at me quizzically.

"Oh? How's that?"

I glanced at Henrietta, whose expression was what you might call wary. "Well," I said, hesitating for a second, "it's still too early to say, you understand, but we've stumbled across some papers at the historical society which might, and mind you I'm only saying might, involve a lot more than the activities of the Mindleberg Mills during the Civil War. Other people, that is."

"Such as?" Henrietta inquired, her tone indicating that she really couldn't care less. Pierre nodded imperceptibly.

"Lee, Jefferson Davis, Judah P. Benjamin. There may be others."

"You say, 'may be.' I've lost you," Pierre put in.

So, as briefly as I could, I told him about the coded letters and the uncoded letters and the obscure, slightly sinister-sounding messages of gratitude these latter contained. By the time I'd finished, Pierre was, to my intense gratification, grinning wickedly.

"Wonderful, Saltire. Simply wonderful. Good old Uncle Marius," he declared happily. He became abruptly serious: "Do you think you're going to be able to decode them or shall we call in an expert to have a look?"

"I'd like to have a go at them myself first. Then, if I run up against a stone wall, I'll yell for help."

"Of course, if it turns out that the old scoundrel really was corrupting the hell out of the Confederacy's tin gods, we may have to exercise a certain amount of discretion," Pierre mused, lighting a cigarette and regarding the tip of it without seeing it. He chuckled briefly. "My God, Saltire, we'll have every ancestor worshiper in the South gunning for us."

"And it would serve you both right," Henrietta said pertly. "If you asked me, I'd say the best thing to do with those letters or whatever they are is take them out and burn them."

"But nobody's asking you, my pet," Pierre answered her

equably. He reached for my now empty glass. "Refill, Saltire?"

"Please." I turned to Miss Mindleberg. "You wouldn't actually destroy something that could have real historical value, would you?"

"What's so historically valuable about character assassination? And besides, what possible difference does it make now, after all this time. Who cares?" she demanded in reply.

"I care, to name only one," Pierre said. "You've probably never given it a thought, my pet, in all your spoiled young life, but the Southern myth, the Southern cavalier fighting for the honor of Southern womanhood against hopeless odds, all that eyewash, all that nonsense has done more harm to the South than the war ever did. It might be a very salutary development if it turned out that some of the plumed knights were human after all, and maybe we could quit sobbing over the past and join up with the rest of the twentieth century. End of speech." He handed me my glass.

No question about it: I was going to enjoy working for Pierre Mindleberg.

"It will certainly add a lot of luster to the family name, and that's for sure," Henrietta said grimly.

"Family name, forsooth!" Pierre shot back. "You could always change it to Mindlemount. Like the Battenbergs. And bear in mind, young woman, that your family name was probably invented by some underpaid, overworked German tax clerk."

"Very funny-ha-hah," Henrietta riposted, showing, I felt, a certain lack of imagination in the repartee department. I decided my best course lay in keeping well out of the family debate and applied myself to that superlative bourbon, which was absolutely the finest I've ever taken aboard. But after a few more genial jeers at one another, Pierre hauled me back into the conversation which became, as they say, general. Yes, I liked Textilia, and no, Henrietta thought Textilia was too "newish," and much preferred the older towns of tidewater North Carolina which, she declared, were "Williamsburgy" without being too damned quaint for words. During the course of these exchanges, we had another round of drinks, and then Pierre heaved himself to his feet.

"I'd like nothing better than to go on shooting the breeze with you two young people," he said, "but the fact is I've got some people from the New York office flying down this evening, and I'm stuck for dinner and business talk, which I assure you will be dull as dishwater. Why don't the two of you run on out to the club for dinner. It's just possible that I may be able to join you later on, but I doubt it. What do you say?"

Henrietta gave me a glance which said plainly that while it wasn't precisely her idea of the bonniest way to spend an evening, it would have to do until something better came along, while I tried to look enchanted at the prospect of spending the next few hours on the *qui vive* lest she attempt to seduce me from the path of duty.

"Now, dammit, Het, you drive carefully, you hear?" Pierre said sternly as we rose to take our departure. "Or at least keep that damned thing at treetop level."

"I promise, Cousin P. And besides, it would never do to scare the wits out of Mr. Saltire. Or on second thought, maybe it would." The tone of Miss Mindleberg's voice was crisp, and it struck me that there were, perhaps, better conditions in which to establish an acquaintance than those in which I found myself. In all fairness, a girl cannot be blamed too harshly for taking a dim view of a man who stands ready to make her family name a hissing and a byword. And for pay, at that.

☞ *10*   *THE CAUSE* of Pierre Mindleberg's ad-
monitions to his cousin revealed itself as
Henrietta led me into the carriage house
astern of the mansion, having declined, rather offhandedly I felt,
my offer of transport in my company Ford. Crouched like a
black panther alongside the stately Rolls which had met Brooke
and me at the station was a hard-topped foreign sports car, what
I believe is called a *gran tourismo*, of a marque unknown to me,
all soaring fenders and wire wheels. My chauffeuse waved me to
the far side of this gleaming artifact, and, with no more difficulty
than is encountered normally by the average submariner going
to action stations, I managed to insert myself into its leather-
smelling depths, while she, for her part, performed what I had
hitherto deemed an impossibility, i.e., the graceful entrance by a
female into a sports car. There was a brief slither, and there she
was. A small plaque on the dash-board informed me that the
car was a Lancia.

The touch of a dainty foot upon the starter produced a subdued
thunder from beneath the vast length of hood, the flick of a dainty
finger produced light, and we were off, in reverse briefly and
then, with a mighty surge, forward. Miss Mindleberg drove expertly, slipping deftly up and down through the various gears,
and contemptuously ignoring the blowzy challenge of an enormous Lincoln convertible which drew alongside, its driver leering
and gunning its engine furiously, when we stopped at a traffic
signal.

"Jerk," observed Henrietta tautly as the giant Lincoln screeched ahead when the light turned green. Otherwise, we spoke little during the drive to the Mindleberg Hills Country Club, which was only a few miles distant and which appeared to have been designed along the general lines of the White House. As we eased into the club's parking lot, I was again reminded of Textilia's abundant wealth by the many other foreign sports cars scattered about; not the little fellows, either, but the big jobs, including a couple of Bentleys. Probably only the underprivileged drove Cadillacs.

Despite the number of cars on the parking lot, the club's cocktail lounge was almost empty when we walked in.

"Everybody's down on the garden terrace," Henrietta explained. "It's always too noisy and crowded. I like this room much better." We picked out a couple of comfortable-looking armchairs, and a Negro waiter drew nigh. "I'm not sure what there is in Mr. Mindleberg's locker," she told the waiter, "but if there's any of that special bourbon of his, we'll have two. With soda." Grinning, the waiter withdrew.

"You could get yourself into trouble," I said. Henrietta gave me the first friendly smile of our acquaintance.

"Pierre's bark is worse than his bite. And you won't run and tell, will you?"

"I'm the soul of discretion. And to be honest about it, I wouldn't object to another sample of the stuff myself. It's pretty fabulous bourbon."

"Bracing yourself against my womanly wiles, is that it?"

"That's the last thing I'd brace myself against," I replied gallantly.

"Why, Mistuh Saltyuh, suh, Ah sweah yew do say the pretties' thin's," mocked Miss Mindleberg, as our waiter silently reappeared, still grinning, with our drinks.

"Tha'ss th' McCoy, Miss Minnelbuhg," he reassured my hostess, and took off again.

"Luck," said Henrietta raising her glass to me. "And by the

way, what do people call you when they get past the 'Mister' phase?"

"Luck," I toasted in turn, and went into my Nick the Gambler routine. Like Brooke, Hetty, as she suggested I call her, agreed that "Bent," while no prize as a nickname, had a less sinister ring than "Nick." "Although, mind you, I have a passion for silent sinister men," she declared. "George Saunders makes me go all giddy, and Robert Mitchum—I could swoon." She looked at me appraisingly for some seconds and then shook her head with a pretty toss of raven locks. "Your trouble is, you look honest. I'd say you were more the Joseph Cotten type, steady, dependable, and so on."

"The real truth is that I'm actually the by-blow of the late German Kaiser. Mother would never say much, of course, but somehow, I knew.

"You poor thing. It must be hell."

"It hasn't been easy, God knows."

We kept up this species of badinage for the duration of our first drink, but, when the waiter fetched us a second, Henrietta grew serious after her first sip, and I went to Condition Yellow: enemy attack imminent, stand by to repel boarders.

"You know," she said gravely, "no matter how much Pierre makes a joke of it, I really am concerned about this thing he has about digging up the past. And as for my parents—it's driving them up the wall." I shifted uneasily in my chair and looked sternly into the depths of my drink. "I wish there was something we could do." I twitched invisibly at that "we."

"But look," I said, all sweet reasonableness, "as Pierre himself said, if we *do* find anything questionable, we'll certainly play it very carefully and with plenty of discretion. And don't forget, these letters may turn out to be nothing at all; in fact, we may not even be able to decode them."

"One, you don't know what constitutes Pierre's idea of discretion. Two, I'd be willing to bet my last dollar those letters will be hot stuff, and three, once Pierre Mindleberg gets his teeth into something, they stay in. He'll get those letters decoded or whatever it is if it's the last thing he ever does. His curiosity is aroused, and once that happens, we're done."

Another inner wince at the second "we." I sat silently for some moments, no reply of an appropriate nature springing readily to mind. Henrietta now took her turn at staring into the bottom of a highball, her smoky eyes troubled. She stubbed her cigarette out in the heavy ashtray which was the principal adornment on the coffee table before our chairs, and accepted another from the pack I immediately proffered.

"I suppose what it really comes down to is my father's being half-Jewish," she said, exhaling a long burst of tobacco smoke, her tone musing. "My grandmother conned *his* father into the Episcopal Church, as I imagine you've heard by now, and I think that sometimes, deep down, he feels guilty about that in a mixed-up sort of way, as though he were somehow faking it on both sides of the fence." I nodded sympathetically. "I mean," she went on, "he's aware that a lot of Christians don't think he's for real, and also that a lot of Jews resent a Christianized Mindleberg. And now Pierre comes along with this scheme to resurrect old Marius Mindleberg, and my father thinks that all over the state the Christians will be saying, 'See? I told you so. It was all the fault of those damned kikes,' and the Jews will be asking, 'Why bring that up, for God's sake?' Am I making sense?"

"I see what you're driving at, but I don't see it happening that way," I told her, feeling slightly dishonest, because she was probably one hundred percent correct in her estimate. "Have you tried this argument on your Cousin Pierre?"

Henrietta nodded grimly. "Let's just say it didn't work. He thinks my father's being stuffy, and maybe he is, at that. And I'm sorry if I sound awash with self-pity. I'm supposed to be exercising my wiles, not discussing the Jewish problem. Let's forget all about Marius, and you tell me what you've written."

"Well," I began, not without a certain amount of relief at this change of subject, "most of it's nothing to brag about . . ."

We left the country club sometime shortly before midnight after a leisurely, and to my pleased astonishment, beautifully prepared and served dinner, and what was my delight when Hetty asked me if I'd care to try my hand at the controls of her car, which, she said, she had picked up in Italy the year before.

"Don't just drive back to the house," she commanded. "You can't get the feel of it in that short a distance. Let's take a run out the Winston-Salem road." For the second time that evening she accomplished the impossible without so much as twisting her skirt, and then, before I started the engine, she led me through the gears and pointed out which buttons did what.

After only one or two false moves on my part, we were off, tooling smoothly down the club's long drive and onto the highway which led to Winston-Salem, some thirty miles distant. In time I sorted out the various dials on the dashboard and found the speedometer, having in mind the zeal of the State Highway Patrol. I'd never driven a car of such power and luxury before, and, looking down the long hood at the white strip of road unrolling before us, I wondered what it must be like to own enough loot to be able to stroll into a showroom and buy such a spectacular plaything, just like that.

And yet, Henrietta Mindleberg did not act, I felt, like a spoiled and immensely wealthy young woman—not, God knows, that I was well acquainted with the breed. Judging from the way she drove, she didn't regard her car as a toy but as a sensitive and beautiful piece of fine machinery, so it didn't seem to be a plain case of conspicuous consumption. And over dinner, I'd learned that she'd gone to the University of North Carolina, just like anybody else, and only in passing had she mentioned that earlier she had gone to a girl's school in Switzerland. There had been no idle chatter of madcap times at Saint-Tropez or Portofino or country house weekends in the Cotswolds or even Bar Harbor. At the moment, she'd told me, she was more or less marking time while she tried to make up her mind whether to take some courses at the Sorbonne or whether to accept the offer of a job from a highly regarded interior decorator who operated out of Charlotte: interior decoration, it seems, was what she did best. In sum, then, the sort of problem any girl in even modestly comfortable circumstances might ponder.

Little I knew.

She sat beside me, staring straight ahead, her semi-Cleopatra features dimly lit by the soft glow of the dashboard dials, and smoked a cigarette, keeping an altogether admirable silence as I acquired an idea of the car's power and sensitive steering.

"What will you do when this is all over and done with, Bent?" she asked then, breaking her silence. "This book, I mean."

"Probably try another novel. It all depends on what turns up, of course. There are a lot of these 'as-told-to' jobs around, and the money's not bad. A boy can live on it, at any rate."

"I don't know—somehow it seems awfully—well, awfully indefinite and hand-to-mouth."

"You're so right."

"I mean, suppose you had to support a family. How would you know you'd have enough to pay the bills? Or put children through school?"

"The problem hasn't come up so far."

"Yes, but suppose it did. Then what?"

"It could be managed," I told her flatly, and perhaps a bit testily, for the truth was that she had touched on a delicate subject: the Micawber philosophy might be satisfactory enough for me in my single estate, but it wouldn't be good enough if I ever did marry. And certainly I had no intention of remaining a bachelor all my life.

"What you ought to be is one of those writers-in-residence,

like William Faulkner was, for instance," Little Miss Common Sense said, after another brief silence. "You know, have a seminar once a week or so, and spend the rest of your time writing."

"Nice work if you can get it. Except that I don't happen to be in that league. But thanks, anyhow, for the compliment."

"You don't necessarily have to be famous."

"No, but it sure as hell helps."

"Well, look at Grantley Paget, for example."

The name rang a very faint bell, but only just, and I said as much to Henrietta. "He's been writer-in-residence at Claiborne for the past three years," she explained. "It's an Episcopal college out near Asheville, not very large but it has a wonderful reputation. Well, Grantley Paget's there. He does these books about the Revolution and the Civil War, biographies mostly, and he's done so well that Tulane's made him an offer, and he'll probably move down there next year."

"Good for him," I said heartily as a thought hit me. "How come you know so much about this Grantley Paget?"

"Oh," said Miss Mindleberg casually. "Of course you wouldn't know. My father's on Claiborne's board of regents."

So-ho! I glanced out of the corner of my eye and saw that Henrietta's face was as innocent of guile as that of a newly joined Girl Scout at her first candlelight ceremonial. I went over to Condition Red: man battle stations and commence firing at will.

"Maybe we'd better be thinking of finding a place to turn around, or I'll be in trouble for keeping you out too late," I suggested, as if the significance of her remark had been lost on me. If this was a bribe offer coming up, I wanted her to spell it out without the help of any leading questions from me.

"With Paget leaving at the end of this year," she went on, still conversationally, "they're looking around for someone to take his place." I spotted a closed gas station, slowed and swung the Lancia in and around the pumps until we were once more headed in the direction of Textilia, and waited while a gigantic tractor-trailer rig thundered past. ". . . at all interested?" she was asking as the noise of the truck's diesel abated.

"I beg pardon?"

"I was wondering whether you might be at all interested," she repeated patiently.

"In Paget's slot at Claiborne? You're kidding."

Henrietta shrugged indifferently. "I was just asking. I've no idea who, if anybody, they've got in mind, but I do know they're looking. Daddy says there's a lovely house that goes with it."

To this I made no immediate reply, having heard, during her remark and over the smooth purr of the Lancia's engine, the high, howling whine of another engine astern going all out and accompanied by the banshee wail of a siren. The rearview mirrors disclosed nothing, however. Henrietta, too, had heard.

"Pull over. Fast!" she ordered crisply. "Don't wait for a smooth spot, for God's sake! Just get off the road."

I swerved the Lancia onto the shoulder amid a great rasping and scattering of gravel as the brakes grabbed and brought us to a halt. And not a second too soon. Out of the night past us hurtled two cars, the front one without lights. Incredibly, the right front fender of the pursuing car, which had its headlights and a spotlight blazing but bore no official markings that I could see in the instant of its passage, was abreast of the first car's left rear bumper and almost touching it. They must have been doing at least ninety miles an hour.

Engines and siren screaming, the two cars vanished over a slight rise a few hundred yards ahead, and a couple of seconds later there came the sound of an unholy smashup, followed after a few seconds by a great flare of flame.

"Good God!" I gasped, shaken to the old core. "The damned fools were asking for it. We'd better go see what's left."

"Roadrunner," Henrietta said briefly as I eased the Lancia carefully back onto the road and toward the disaster scene. "The second car was an A.B.C. car—State Alcohol Board of Control, that is—chasing a roadrunner with a load of moonshine."

Topping the rise and feeling slightly sick in anticipation of the grisly mess that undoubtedly lay just ahead, I saw the second car parked on the right shoulder of the road, apparently undamaged and gaudily lit by the flames of what had been the first car, which was upside down and some fifty feet away in the field adjoining the highway. Three men stood just in front of the undamaged second car, chatting unconcernedly as I drove slowly past and pulled over. "You'd better wait here," I told Henrietta, getting out of the car. "They probably couldn't get anybody out of that wreck, and it might be pretty messy."

"Gawddammit, Phodie, whut'd yew hev in thet cyah, ennehhow?" someone was asking as I approached the group.

"Bran' new Olz, bah Gawd. I swayuh to Gawd, Henneh, Ah don' know how in hayull y'all eveh kep' up. Ah knew damn good an' well Ah should of stuck to mah ol' Merc."

"Anybody need help?" I asked, feeling some bafflement at this undisturbed chat in the presence of hideous death. A portly man in a rumpled suit of civilian clothes stared at me in astonishment, as if my query failed to make sense. "Anyone hurt?"

"Huht? Heah? Whah, hayull no, frien'. Sorreh ef we put yew t'enneh trouble. Ol' Phodie heah—" he motioned genially to a tall, horse-faced young man, whose garb was in considerable disarray and who grinned at me in an embarrassed sort of way— "ol' Phodie wuz jus' fetchin' a li'l Wilkes Counteh oh-be-joyful down to the citeh an' we had to give him a li'l ol' nudge to make him slow down. Ain' thet right, Phodie?" The horse-faced youth nodded happily.

"Give yew a damn good run foh yoh moneh, though, di'n Ah, Henneh? Neahleh run th' ass raht off'n thet Plymouth of yourn."

"Well," I said uncertainly, "as long as you don't need any help or want me to call an ambulance . . ." My remark elicited a burst of merry chuckles as the combined forces of law and dis-

☆ 78 ☆

order appreciated its patent absurdity, and I took my departure in some confusion and with a sense of injured dignity. I had done no more than would have any civilized person, only to be treated like an interfering busybody. There was a muffled explosion and the sound of shattering glass from the burning car.

"Hoo-eey, Phodie," hooted one of the officers of the law, "yew shorely to Gawd must of been carryin' some high-proof stuff this tahm." This sally produced another great guffaw of mirth as I slid into the Lancia.

"Anybody killed," Henrietta wanted to know as I started the engine. I told her what had happened and she, too, laughed happily. We had just been witness to, she explained, another in the endless series of contests between the representatives of the state's alcohol control unit and the bootlegging syndicates which operate mainly in the mountains of western North Carolina and dispose of their product mostly among the poorer Negroes of the Piedmont cities. The stuff is delivered in specially altered stock cars, fitted with heavy truck springs and souped-up engines.

"Why, some of the finest stock-car racers around began as roadrunners," Henrietta advised me. "And generally speaking, both sides, the law and the runners, get along just fine when one isn't chasing the other. Sort of an informal code duello, as I understand it. Oh, every now and then someone gets killed, but mostly it's simply good, clean, country fun."

"Fun or not, they could have killed us, driving like that at that speed," I protested bitterly as we pulled away. Henrietta shrugged.

"You can get hit by a taxi in New York, too," she countered.

There seemed to be little point in arguing the issue, but the incident had confirmed my suspicion that there was a great deal about this section of the country that I didn't understand and, for that matter, didn't want to understand. I could sympathize with the old Romans, running their far-flung provincial cities with proper, civilized Roman procedures and knowing all the time that the barbarians were there just out beyond the walls, stomping around in the darkness, yelling.

In any event, the affair had served to distract our conversation from the subject of the soon-to-be-vacant position of writer-in-residence at Claiborne College, and I was left to wonder whether Henrietta had been edging warily toward a more direct approach. I was also left to wonder precisely how I would have dealt with such an approach, and it was to this matter that I gave no little thought after I had dropped Miss Mindleberg and her car at January Hill and drove slowly home in my company Ford.

"I've loved it. We must do it again, soon," Henrietta had declared as I took my leave of her. "And I promise I won't worry you about old Marius or his letters."

I'll just bet you won't, I told myself. "I'll look forward to it," I told Henrietta, and meant it.

And where, I pondered, as I steered the Ford down the long drive, do we go from here?

All in all, it had been quite a day.

☞ *11*   *MUCH* as I wanted to have directly at the coded letters, there were other duties to be done, and the morning after my unnerving evening with Hetty I set about them. With Syd Cheek's approval, since she would be dealing with personal family papers, I assigned our Miss Jermyn to the task of sorting out the documents which remained in the historical society's attic, and extracting those pertinent to our project. A phone call to Miss Liddie assured that Thomas would fetch the various cartons and files down from their dusty aerie so that Miss Jermyn might work in comfort. A Miss Brownhill appeared to assume Miss Jermyn's secretarial chores, and she, too, was a member in good standing of the Golden Quarter Club. In his quietly efficient fashion, Cheek was ensuring that, for me at least, there would be no needless distractions around the office to divert the attention from the work in hand.

Another visit took me to the offices of the Textilia *True Democrat*, the city's excellent morning newspaper. There I met Dave King, the executive editor, an amiable, ruggedly ugly man with an air of vast detachment who, it developed, viewed the municipality's forthcoming observance of the Civil War Centennial as a howling waste of time. He received me in his large, comfortably cluttered office, where I explained who I was and what I was up to.

"Mind you, I have no quarrel with Pierre's history book," he growled around his cigar. "That could conceivably have some lasting value. No offense, Saltire. But for the rest—well, there's simply nothing here to centennialize about. We didn't produce so much as one Confederate brigadier, and the Dancey County Light Infantry Guard spent most of the war guarding the arsenal over at Augusta, Georgia, until they heard Sherman was on the way, at which point they resigned from the war and came home." King snorted. "No, Saltire, our trouble is our professional Confederates: they're bound and determined to have their sentimental orgy, God help us all. You ever heard of a nut named Ploughman; runs the local Civil War Round Table?"

"I'm supposed to be an honorary member."

"Bunch of nuts," King declared fiercely, stubbing his cigar into an overflowing ashtray. "Ploughman's the chief nut. He and his gang are sponsoring some kind of a community pageant and a high-school essay contest. The Daughters of the Confederacy are in on the deal, and the two outfits have pressured City Council out of some cash for a parade and decorations downtown. And we're all supposed to grow beards and wander around in period costume. Now ain't that just the cat's pajamas?"

"Sounds like loads of fun."

"What scares the bejaysus out of me, Saltire, is what would happen if this town really had something to celebrate. The place wouldn't be fit to live in. But you didn't come here to listen to me bitch and holler. What's your problem?"

"I was hoping you might have somebody on your staff who could use some extra cash for spare-time research. I need somebody to go through your files."

"That ought to be easy," King replied, reaching for his phone, with the result that shortly afterward I had completed arrangements with a tall, gangling youth named Spenser, a newcomer to the *True Democrat*'s copy desk, who agreed to search the paper's bound files for anything having to do with the operations of the Mindleberg Mills during the late War of the Rebellion.

"Good kid. He'll do a nice job for you," King told me when Spenser had left the office, beaming. "Just got married, and the money will come in handy." He cocked his head and squinted at me speculatively. "You met Pierre yet, Saltire?" I said that I had, and been much impressed. "He's quite a guy," King agreed, "but I'd hate like hell to cross him."

"He bites?"

"I don't honestly know. Nobody's ever seen Pierre really mad enough to lose his temper. And that, my friend, is what makes me feel I'd hate to cross him."

"I see what you mean," I said.

When I got back to my office, Brooke had something to tell me. Our Miss Jermyn had telephoned from the historical society to advise that Miss Henrietta Mindleberg had put in an appearance and, standing tactfully but firmly on her rights as a member of the family, had insisted on lending a hand in the job of sorting out the papers. "Miss Jermyn said Miss Mindleberg seemed surprised to see her there," Brooke said in conclusion.

"Miss Mindleberg is a fast worker," I observed. Out of the mouths of babes . . . But I saw nothing to worry about: unless I was very much mistaken, Hetty would find no more of Marius Mindleberg's papers. The black tin trunk, I felt strangely certain, held the really significant facts about the man, and I therefore told Brooke that on no account must the trunk be permitted to leave the premises.

During this period, too, what Dave King had called the professional Confederates occupied a certain amount of my time, and I abided by Brooke's advice to humor them at all costs.

The first to call was Mrs. William Lacey Bredalbain, commandant-general of the local Daughters of the Confederacy and a woman who had clearly put the foundation garment industry to the ultimate test. It would be an exaggeration to say that Mrs. Bredalbain creaked as she walked, but I got the distinct impression of guy wires straining under incredible tensions—like the framework of the dirigible *Macon* just before the great ship broke up off California—when she seated herself in my office. She had come, she told me, to offer the services of herself and her organization in the splendid work upon which she understood me to be embarked. I thanked her kindly and said that, at the moment, there were no chores worthy of her or her organization's talents waiting to be performed. She did not appear pleased.

"Our genealogical committee has compiled the family history of every single member of the Dancey County Light Infantry Guard," she said firmly. "Surely a book such as yours should include at least a portion of the notes we have gathered."

"Very possibly," I agreed tactfully. "Very possibly, indeed."

The commandant-general gave me a thin smile. "We think very highly of family in North Carolina, Mr. Saltire. The war left us with little else to treasure but our good names, I'm afraid."

I looked out of my window at the distant vista of the Mindleberg Mills, and the nearer prospect of the Piedmont Furniture Company's huge plant churning out its daily production of Early American by Carolina Craftsmen. "Textilia seems to have come through pretty well," I said, like a fool. Mrs. Bredalbain's smile was a glacial crevasse

"Materially, perhaps, Mr. Saltire, but spiritually . . . ?

"I believe you are a Northerner by birth and upbringing?"

I admitted the charge as Mrs. B. got to her feet, and this time she did creak slightly as the crew ran aft along the catwalks to trim ship. She gazed down at me magisterially. "I think I should tell you, Mr. Saltire, that our Advisory Committee on Patriotic Literature will give your book a very careful reading."

"I sincerely hope so," I replied, not getting the drift.

"In fact, you might even wish to let our committee read your manuscript before it goes to the printers," the old biddy went on coolly. "They could point out any possible errors that might have crept in."

I got the drift, but, as Brooke had pointed out earlier, there was no reason to make enemies at this stage of the game. "I'll certainly relay your very kind offer to Mr. Mindleberg," I said, eliminating the problem. Mrs. B. favored me with a less chilly smile at this evidence of my sweet reasonableness, and sailed majestically out of my presence, still miraculously intact. Brooke drifted in from her office, grinning, as the door closed.

"Nicely fielded, Saltire," she declared. "Hope you don't mind me eavesdropping."

"You can eavesdrop on me anytime, Miss Hastings, anytime at all. What do you say to lunch?"

Mrs. Bredalbain's visit was followed by one from a fierce, ancient man who identified himself as Dr. Alexander Renshaw Cates, professor emeritus of Bible history at the Dancey College for Women. He had brought along the wartime diaries of his father, the sometime First Sergeant of the Light Infantry Guard, he said, fixing me with a baleful glare, his aged eyes aglow with what I instantly recognized as the hot fires of lunacy.

"There is a canard extant," he declared harshly, "that the Light Infantry Guard deserted its post of duty at the Augusta arsenal upon the approach of Federal forces. That, sir, is a vile and vicious lie!" He shook the diary at me. "Here, young man, are the true facts, as set down by my father. The Guard did not desert, but rather discharged its moral responsibility by returning here to defend its home and the honor of its women. It is high time the truth of the matter were known."

"I'm sure it is, sir."

"You'll say as much in your book, young man?"

"Actually, Dr. Cates," I said in my most diplomatic tone, "the book we have in mind will not touch too heavily on the activities of the Guard. We are more concerned with what happened right here in Textilia. Of course, the Guard will have its proper place as the community's contribution to the Southern military effort, but once it has left the scene, so to speak, its work in the field will no longer be germane to the central theme."

"Ha!" Dr. Cates was a war-horse among the trumpets. "I might have expected it. The Jew-controlled press isn't interested in the truth. They *want* the people to believe that white Christian Southern men were cowards."

As there was no sane reply to this observation, I remained silent.

"The Jews control the Pope of Rome," Dr. Cates went on by way of explanation. "The Pope of Rome stands for the mongrelization of the races and thus turning this country over to the Communists. How can you bring yourself to work in league with these people, young man? That is what I ask myself."

"I wish I had known all this before I came to work here," I replied with great sincerity in the spirit of intellectual inquiry and the hope of ascertaining where this septuagenarian booby would take it from here.

"You have it in your power to expose these anti-Christs, Mr. Saltire. Rise up and smite them, hip and thigh."

"I'll certainly think it over," I said courteously, rising. "Hip and thigh, by George!" I slapped my desk briskly.

"Then you'll write the truth about the Guard, young man?"

"Nothing but, sir, nothing but."

"The Lord will bless you."

"Let's get the Christ out of Christianity, that's what I always say, Doctor."

The old boy blinked. "Eh? Oh! Yes. Quite. Very well put, young man," he mumbled uncertainly, getting to his feet. He put the diary on my desk. "All the facts are right in there. I bid you good morning, Mr. Saltire."

After Cates had left, I went into Brooke's office. "You just missed a beaut," I told her, and described my conversation with the professor emeritus of Bible history. She did not share my amusement.

"I may have missed a beaut," she said bitterly, "but you missed the point. Your Professor Cates is part of what's wrong with the

South, Bent. Stop and think of the hundreds, maybe thousands of adolescent female minds that miserable old man has soured, and then think of all those females teaching the same bigotry to their brats. It's enough to make you sick."

"Maybe we ought to warn the Pope of Rome," I suggested.

" 'Tain't funny, Saltire. You should have heaved the old coot out of your office."

"I am always kindly to loonies, Miss Hastings. It is a part of my essentially noble nature. I'll toss you for a Coke."

Finally, there came John R. ("Rebel Jack") Ploughman, a vice-president of the King Cotton Life Insurance Corporation, and chairman of the Textilia Civil War Round Table. He was a large, unhealthily ruddy man with a voice like drawling thunder and the patently insincere guffaw of a man who, in the course of his successful career, has advised untold scores of widows that Junior's college education was assured, thanks to Dad's foresight in purchasing a King Cotton annuity program. He barged into my office one afternoon, beaming hugely, and nearly crushed my right hand in his manly, Kiwanian grip. It came as no surprise to perceive in the buttonhole of his lapel the jeweled halberd insignia of the Saracen Knights.

"Looking forward to knowing you, Saltire," he declared heartily, sitting down squarely and with great force in one of my armchairs. I recognized it as an old insurance man's trick, suggesting that he was there to stay, by God, until he finished his spiel and that only dynamite or heavy winches could remove him. "Hope you'll find time to make it to the Round Table. Got a great bunch of men, all serious students. We're hoping you'll see your way clear to maybe giving us an interim report on how you're coming along." To which I replied that we were still getting things organized and that much research remained to be done.

Rebel Jack nodded sagely. "Had an idea that's the way it might be. Brought along a couple of items you might find useful."

He hauled a couple of fairly hefty pamphlets from his coat pocket, and handed one across my desk. "Little thing I worked up a few years back," he said as I saw that it was the *Survey of Positions Occupied by Battery C, 24th North Carolina Volunteer Artillery.*" My expression apparently told him what I was thinking. "If you're wondering about the connection," he went on, "it's simple, but not many people know about it."

"Oh?"

Rebel Jack leaned forward conspiratorially and lowered his volume. "As you'll probably discover for yourself, Saltire, the Mindlebergs have a skeleton of sorts in the family closet: old Solomon's son, Marius. Seems the boy was pretty much of a dead loss when the war came along. Well, sir, when Marius finally took off for parts unknown, old Sol felt he ought to make some sort of a gesture to make up for the boy's behavior, see? So what did he do but put up the money for an artillery battery being organized over in Yadkin County. The old man wasn't one to brag and hardly mentioned it to a soul around Textilia, but it's all in the record.

"There, now, I'll bet I've told you something you didn't know," Ploughman concluded, smiling archly.

"You certainly have. So far I haven't come across a mention of it. Thanks very much."

"Don't give it a thought." Ploughman's smile grew modest. "I've autographed it for you. Be sort of a little souvenir of your stay here. Now this other thing," he added, extending the second pamphlet, "is something that doesn't have anything to do with Textilia, but I think it's so important that I distribute these at my own expense to every high-school senior who graduates here. It runs into money, but by God, Saltire, it's worth every red cent it costs me. Pretty well states what most of us around here stand for."

The second pamphlet's cover bore crossed Confederate flags

and the title, *Facts the Historians Leave Out! A Youth's Confederate Primer*, by John S. Tilley."

"Sound stuff, eh?" I inquired, playing it straight.

"Might give you a couple of new slants."

"They don't call you 'Rebel Jack' for nothing, do they?" I asked
jovially. Ploughman beamed some more.

"Well, I'll tell you, Saltire, if it had been me instead of Robert
E. Lee at Appomattox, you Yankees would need a passport south
of the Potomac today," he declared with a merry chuckle. "Yessir, you'd need a passport to visit God's country."

"In that case, I'm glad it was Lee," I replied, suavely as a third
secretary of embassy, and Rebel Jack and I parted as amicably as
Marse Robert is said to have left Grant at the McLean residence,
honorable foemen with no hard feelings.

A Youth's Confederate Primer, as a casual perusal disclosed,
proved conclusively, or at least to the satisfaction of John S.
Tilley, that the Southern Confederacy should have won the war
on moral and legal grounds.

Nevertheless, Ploughman had contributed a nugget of fact, and
I phoned Miss Jermyn to tell her to be on the alert for anything
pertaining to Battery C, 24th N.C. Vol. Arty., C.S.A.

Marius Mindleberg, I reflected as I hung up, must have been
an authentic wrong 'un, and it was high time I got around to those
coded letters and discovered just what the hell Marius had been
up to which required a whole artillery battery by way of soothing syrup. Even at 1860 prices, cannon couldn't have come
cheap.

Brooke came in as I was musing in this wise, and inquired
where my thoughts lay.

"I was just wondering how you'd go about ordering four brass
cannon," I told her, having in mind the late Robert Benchley's
splendid essay on bridge-building. "What would be your first
move?"

☆ 89 ☆

"Simple," replied this eminently sensible young person without hesitation. "I'd go to a cannon store."

"I admire your thinking. You're the sort of girl who can tell me what a mighty looks like."

"A mighty?"

"Surely you've heard of mighty hunters, Miss Hastings."

☞ *12* MY profoundest advice to any young man contemplating a career in cryptanalysis is: Don't.

I understand, as a matter of fact, that some people practice, if that is the word I'm groping for, cryptanalysis as a hobby, and all I can say is that if I were a member of any of their immediate families, I'd be worried sick.

To begin with, you have to be terribly good at mathematics, and for me mathematics becomes incomprehensible after long division. Then you must have an enormous amount of patience, and again I'm not oversupplied in this line. The second you start getting the least big edgy and impatient, you start making mistakes, and the trouble is that these mistakes usually don't show up until you've worked for hours and arrived nowhere. Just to foul things up a trifle more, every so often, I suppose by sheer dumb luck or the operation of that theory which holds that a dozen monkeys at a dozen typewriters will eventually write Shakespeare's plays, you turn up an actual word right in the middle of what is otherwise purest gibberish. Got it! you cry in triumph, but of course you haven't. Nevertheless you keep trying until, hours later, you realize that your word is a fluke and that the only thing for it is to start all over again from the beginning. *That's* when you discover your original mistake.

But with the help of God Almighty, the *Encyclopædia Britannica,* a book entitled *Elementary Cryptanalysis* (and never has the word "elementary" been more loosely employed), by a man named H. F. Gaines, which the Textilia Public Library succeeded in borrowing from its New York counterpart, gallons of highest octane black coffee and reams of scratch paper, I attacked Marius Mindleberg's cipher and finally, as we cryptanalysts like to put it, cracked the damned thing. Brother Gaines and the *Britannica's* man, W. F. F., supplied the technical information, but God Almighty was responsible for the hunch which did the deed.

The morning after my visit from John R. Ploughman, a succession of minor interruptions convinced me that if I were to do any real work on decoding the letters it would have to be done away from my office, and to this end I took the black tin trunk out to my apartment, stopping by the library on the way to borrow whatever books they might have on the subject of cryptography. Except for the *Britannica* article on "Codes and Ciphers," they had nothing, but as a special favor they allowed me to borrow the pertinent volume—Castir to Cole—from their reserve set and promised to see what they could obtain from New York.

W. F. F. advised that something he called the Vigenère Cipher was a favorite with the Confederate armed forces. (He also noted, with a sneer, that the Federal cryptanalysts broke it with ease whenever the Confederates used it, to which my only reply is that my hat's off to those Federal cryptanalysts, and nuts to W. F. F.) For lack of a better lead, then, I began with the assumption that this was the cipher Marius had employed. But this cipher requires a key word, and this I had no way of knowing.

For two whole days I labored and sweated to the exclusion of all else to no avail, trying out various possibilities, none of which worked, except that once I got the word "feeble" to emerge from the goobledygook. It was, of course, a fluke.

The third day of my travail the Gaines book arrived by special messenger, but all Gaines succeeded in doing was to compound my already monumental confusion with his glib chatter of polyalphabetic systems, nomenclators, nulls and variants. I was still no closer to a solution, and wouldn't be until I figured out the key word which would unlock Marius's secrets. I rechecked W. F. F. and discovered that I had overlooked the hideous fact that more than one key word could be employed, provided both sender and receiver knew what they were. Which meant that it was entirely possible that each of the coded letters might have a different key.

That same afternoon Brooke dropped by the apartment to ascertain whether I was still among the living. I received her, nattily attired in slacks, bathrobe and two days' growth of beard.

"You look like hell," she commented brightly as, herself impeccable in a little black suit, she stepped into the litter-strewn chaos of my living quarters. "Or General Grant. I can't make up my mind."

"It gives my face a rest," I said defensively, rubbing the stubbled jaw. "Anything come up at the office?"

"Nary a thing. I've just got to the installation of the second steam boiler in the old Number One Plant—a momentous day in the annals of the American textile industry."

"I wish I had your problems. How about a drink?"

"You go shave. I'll mix the drinks," Brooke said firmly. "You have any preference?"

"Just make them strong," I replied, moving to comply with her bidding. It occurred to me that I still didn't know anything about her dinner date, and I wondered if, during the days just past, she had had others. So enmeshed had my affairs become with my efforts at cryptanalysis that I had given little thought to more personal matters. All work and no play makes Jack a dull boy, I advised myself as I plugged my razor into the outlet provided by the bathroom mirror. Easing the razor against my chin, I stared mindlessly at one of the Mindleberg letters which I'd propped on the little glass shelf beneath the mirror earlier, following an unsuccessful attempt to plumb its mysteries while I lay immersed in a soothing tub. Its envelope was attached to it by a paper clip.

Now why had I bothered to clip envelope to letter? Because I am a neat and tidy fellow who likes to keep everything just so,

I told myself smugly; the right letter with the right envelope. Yes, but what about the envelope itself? I mean, why should it have been as carefully preserved as the letter it enclosed? It would have been much simpler to throw it away and thus conserve storage space. The tin trunk afforded protection enough. And hadn't I read somewhere that there had been a severe paper shortage in the Confederacy, so severe that people wrote letters both vertically and horizontally on the same side of the same sheet of paper?

I realized that I was shaving the same side of my face over and over again, and switched sides.

In view of the paper shortage, wouldn't it be reasonable to suppose that old Solomon Mindleberg, as a patriotic citizen, would have reused the envelopes he received, as the British did during the Second World War? But he hadn't, and the envelopes had been saved. Why? There must be some compelling reason.

I picked up the envelope from the shelf and held it up to the light. No secret writing inside. All of the letters were identically addressed, I knew, and all of the envelopes pretty much of a muchness so far as dimensions and quality went. Then what . . . ?

"I've got it!" I yelled over the razor's busy buzz. "By God, I've got it!"

"Is anything wrong?" I heard Brooke call anxiously from her labors amid the bottles in the kitchenette. By way of reply, I yanked the razor's cord loose, grabbed my bathrobe and burst out of the bathroom, the letter still clutched in one hand. Brooke emerged from the kitchenette, drink laden, her expression startled as she observed my dishabille. I shrugged into the robe as I slid into my desk chair and grabbed a pencil.

"Are you all right?" she asked, putting the drinks down on the coffee table before the sofa.

"The postmark," I gabbled. "Been right here in front of me all the time. It's got to be the postmark."

"What's got to be the postmark?"

"The key. Look—oh, hell, you wouldn't understand—I mean, you would, of course, but you haven't been working with this thing," I said, adding the last bit hastily as I saw Brooke bridle ever so slightly. "This cipher," I went on, "assuming it's the right one to begin with, uses a variable key which both the sender and receiver must know. It could be, for instance, a certain word on a certain line of a certain page of a certain book, and they can agree beforehand that the word, or the line or the page, or all three together will change every so often. See what I mean?"

Brooke nodded, her expression dubious. "I'm with you so far. I think."

"All right. The trouble is, that system is awkward. One guy or the other might lose his copy of the book, or forget to make the right changes at the right time. Too much chance for human error."

"It sounds terribly complicated."

"Ha! *This* is what the experts call a simple code. But the point is, Marius sent the key word right with the letter. That is, if my theory works out. No sweat, no fuss or muss, no books or time-tables of changes. In other words, the postmark of each letter is the key which deciphers it," I concluded triumphantly.

"I'm not sure I'm still with you now," Brooke said slowly, "but I think I see what you're driving at. Are you going to try it out now?"

"Right now, if you'll pass me a martini. And if it works out, Miss H., I'll buy you the damnedest dinner we can dig up in this town. You sit down and have a cigarette while I have at it."

So saying, I bent to my labors over my Vigenère Table, which is what they call the square of scrambled alphabets by means of which you can put what is known as "plain text," or clear English or French or what-have-you into cipher and take it out again. The letter I had fetched from the bathroom was postmarked Alexandria, Virginia, and I decided to try "Alexandria" as my key.

Brooke, admirably calm in this crisis, sat herself down on the sofa, lit a cigarette and started leafing through a copy of what I must confess was one of the gaudier girlie magazines which, in a madcap moment, I had picked up at a downtown newsstand, intrigued by the improbably pneumatic bosom of the young woman adorning its cover. Under normal circs. I would have tucked it away out of sight. From time to time, I heard Brooke giggle.

It was miserably tedious work, but by the Lord Harry! it paid off! As slowly as a glacier forms, the incomprehensible jumble began to take on meaning as I sorted out each letter and traced its tortuous way through the table.

My test letter was dated July 25, 1861, and as the sense of what I was deciphering began to emerge I realized that either I had stumbled across some sort of fantastic cryptological coincidence—a possibility which logic immediately rejected—or, in Marius Mindleberg, a character infinitely more devious and fascinating than anybody had supposed.

Old Marius had been a spy, no less.

I reread what I had deciphered:

> *Utter confusion here assures success of my mission. Have signed Federal loyalty oath and will go north soon to continue operations as ordered. Expect no difficulty. All here believe me a staunch Union man. Benjamin will know my whereabouts in emergency. Yrs. M.*

"Well, what do you know?" Brooke said, suitably impressed when I showed her the results of my toil. "Wouldn't this explain those notes from Lee and the others?"

"It might, if it turns out that he really was some sort of a secret agent. Benjamin must be Judah P., which would figure. On the other hand, old Solomon might have decided it would be smart to have a foot in both camps and sent Marius North to look after his interests there. Benjamin could be the name of some trusted chum, in that case, right? I think we ought to work out a few more of these letters and find out what gives."

But on this point Brooke grew firm. "No you don't, Bentley Saltire; no more work for you today, my friend. These letters have kept for a hundred years; they'll keep until tomorrow. My bet is that Marius really was a kind of spy and that you've just possibly got a hero on your hands, but for this evening you're going to march back inside that bathroom, finish shaving, get dressed and take me out to the damnedest dinner we can dig up in this town, as you so charmingly phrased your invitation."

"But dammit, Brooke—" I protested feebly.

"No more, you hear? Tomorrow you can get back to work, and maybe we could get Miss Jermyn to help, if you can show her how to work your whatchamacallit."

"Vigenère Table," I said sullenly.

"Whatever it is."

"You win," I conceded. "But I think I deserve another martini. Anything left in the jug?"

"Just about enough for one each apiece all around. But only one. After that, you get dressed." Brooke refilled our glasses and I joined her on the sofa. She raised her martini: "Congratulations, Bent."

"Shucks, ma'am, 'tweren't nothin'."

"I mean it," she said simply, and then grinned as she picked up the girlie magazine from the coffee table. "I've been looking at your lurid pictures. Hope you don't mind."

"I blush."

"Why, for heaven's sake?"

"Well, you'll have to admit it's not the most improving literature a boy could have floating around the house. And for you it must be as interesting as shower night at a girls' camp." I gazed fixedly into my glass.

"Mind you, I can understand why men buy this sort of thing," Brooke resumed thoughtfully. "It's perfectly natural, after all."

She laughed, her tone unexpectedly bitter. "Paul used to get magazines with pinup boys in them."

"You're kidding."

"No, really. You must have seen them around."

"The boys or the magazines?" I inquired rudely, unhappy with the introduction of her former husband into the conversation. But Brooke ignored this boorishness and was again leafing through the magazine, looking amused.

"Now honestly," she said, holding it up for me to see. "That's a little much, don't you think?"

"It depends on your viewpoint."

Brooke laid the magazine back on the coffee table and took a sip of her drink. Her gaze, over the rim of her glass, was the same appraising look she had given me in the bedroom aboard the Rebel Raider, and abruptly I sensed that we twain might well be once more approaching a new phase in our hitherto straightforward relationship. The nerve ends began to tingle pleasantly as she held out her empty glass. "On second thought," she murmured, "maybe we could spoil ourselves and have just one more."

"By all means," I replied heartily, and withdrew to the kitchenette, there to work my merry magic.

"Cheers," Brooke toasted, sampling the fresh batch upon my return. I returned the salutation, and her expression became grave. "Can I ask you something?" Her voice was low and level, and I promptly matched my expression to hers.

"You can ask me anything, Miss Hastings."

"Would you be shocked if I told you that I've posed for pinups?"

I absorbed this for a second. "Shocked? Not in the least, and not surprised, either. You're a right handsome figure of a woman, Miss H.," I said, and would have added more in a similar vein had I not observed that Brooke was, absurdly, close to tears. "Have I said something wrong?"

"Suppose I told you they were more than just pinups?" Brooke's voice was unsteady, but her eyes were still on mine.

"You mean what they call art studies?"

She nodded, her mouth trembling. "Not the awful kind, Bent. Not that. But nude."

"I'd say you must have had your reasons," I told her gently. "Do you want to talk about it?" And the tears came.

"Paul was between shows, and we were desperate for money." Brooke's words came in a tearful torrent. "Then, one afternoon Paul came home and said he'd bumped into a friend who was a fashion photographer who paid top rates for models. He said it would be money for jam; that he'd come along to look after me . . ." Brooke took a deep, shuddering breath. "Oh, Bent, it was horrible. I was still in love with Paul, then . . . he told me he'd leave me if I didn't go through with it. So I did, and . . . and he just stood there and watched . . ." Brooke leaned forward, burying her face in her hands and sobbed like a little lost child.

"Brooke," I whispered. "Brooke, it's all past now. And it doesn't make the slightest bit of difference in the world to me, for Pete's sake." She came into my arms, seeking shelter from the storm, and pressed her cheek against my chest. I kissed the top of her head very softly, and at the touch of her hair on my lips I realized, numbly and yet with cold clarity, that what I was feeling at this instant was an emotion I had never felt for Ardyth, thank God.

"This may be one hell of an occasion to tell you," I said quietly, "but the fact is, I love you, Brooke."

She looked up at me and I seized the opportunity and kissed her, not hard nor passionately, but as gently as I could so that there could be no possibility that she might think I was trying to take advantage of her disclosure to get her into bed. Bed was the last thing I thought of at that moment. She responded very quietly and then drew her lips away.

"I was hoping you'd say that, Bent. But I had to tell you; I had to know how you'd feel."

"Now stop thinking about it, Brooke. Put it right out of your mind." The import of what she had just said finally hit me. "You were hoping . . . then that means . . . ?"

Brooke nodded. "Yes," she said. "From the moment I watched you stomping through Penn Station looking like a thundercloud in a gray flannel suit." She managed a smile, and began dabbing at the tiny rivulets of tears which ran down both sides of her small nose. "I'm sorry," she sniffed, and I kissed her again, and this time we kissed in earnest.

But she said no when I asked her to marry me right away. We had lighted cigarettes and sat for some moments in silence, aware of the vast change in the relationship between us and what it implied. "Not right away," Brooke said wistfully. "It wouldn't be fair to either of us, Bent. Please, let's give this a month.

"Oh, Bent, I want to marry you now, this instant, please believe that, but we've both been hurt before. You think you love me; maybe it's just sympathy. I think I love you, but maybe with me it's just loneliness and the need for a man's shoulder to weep on, and this time I want us both to be so sure that nothing, nothing in the world can make us change our minds. Does that make sense, my dearest?"

I had to admit that it did. I'd seen too many of my friends louse things up, and no matter how lightly they appeared to take the breakup the whole incident invariably left deep, nasty scars, and I didn't care for the scar tissue of brittle harshness and cynicism that followed. Brooke was an exception who shouldn't have been: not after a complete bastard like Paul Kenyon. And even though Ardyth and I hadn't been married, our shattering split had left me with some long, not especially pleasant thoughts about the viability of the institution.

"At least I can start off by proving I'm a man of my word," I said as we stubbed out our cigarettes. "I can't promise you pheasant under glass, but if we hurry I'll be able to pick us up a bottle of champagne at the A.B.C., or maybe even two. I think some sort of celebration is in order, Miss Hastings. Do you agree?"

"I couldn't agree more, Mr. Saltire. And I like a man who keeps his word to a lady. Oh, Bent, I do so want us to work out."

"G'night, Bent," Brooke said happily, putting the key into the lock of her apartment door. "It was a wonderful dinner."

"It was a ghastly dinner and you know it, but with you there it had overtones of splendor," I replied gallantly. "I love you, Brooke Hastings."

"Same to you, Bent. I think." And she was gone.

I returned to my own apartment borne on a cloud of euphoria, of which the least ingredient was the champagne with which we had been able to render palatable the produce of the kitchens of The Sirloin of Beef, Textilia's version of a steak house. A quick nightcap and to bed, eager for sleep and thoughts of my Brooke. As the head dented the pillow, I realized that I still hadn't learned how Brooke had enjoyed her mysterious dinner date, and decided that it didn't really matter anymore. What was far more important was the fact that we were in love.

But the mind is a peculiar beast. Or at least mine is.

Instead of beautiful thoughts, I got blue movies. What degradations had Paul Kenyon obliged my darling to undergo? And did she really *have* to undergo them. Wouldn't a decent, self-respecting girl have simply up and walked out? Was it possible that Brooke had actually enjoyed herself at the time and only later come to rue her participation in the modeling sessions?

I tried thinking of home and mother, but things only got worse and worse as the gray cells frothed turgidly, conjuring up blurred, flickering visions of unimaginable orgies.

Suddenly my telephone rang, terribly loud, like the voice of Jehovah telling me to knock it off. I leaped up and, as an enormous pain shot up from my left foot, so did my brass wastepaper basket, to soar gracefully across the room. Shouting a mighty oath, I half-staggered, half-fell across my desk, scrabbling for the source of the infernal din, which fell to the floor.

☆ *101* ☆

It was Brooke. "Are you all right?" she asked, her tone anxious, presumably at the strangled sound of my voice.

"Perfectly," I gritted courageously. "Are you?"

"Perfectly. I just called to say that I take back the 'I think,' Bent."

"Really and truly?" I yelped as pain vanished.

"And Bent . . ."

"Yes?" The heart paused in its function.

"About the other evening . . . last week . . . that dinner date. I went out to some people named Hurst; they were old friends of my parents."

"Shucks, Brooke, I—"

"See? No secrets."

"No."

"G'night, Bent. I love you."

"Me, too. I mean, I love you, Brooke."

"I'm glad."

We hung up, and I went back to bed and slept like a log as I hauled the serum to Nome, helped nice old ladies across the street and was elected to the United States Senate simply because I was such a damned noble fellow. Somewhere along the way I also paused long enough to knock the daylights out of a faceless, whimpering creature who could only have been Paul Kenyon. Thrashed the swine within an inch of his miserable life.

☞ *13* *MUCH REFRESHED* by my night's easeful rest, I went hard at it the following
morning. Until now, I had worked on let-
ters, half a dozen at most, selected at random in the hopes of
finding one I could decipher. But now it was important to ascertain whether Marius had been, as it seemed, some sort of espionage agent for the Confederacy, or whether he had merely been
acting in his father's interest. This latter possibility, in view of
the notes from the Confederate brass, seemed remote. Since the
packets had been assembled in chronological order, there was no
difficulty in finding the first letter Marius had written to old
Solomon Mindleberg. It was one bearing a Richmond, Virginia,
postmark, dated June 15, 1861. I went to work putting it through
my Vigenère Table:

> *Commission and orders received. To Alexandria this week
> and thence to New York. As agreed, will advise you of all
> movements and information transmitted. Vital you keep
> these letters for future of our good name. C.S. government
> can give me no help if I am arrested. Believe nothing re-
> ported of me in the South. I work only for its ultimate good
> and am doing my duty. M.*

Clearly, then, Marius had been a spy. And the coded letters
to his father were a kind of insurance policy, so that if something
went wrong, old Solomon could step forward and say, "See, my
son wasn't a traitor after all, but a hero, and here's the proof."
Possibly, too, Marius had taken into account the possibility that
the Confederacy would lose the war, in which case it would be

more important than ever that he should have some means of clearing his name. Or would it? The Reconstruction Era wouldn't have been a healthy time for a Confederate ex-spy to disclose his identity.

Yet even after the worst of the Reconstruction, Marius hadn't come home, nor had Solomon revealed his son's secret. Why? The question nagged me briefly until I decided that there was probably some perfectly logical explanation tucked away somewhere among the letters still to be deciphered. The important thing was that I seemed to have discovered an honest-to-God, totally unknown Confederate hero of the most romantic sort, a Rebel Pimpernel.

I sat staring at my handiwork, but my exultation was tempered with just a trace of disappointment: it would have been much more fun if Marius really had been a real, prismatic, revolving son of a bitch, with half the Confederate cabinet in his pocket. How the professional Confederates would have screamed and yelled! Lordy, Lordy!

On the other hand, Textilia now had something to centennialize about. In spades. And Cousin Theodore Roosevelt Mindleberg would be ecstatic. Which, in turn, would hardly rejoice Pierre.

Nor did it. "Damn!" was his comment when I telephoned him to announce my finding. "You're absolutely positive about this, Nick?" I said that no, I wasn't absolutely positive and couldn't be until all of the letters had been deciphered, but that it surer than hell looked as if Colonel Marius Mindleberg had been one of the brighter gems in the Confederate diadem. "Damn," said Pierre again, dispiritedly. "Who else knows besides yourself?"

"Just Broo—, just Miss Hastings."

"Hmmm. Let's keep it that way for the moment, Nick. Can she help you with the deciphering?"

"She's got an awful lot of work piled up. I thought of maybe putting Miss Jermyn on the job for speed's sake, and—"

"Good God, no! Nothing personal, of course; she's an old and valued employee, but she's got a mouth a yard wide. Let's see now: I can't spare you Syd Cheek, although he'd be the ideal man for the job, and Sam Hoopes can't leave New York, and . . . wait a second! Why not Hetty?"

It didn't register for a moment. "Hetty?" I asked blankly. "Oh! Hetty. Miss Mindleberg. Why, I don't know . . . I mean, I thought that . . . well, what about her father?" I was stalling to get my thoughts in a row: how wise would it be to have Hetty Mindleberg working in my apartment? Suppose Brooke got the idea that the scheme was my brainchild? Or suppose Hetty got it into her head, purely in the spirit of girlish sport and the hope of annoying Brooke, to make a casual play for my lily-white body. There were ramifications fraught with danger in the setup.

"Teddy?" Pierre chuckled in response to my question. "Don't worry your head about my plump cousin, Saltire. And don't worry about Hetty, either; I'll see to it that she doesn't say anything about these letters until we're ready. Okay?"

"Yessir," I agreed, all coward.

"By the way, you're not doing any of this work downtown, are you?"

"No, sir. At my apartment."

"Fine. Carry on there, and I'll send Hetty along."

"Yessir," I replied unenthusiastically, cursing myself for a weak-kneed craven as Pierre hung up, presumably well satisfied with his arrangements, which is more than I could say for myself. Well, there was nothing I could do about it except hope for the best, but to forestall possible complications I telephoned Brooke at her office and told her what had transpired. She was, to my dim unease, perfectly fine about it.

"Why of course it makes sense, Bent, and she seems to be an awfully intelligent girl. Plus which it keeps everything in the family, so to speak, and I agree with Pierre that at this stage we shouldn't say too much. I just wish I could be helping you."

"That makes two of us. Will I see you this evening?"

"If I get out of the hairdresser's in time."

"You're going to a beauty parlor tonight, for God's sake!"

"It's the only time they could fit me in."

"Ridiculous. What women won't do for vanity," I chided.

"Not vanity, Mr. Saltire. You." To which there was, of course, no adequate reply. I rang off in a small glow of masculine complacency, marred only slightly by Brooke's perfectly fine attitude. She might at least have betrayed some trifling edginess at the idea of my being closeted for some days in my apartment with the glamorous Henrietta Mindleberg thrusting heaven only knows what voluptuous temptations in my path.

At which point, the beauteous Henrietta herself rang up.

"Pierre's just told me the happy news," she announced brightly. "I think you're an absolute marvel, Saltire darling." My collar, unbuttoned for comfort, seemed to have buttoned itself. "When does the afternoon shift report in, Boss?"

"Anytime it suits. Maybe you'd sooner start tomorrow?"

"The sooner the quicker. How's your gin supply?"

"I beg pardon?"

"Well, you're not going to make me work all afternoon without offering me a drink, are you?"

"Wel-l-l," I hedged uneasily, "we really do have one hell of a lot of work to get through and I'm not too sure whether—"

"I'll be there in less than an hour," Hetty declared in the voice of a woman who would stand no further shilly-shallying. "Get the ice out."

But to my pleased astonishment, that first afternoon worked out exceedingly well. Hetty appeared within the hour, attired in a discreet print dress which would have fetched a murmur of motherly approval from the dean of any sound secretarial academy, and, although she insisted that I mix us each a gin and tonic to be getting on with, she was thereafter all business. And smart, smart as a whip. She grasped the workings of the Vigenère Table before I had finished the first half of my explanatory lecture, and had constructed one of her own without a mistake in less than an hour, a feat which had taken me a full morning. Then we went to work, and by the end of the afternoon we had completed the deciphering of two more letters and the pattern of Marius Mindleberg's operations began to emerge from the shadows.

He was, he wrote to his father, instructed to go North in the guise of a Southern Union sympathizer, and once there to establish an espionage organization based in New York City. Further orders would follow, assigning the organization's various missions.

"Just like Eric Ambler," Hetty said, her black eyes sparkling, when we compared notes, preparatory to closing up shop for the day. "I can't wait to see what the next chapter is all about."

"What *will* be interesting is whether or not Marius was the kingpin up North, or whether he reported in to some other joker who was," I said, stretching. "I think, on the whole, that we owe ourselves another gin and tonic. What say?" Hetty glanced at her watch.

"Second the motion, but it can't take long. I've got a date."

I went off to mix our drinks, quietly pleased at this further evidence that I did not figure large in Hetty's plans. She had made no mention of the writer-in-residence business, either, and it seemed unlikely now that she would in future, for with Marius transformed from villain to hero there was no longer any need to dangle hints of bribery before me.

When I returned to the living room with our drinks, there was Hetty, settled gracefully on the sofa, looking at that damned girlie magazine. What with the events of the previous evening, I had completely overlooked it and left it lying on the coffee table. Like Brooke's, Hetty's expression was one of faint amusement.

"I never have understood why they just don't pose in the altogether instead of these ridiculous costumes," she observed critically. "Or do men get some sort of fetishist pleasure from these little bits and pieces of cloth?" She flipped over a few pages as

I put her drink down, my boyish cheeks flushed a dull red with embarrassment. She giggled abruptly: "Listen to this: 'unusual adult club for people with imagination. Details twenty-five cents.' What on earth do you suppose they're up to?"

"I wouldn't have the foggiest notion," I returned stiffly.

"Why, I'd have thought you'd be a card-carrying member of all sorts of unusual adult clubs," came the arch riposte. I wasn't at all liking the direction our little chat was taking, but for the moment felt powerless to change it. Hetty was having too much fun watching me trip and stammer.

"I'm not a joiner, thank you very much," I advised her.

"I'll bet you'd like to, deep down."

"Not deep down or anywhere. Nor anywhere."

"Hmmm," was Hetty's only response as she turned another page. "Are wasp waists what I think they are, or something unspeakable? You can tell me, Saltire."

"Look, I just happened to pick out that damned magazine downtown mainly because I couldn't imagine that the girl on the cover was for real, that's all."

"And is she?"

"Must be. You've seen the shots inside the book."

"The poor thing," Hetty murmured sympathetically. "Imagine what she'll look like in another ten years." Then, to my bewilderment, she gave me a dazzling smile, warm and friendly. "You," she said, "are a very funny man, Bentley Saltire, and I think I like you that way."

"Well, gee, thanks a whole heap."

"No, I meant that, Bent. In your own oddball way you're what my Aunt Julia used to call 'the soul of honor,' bless her heart. It was the highest compliment she knew, too."

Which left me standing there with my teeth in my mouth. What the hell was she getting at? One moment she was twitting me with being a satyr; the next she was calling me the soul of honor, and what do you say in bright reply to that? As if sensing my confusion, Hetty finished her drink and stood up.

"See you in the morning, Bent," she said as I helped her into the light topcoat she'd worn over her dress.

"Fine," I said vaguely. "That'll be fine."

Whereupon, to confound me utterly, Hetty kissed the tip of a forefinger and laid it swiftly but gently against my cheek as she walked past me toward the door. Her smile would have reflected considerable credit upon La Gioconda.

☞ *14*　　MORE than a little bemused by the manner of Hetty's exit, I fixed myself another gin and tonic and sipped it thoughtfully. Her departing smile could have meant almost anything. Or nothing, and the latter was the more likely interpretation.

I phoned Brooke's apartment and got no reply, which meant that she was still in the hands of the beauty merchants, and, very probably, there was little point in continuing to plan on taking her to dinner. The evening stretched ahead like a Sahara of sorts. Consultation with the *True Democrat*'s television schedule disclosed that the only programs worth watching over the local transmitter had been superseded by live coverage of the closing sessions of the 57th annual convention of the Piedmont Baptist Association, then meeting in Greensboro, a pietistic spasm I had no desire to witness. The city's motion-picture theaters offered little better in the way of sprightly entertainment. Whereupon I determined to make my own supper and spend the evening intelligently, and to this end extracted from my tiny refrigerator one of the frozen meat pies I had purchased for just such an occasion, and popped it into the oven of my even tinier stove without reading the instructions on the label. Rather, my thoughts were concerned with how the rehabilitated Colonel Marius Mindleberg should be presented to the public.

A dignified press conference seemed to be the obvious answer, with Pierre serving as the family's spokesman. But, in the light of the natural cynicism of the press, this might be regarded as a bid for personal or corporate publicity, and the true worth of the story thus rendered suspect. It would be wise, therefore, to have the facts presented by someone unconnected with either family or industry, preferably an academic, if possible an academic who was also a recognized authority on the history of the Civil War. In addition to the press, we could invite some of the top writers on the period as well, to lend tone and gravity.

I was finishing my drink as I filled in the details of the press conference, not forgetting to lay on limousine service from the airport for the convenience of visiting dignitaries, when my nostrils were assailed by a fearsome fragrance. Previous (and, clearly, totally valueless) experience informed me immediately that my frozen meat pie had gone up in flames, as, indeed, it appeared really to have done when I dashed to my stove and flung open the oven door. With the aid of a couple of kitchen tools I was able to extricate the charred remains from the fiery furnace and heave them into the sink. I turned on the cold tap, added a cloud of steam to the already present smoke, assured myself that the pie would not burst into flames again and retired disgusted to the living room.

I tried phoning Brooke again, with no better luck, and called down God's terrible wrath upon all beauticians everywhere. Beauticians, forsooth! Why not hair arrangement engineers? And why couldn't they keep normal hours instead of insisting that their victims appear during dinnertime? Besides, what was the big hurry? Especially in Brooke's case; she needed the services of a beautymonger like rocks in the head. Why couldn't she have fixed her appointment for a later date?

My irritability stemmed from the plain fact that I was hungry. Lunch had been a pickup affair assembled from various oddments of cheese and cold cuts in my refrigerator. Going to one of the downtown restaurants at this hour would doubtless result in my finding that everything on their always meager menus was sold out except, of course, the breaded veal cutlet, a dish in seemingly inexhaustible supply and one which, as prepared by the Hellenes who dominate the Southern public messing industry, could be the answer to the problem of a light body armor for infantry troops. The country club dining room, while excellent, would oblige me to dress appropriately, and even if I dined informally in the men's bar there was always the chance of running into Rebel Jack Ploughman and his dreadful bonhomie.

It was then that I bethought myself of Fat John. With a view to the morrow and the need for a good night's sleep, it would be folly of the highest order to consider his dipped ribs, but Brooke had mentioned something called Brunswick stew, and this might well suffice my simple needs, which were no longer to be denied, as a series of melodious gurglings from somewhere in the region just below my diaphragm now testified.

Thus it came to pass that within twenty minutes I had parked my company Ford beneath one of the soaring wings that flared out from Fat John's charcoal pits. I was too early for the post-movie crowd, and only two other cars were on hand, both parked near the wing's outer extremity. From them emanated the cacophony of two radios attuned like twin souls to the local station which specialized in the broadcast of "country" music, allegedly derived in an almost straight line from the Elizabethan ballad, which I find hard to believe. I was listening to this incredible noise, pondering its significance for our time, when my thoughts were interrupted by a remembered voice: "Hut'chuh lak, honeh?"

It was the poor man's Jayne Mansfield, leaning with ripe insouciance against my door, her plumply rounded chin moving in sensuous rhythm as she savored the succulence of her Wrigley's. I asked if the establishment served Brunswick stew, and she favored me with an incredulous stare.

"Brunzik styew? Mah Gahd, yeayus. Y'wantchuh bowl, honeh?"

"Please." And away she swayed. I observed that below her firmly fleshed thighs she was just slightly knock-kneed. Shutting, as best I could, my ears to the lamentations and roarings from my distant neighbors, I gave my attention to the current issue of *The Carolina Israelite* and the editorial meditations of Mr. Harry

Golden, its proprietor. I was deep in the East Side, immersed in lower-middle-class Jewish family life, when the Earth Mother reappeared, bearing a tray.

"Yuh din' oaduh one, but Ah broughtcha Coke ennehow," she informed me winsomely as she fastened the tray skillfully to the car door. I put aside the *Israelite* and thanked her for this kindliness. She appeared to be in no hurry to return to her post of duty. "Yuh nevuh trahed Brunzik styew buhfoah, honeh?" she inquired in tones of sincere concern. I conceded as much, and she shook her blonde locks in dismay at my unenlightened state. "Now how 'bout thet?" she observed, and then her conversation took a more personal turn. "Whehbouts is yuh laydeh frien', honeh?" she asked.

"There you've got me," I replied in my frank and open fashion.

"Wayull now, jus' emagin thet," said Cuddles in mock wonderment. She leaned over my tray in such a manner that I feared that my salt cellar would vanish into her cleavage, and gazed at me in what can best be described as challenge, her baby-blue eyes hooded. "Ah'm goin' off shiff inna coupla minutes. Howjuh lak tuh drahv me home afteh yuh fennesh eatin'?" Her smile, despite the Wrigley's, was blowzily seductive.

It cannot be denied that at this juncture I should have firmly but courteously declined the opportunity thus presented, on the grounds of a previous business engagement, and fled. But my curiosity was piqued and, let the truth be stated, the primal senses not entirely unstirred by the series of rich curves of which Cuddles seemed to be completely composed. There could be no great harm, I told myself lightly, in acquiescing to her suggestion.

"I'd be delighted to," I said, at which her smile became downright brazen.

"Yew won' be sorreh, honeh," she murmured. "Yew ken pay yuh check now, en' Ah'll take et oveh to th' dayusk, en' then Ah'll be raht back, y'heah?" I gave her the payment for my food, and her walk back to the counter was even more of a performance than her earlier stroll in that direction. Cold common sense immediately and harshly asked me what sort of foolishness was this, and urged me to dump the tray and get out of there fast. But, argued my Creative Nature, is not everything grist to the artist's mill? Did I have the right deliberately to reject this insight into a simple society of which I had no knowledge? Suppose the demands of some future opus required the delineation of just such a girl from the less privileged classes? Cut the comedy, yelled Common Sense, and start the goddamn engine. But stay a moment, called the Muse, and debate would have been hotly resumed save for the reappearance of Cuddles, wearing a light cotton raincoat and minus her drum majorette's shako. She still wore her white boots, however. Without a word, she disengaged my tray, placed it on a service table on the walkway between the parking spaces, and returned to get into the front seat beside me. "Le's go," she said amiably, leaning back comfortably and, I was pleased to note, at a maidenly remove. I backed the Ford from its position and set out I knew not whither.

"You'll have to give me directions," I said as we paused at the entrance to the street upon which Fat John's parking lot fronted. "I don't know Textilia too well."

"Yew know th' Asheburra Pahk? Wayull, yuh get onna Asheburra Pahk en' keep on a li'l ways out. Okay?"

"Got it," I replied, feeling some slight dismay, since the Asheboro Pike lay in exactly the opposite direction from my return route to the Mindleberg Arms.

"Hut'cho nayum, honeh?" Cuddles inquired casually as we drove through Textilia's somewhat seedy southern outskirts.

"Sal—," I began, and for once the subconscious managed to reach the bridge and take command in time, "—kins," I finished. "Jerry Salkins. What's yours, if I may ask?"

"Whah sh'un yew ast, fuh hevvinsake? Ah'm Bonneh Jean Clodfeltuh, but yew ken cawl me Bonneh, 'fyew lahk." With which, Bonnie Jean performed a movement termed, by the Pennsylvania

Dutch of my native heath, "rutching," a kind of gluteal spasm which brought her several inches along the seat in my direction. The motion caused her raincoat to part, and by the dim light of the dashboard I was enabled to perceive that she still wore her service uniform of very tight scarlet silk shorts and even tighter bodice. "Ah could showleh use uh ciguhrette," she murmured.

I produced my pack from my coat pocket. She took one and set it afire with the car's lighter, exhaling a long, satisfied jet of smoke from her nostrils. From the corner of my eye I had observed her inhalation and involuntarily tensed in the expectation that her bodice would burst asunder with a giant twang, but somehow it held together despite the huge pressures to which it was subject. Bonnie Jean could have given the wench on the cover of my girlie magazine aces and spades. By now, we were out in the country and I began to worry mildly about how much farther we might have to drive.

"Take yuh nex' layuff," Miss Clodfelter bade me, as if divining my thoughts, and I swung the Ford down an unpaved road. "Rah' cheah," she added as we approached a ramshackle, one-story structure with several windows dimly aglow. I drew up in what amounted to the front yard of this establishment, stopping by the dark ruins of an ancient Packard sedan, the rear half of which had been carelessly lopped off to make way for a home-made truck bed, resting on rusted and tireless wheels. "Tuhn ahtcho lahts en' come awn in uh whahl, 'fyew lahk," suggested my fair companion.

I'd come this far, so what the hell? Why not see what happened next?

"Why thanks, I'd like to," I replied manfully, turning off lights and ignition. No sooner had I done so than Bonnie Jean, her voice husky, muttered, "Come heah, honeh," and drew me into an embrace which bade fair to suffocate me as she gave me a kiss of the sort usually described as naughty. It was also almost overwhelmingly Doubleminty. I must confess that instinct got the better of me, and I responded with more enthusiasm than was perhaps necessary under the circumstances, especially when she seized one of my hands and guided it to press against one bulging half of that taut bodice. Then, with a merry laugh, she drew away. "Come awn in, en' Ah'll fex us a li'l drenk."

As heedless of the consequences as Captain Smith driving that great ship *Titanic* into the ice fields at full ahead, all engines, I followed Bonnie Jean into the house, and we entered what was presumably the parlor. A hideous floor lamp, incorporating a smoking stand in its base and topped by a plastic shade for which there exist no adequate adjectives, provided the only light, full forty watts of it. A set of overstuffed, blue plush furniture, much worn, was placed stiffly against the walls, and before the sagging sofa stood a coffee table whose exposed surfaces were entirely plated with blue mirrors, all chipped.

"Ah lev heah with mah ayunt en' huh daughtuh," Bonnie Jean observed, casually flinging her raincoat onto one of the armchairs. "Mah ayunt's kinda real broad-mahnded, 'fyew unnehstan' whut Ah mean, honeh," she added, giving me a brazen grin and walking toward me, arms extended. This time she nearly toppled me backward as she brought her pelvis smartly against mine in a burlesque-type bump and grind. "Man, Ah lak th' way yew kess," she murmured shortly, ungluing her mouth. "Lemmeh go inna kitchen en' fex us a li'l somethin'. Yew jus' set down onna damport, en' Ah'll be raht back." She left, rump a-roll.

I sat down as directed. An unspoiled child of nature, I reflected, pursuing her simple pleasures as thoughtlessly as do the creatures of the wild. I glanced at the dog-eared magazines scattered haphazardly about the top of the coffee table and noted idly that Bonnie Jean's literary taste ran strongly to biography, with a distinct preference for those of cinematic celebrity. Gazing at my surroundings, I was struck by the parlor's resemblance to a dentist's reception room or some similar public chamber. The only decorations I could see were a couple of gilt-framed photographs of Cary Grant, smiling, and the late James Dean, scowling. Atop the elderly television set was one of those cylindrical lamps which, when alight, depict Niagara Falls surrounded by burning forests, all in glowing color and motion.

The door to the kitchen opened and Bonnie Jean entered, clutching a tumbler in each hand, to advance with slow and sensual gait to the coffee table where she set down her burden and then joined me on the sofa. I leaned forward, took my tumbler in hand as I assessed its probable authority, and turned to raise it in toast to Miss Clodfelter. She was deftly removing her bodice.

"Come awn heah, lovuh," she commanded throatily, leaning back to better display a bared bosom capable, I vow, of nourishing armies. I set my tumbler back on the coffee table with a crash as the mind reeled, and I realized that Bonnie Jean was still talking, cupping her massive endowments in her hands: "W'un yew lak a li'l ol' poontang, honeh? Li'l Bonneh Jean'll gev yew uh real good tahm fuh jus' fahv dolluhs. Fahv li'l ol' dolluhs, lovuh, en' ennehthin' goes, jus' ennehthin' yew lak . . ."

Had, by God!

Had like a beardless freshman, like a complete damned fool, had! Oh, Saltire, you total jerk, you randy Boy Scout!

Brushing Creative Artistry aside with a powerful blow, Common Sense seized the wildly spinning helm, set me back full astern and swung hard to starboard as the watertight doors slammed shut. I stood up as one galvanized, with but one thought uppermost in the turbidly sloshing gray matter—flight. "Look," I gargled, my voice a castrato's yelp, "I'm terribly sorry, but let's forget it, shall we? I mean, I'll just take off, okay, and we'll just forget it, right?"

From her wantonly sprawled position, Bonnie Jean stared up at me in disbelief as a wild surmise gleamed briefly in her baby-blue eyes, which suddenly took on the sheen of baby-blue ball bearings. "Yew mean yew don' wan' no poontang, buddeh-roh?"

she asked, her voice edged with industrial diamonds. "Bes' fahv-dolluh poontang in Textahlyuh, en' yew don' wan' a li'l piece?"

"Look," I counter-tenored frantically, "it's getting awfully late, and I've had an awfully big day and I'd better be getting back to town, so let's call it off, shall we, Bonnie. I mean, I wouldn't be much fun now, would I?"

Miss Clodfelter's ripe lips curled in contempt. Suddenly, with a couple of vicious jerks, she removed her shorts to display a vista that staggered the imagination. "Whah yew sonnofabetch," she said amiably. "WHAH YEW MIZZUBBLE SONNOFABETCH!" she continued, upping the volume by roughly a hundred decibels, and did another burlesque bump. "YEW DON' WAN NONNUH THIS? HEY! LU, HONEH! COME AWN IN EN' LOOKUH THIS MIZZUBBLE SONNOFABETCH WON' SPEN' FAHV DOLLUHS AWN POONTANG! YEW, TOO, BETTEH MAY!

Oh for God's sake!

A door I had not hitherto noticed at one side of the room crashed open to disclose a lady wrestler wrapped in a faded pink flannel dressing gown and grasping a bottle of gin in the fashion so often seen in Western movies—by the neck, ready to break off the bottom and convert it forthwith into a deadly weapon. Her expression was stern.

"Betteh May's got uh customuh," the lady wrestler advised. "Now whus'suh matteh heah?" she went on, staring at me grimly as a public prosecutor engaging a hostile witness. "Hut'chew done to Bonneh Jean? Yew some kahn of puhvuht, mebbe?"

"I haven't done a damned—" I began my defense.

"Screw him," Bonnie Jean interrupted harshly, rising from the sofa, bosom jiggling angrily. "Ge'ss me alla way outcheah, ge'ss me to strep nekkid so's he ken get a free look, en' then won' pay out a gawddamn nickle fuh uh li'l fun."

"Wayull gawddamn," said the lady wrestler, or Lu, as I gather was her name. "Look, frien'," she continued, addressing herself to me most reasonably, "yew gotta unnehstan' Bonneh Jean's gotta levin' t'make. She coulda brought anuthuh fella home tonaht en' made husseff fahv dolluhs. Instead, she brengs yew home en' streps buck nekkid, en' now yew say yew ain' about to spen' no monneh. Now does thet seem fayuh to yew, frien'?"

"Look," I babbled, reaching for my wallet, "it's not a question of money, believe me. I'll be glad to pay you five bucks. Here. Five bucks. And I'll just get the hell out, okay?"

"Et's yoh monneh, frien'," Lu said equably, taking the bill from my palsied fingers. "Yew entitle to stay, 'fyew change yoh mahn."

"No, thanks just the same."

"Bonneh Jean's hot as a two-dolluh pistol, once she gets goin'," Lu said wistfully, leering.

"Don' seem raht t'take fahv bucks en' not put out," Nature Girl muttered sullenly, glaring at me.

"Well, good night, ladies." I lurched blindly for the door.

"Ah'll bet he couldn't of ef he trahed," the irrepressible Miss Clodfelter flung after me as I caromed out of the house. "Ah'll bet he ain' got nuthin' t'do et weth, tha'ss whut Ah'll bet," she added, quite unnecessarily, as the door crashed shut behind me, and from behind the matchboard paneling there came the sound of loud, lewd female glee as the ladies shared their little joke at my expense. I stumbled, blind in the pitchy darkness, toward where I remembered leaving the Ford, stepped on a couple of tin cans, kicked some unknown object, and slammed into the antique Packard, a raw metal edge of which caught my coat sleeve and slashed it expertly from wrist to elbow before letting me go to stumble the final few feet to my car. I leaped into it, giving myself a stunning blow on the forehead as I misjudged the door's height, and was fumbling with the ignition key when the front yard of that wretched house was illuminated by a shaft of light from the door, which had been flung wide to reveal the unclad silhouette of Bonnie Jean.

"DON' YEW GO WETTIN' YUH BAYUD WHEN YEW GET HOME, LI'L BAYBEH BAWEH! NOW RUN ON HOME TO YUH MAHMUH, BAYBEH!"

she roared into the silent, starlit night as the Ford's engine sprang to life. My last glimpse of the amoral nymph caught her with her thumb to her nose as she gave me a final, mocking, triumphant bump.

Baby Boy got the hell out of there.

15 ☞ SO DISTRAUGHT was the mind by its encounter with rural depravity that I took a wrong turning at the end of the dirt road leading to Bonnie Jean's bucolic bagnio and drove several miles in the direction of Asheboro before realizing my error, which gave me even longer to heap reproaches on my head for my folly. What else, I asked myself bitterly, should I have expected? Hadn't Brooke precisely analyzed Bonnie Jean's probable source of additional income? But why had I accepted the wench's invitation in the first place, and, having taken her home, why had I gone into the house? I had been curious about the girl, that was all; and even if she had volunteered her massive favors for free, I wouldn't have taken advantage of the offer, I told myself virtuously. After all, I was practically engaged.

But what a damfool thing to have got into!

The night before, it had been blue movies in my head. Tonight's late, late feature showing was the United States Army Training Film, *Venereal Disease*, followed by a manly talk from the regimental chaplain. The last recollection I have is of the Padre telling us that the best prophylactic kit in the world was self-control and respect for womanhood. Then simple exhaustion brought the mercy of sleep.

As is generally the case, things looked considerably brighter in the morning, and I was able to appreciate some of the more absurd aspects of my escapade. Perhaps one day, long after we were married, I would tell Brooke of my evening with Bonnie Jean and subsequent ridiculous doubts and fears, and we would laugh merrily. As we tucked our tow-headed twins into their cribs.

But by a sustained and all-out effort of will, I was able to put the events of the preceding evening from my mind by the time Miss Mindleberg arrived to begin work for the day. For this occasion she had elected to discard the Girl Friday secretarial uniform in favor of that of the All-American (Intelligent) College Woman, to wit, shapeless, neutrally colored sweater, olive flannel skirt, ribbed black cotton hose and cordovan loafers. Her gleaming black tresses were done up in a no-nonsense bun, and she wore almost no makeup. We set briskly to work.

"Well, what do you think?" Hetty asked when we broke for a midmorning cup of coffee and a turn around the cobbled courtyard to get a breath of air.

"I'm beginning to believe that your father can quit worrying about his Uncle Marius," I said. "Have you mentioned the letters to him yet?"

Hetty shook her head. "Pierre made me promise not to, and I think he's right. It would be horrible to raise Pop's hopes and then pull the rug out from under." She laughed happily. "You know, it's funny. Daddy sent me over here to try to con Pierre out of even mentioning Marius, and here I am, making a hero out of the old coot. Thanks to you, Saltire. We Mindlebergs owe you a large vote of gratitude, Bent."

"By pure accident, if at all. Somebody would have stumbled across that tin trunk sooner or later and the truth would have come out."

"It wouldn't if I'd done the stumbling," Hetty rebutted with great firmness. "Me, I'd have burned the whole caboodle."

At lunchtime, we telephoned a delicatessen for beer and sandwiches, and pressed valiantly on. By the end of the afternoon there was no longer any possible doubt: Marius Mindleberg had been the Confederacy's master spy in the North. Step by step we followed the organization of his espionage apparatus, and learned that, in addition to directing his network of agents, Marius had the job of speculating in the New York stock market, using secret Confederate funds, with the mission of creating a financial panic. In sum, Marius was no bush leaguer, and his reports were, even at this late date, horrifyingly accurate, as I was able to verify in part by means of a vast work entitled *Battles and Leaders of the Civil War*, which had arrived in all its numerous volumes via the historical society's redoubtable Thomas, accompanied by a note in Miss Liddie's copperplate script saying that I might find them useful for reference.

"Time to splice the main brace," I told Hetty at the end of the afternoon.

"High time," she agreed. "Well, do we tell Pierre this is it, or do we decode some more letters?"

"No, this is definitely it. Let's give him a call right now and give him the good word."

Hetty shook her head. "No use now. He's gone up to New York. He said he expected to be back late tonight or early tomorrow, depending on when he could get away."

"Well, one day won't make any difference," I sighed comfortably, withdrawing to the kitchenette to fix our drinks. "What'll it be, gin or whiskey?"

"Martini, please."

"Martinis it is," I cried amid the tinkle of ice cubes.

"How'd you like me to cook supper for you, Saltire?"

"What was that?" I called. "You said cook supper?"

"That's right," Hetty said, appearing at the entrance of the kitchenette. "I'll bet you didn't know I'm practically a *cordon bleu*. Besides, I don't feel like going back to Pierre's for dinner; there's nobody around and that butler of his gives me the creeps. He always reminds me of Boris Karloff in blackface."

We took our nicely frosting martinis into the living room and sprawled in the armchairs to savor the reward of our labors.

"I'll finish this and then dash out and pick up something at the store," Hetty announced. "Do you have any pet hates?"

"Parsnips. I can't stand 'em."

"Who can?"

Her drink finished, Hetty left on her mission of mercy and I refilled my own glass with the remnants in the martini pitcher. Miss Mindleberg's sudden decision to deal with the supper problem had taken me unawares, and while I saw no objections to the idea it did occur to me that Brooke might not be too happy with all this cozy domesticity. Of course, I could simply stroll down the corridor to her apartment and ask her to join us, but it seemed likely that this was not precisely what Hetty had in mind, and that a certain amount of unease might pervade the atmosphere. There was, I felt, little point in complicating what was essentially a very simple, open and above-board situation.

There was a knock on my door, and I opened it to find Brooke there.

"Come on in and have a noggin," I invited eagerly. I could then explain matters, and suggest that she stay for supper. Hetty could hardly object if Brooke had just happened to pop in.

"Sorry, my pet, but I haven't got the time. The Hursts have asked me out for dinner again, and I'm supposed to spend the night. They're looking after me like a mother hen, the sweet things. You'll have to meet them, Bent. What I stopped by for was to give you your mail." She handed me a batch of letters.

"Just one teensy little jolt?" I urged, disappointed.

"Not this evening, darling. But I'll take a rain check until tomorrow, okay?"

"Done. Do you want to use the Ford?"

"If you don't have any plans for it."

"Catch," I said, tossing her the car keys. "Better check the gas, though. And drive carefully, please. I need you."

"Will do. Do I get a kiss for luck?"

"You do," I said, and did, completely forgetting the possibility that I might well be a Typhoid Mary of the socially diseased, and then she was off down the corridor, heels tapping briskly on the genuine flagstones, and I felt a better, finer man.

I looked over my mail. A couple of bills, forwarded from my former residence in far Connecticut. I wondered how Mrs. Patricia Thirsby was getting along and whether she had found a new literary mentor. There, but for the grace of God . . . The monthly newsletter of the Textilia Civil War Round Table, and a brief note from my agent, Sam Brewer, telling me he'd had a nibble from a foreign publisher for the rights to my first and spectacularly unsuccessful novel. And finally, a letter on heavy, expensive stationery bearing the great seal of Claiborne College, richly engraved, and the legend, "Office of the President."

It was a formal announcement that, due to the departure of Grantley Paget, the college's board of regents was seeking a qualified occupant for the post of writer-in-residence, and invited inquiries from professional authors. Across the bottom was a typewritten note:

Dear Mr. Saltire:
Your name has been advanced by Mr. Theodore Mindle-
berg, of our board, with the highest possible recommenda-
tion. I would like very much the opportunity of discussing
this with you personally.

The note was signed by H. Wilfred Cecil, Ph.D., the president.

"The highest possible recommendation," eh? I was willing to bet Henrietta's father had never read a word I'd written. I was also willing to bet that Dr. Cecil's eagerness to have a heart-to-heart talk would fade swiftly, once Theodore Roosevelt Mindleberg learned that Marius was a hero instead of a heel. But common courtesy demanded a reply, and I tapped one out on my portable, thanking Dr. Cecil and advising that I would give the matter due consideration. It would be best, on the whole, to leave the whole business unmentioned when Hetty returned, I decided, and thus avoid any possible embarrassment.

I had just returned from popping my note into the lobby mailbox when Hetty arrived, burdened with a large paper bag stuffed with goodies. She had also changed her costume, for the light tweed topcoat she had worn earlier had given way to leopard.

"I just stopped by the house to make myself presentable," she said, unloading the groceries in the kitchenette. I helped her off with her coat and felt the eyeballs bulge momentarily; beneath it she wore a very simple, strapless black velvet cocktail dress which fitted her like a coat of paint. "Sexy, aren't I?" she asked, giving me a merry leer. "I can be Plain Jane for just so long and then the beast in me takes over. Now, does this establishment boast such a thing as an apron?"

"Alas, no."

"Never mind. I can make do with a dish towel."

I mixed us a fresh batch of martinis, and we sipped them as Hetty set about her preparations, and from the masterful manner of her approach it was obvious that she hadn't been kidding about her prowess in the culinary art. In addition to groceries, the shopping bag also produced a couple of bottles of wine, and within a quarter of an hour the kitchenette was redolent with zesty, flavor-filled aromas, and it was time to renew the martini supply. Dinner would be served in roughly forty-five minutes, Hetty declared, as we retired to the living room to allow the stove to get in its licks.

Now the point is, forty-five minutes is, no matter how charming the company, a long time to spend with martinis, and much too long if you happen to *like* martinis, which I do. Not that I got myself crocked, you comprehend, but by the time Hetty prepared to dish up I was feeling little or no pain and the judgment was to a certain extent blurred by a conviction that all was eminently right with the world.

Dinner was marvelous. Hetty had done something with sweetbreads and white wine, and served the resultant dainty with asparagus and a hollandaise sauce beyond reproach. We topped off our repast with a couple of snifters of brandy and cups of powerful coffee, and I took the occasion to compliment her on her skill.

"If I really had wanted to impress you, I would have made a soufflé," she observed, leaning back in the sofa to stretch luxuriously, catlike and sensuous. The effect was nothing less than sensational. "I think I'd like another drop of brandy, please," she murmured, unstretching. I poured. "À votre santé," she said, taking a sip, her black eyes speculative.

I had tuned the radio to Textilia's one FM station not wholly committed to country music and evangelism, and the apartment throbbed pleasantly to something that may have been Vivaldi as we chatted inconsequentially and the brandy in my stomach began to juggle atomic structures with the gin and vermouth. The consequence of this nuclear exchange was a feeling of immense worldliness, and I allowed a series of whimsical, tired smiles to hover about my lips—I had run with the bulls in Pamplona, lain with innumerable Italian contessas, shot my black tiger in wherever the hell it is you shoot black tigers and eaten the good tripe of Normandy (Normandy?) as we watched the sun rise over the chimney pots of Paris. (And with a dim start, I realized that I had affected this same air of detached disenchantment and unshockable cynicism with my sometime flame, Ardyth . . .)

"I've got a surprise for you, Saltire," Hetty said as she set aside her empty brandy snifter. "I wasn't going to let you have it if you didn't tell me what a good cook I am."

"Nothing you could do would surprise me, Hetty," I murmured, remembering those madcap nights at Juan-les-Pins, the great Duesenberg thundering down the coast road toward the little inn where the gypsies played 'til dawn and the wine flowed red as rubies. Ah, Christ. . .

"If you'll run out to my car, you'll find a couple of bottles of bubbly," Hetty said. "They're in an ice bucket behind the seats."

"*Zu befehl, Gnadige Fraulein*," I replied, rising and clicking my heels and bowing stiffly, like George Saunders.

The fresh air of the courtyard only intensified my mood: it had been this way on that night before we went over to the attack along the Piave, the same stars flickered overhead and there was the distant thunder of the Austrian heavies, as played by a freight train of the Potomac, Richmond & Jacksonville. I found the champagne and returned to my apartment with it. It seemed perfectly in keeping with the moment that Hetty should have turned off one of the two lamps which supplied illumination. The music from the radio had changed; now it was flamenco guitar, very sad.

I opened the champagne and poured it into two tumblers, the only clean glassware remaining of my limited stock, after which I joined Hetty on the sofa. "*Prosit*," I toasted, keeping on with the Saunders bit. Hetty giggled.

"I love the way it tickles my nose," she said, sipping.

"You're so very young, my dear," I said gravely as the pain came stabbing across beneath the gaudy, useless rows of ribbons on my tunic . . . I couldn't take many more like that. I lit a cigarette and inhaled deeply. The pain passed.

"But not too young, Saltire," Hetty said, her voice suddenly and curiously husky, and put her glass down on the coffee table. "Don't ever make that mistake, my sweet." She leaned toward me. "You won't, will you, Saltire?"

Ah, God! we would be going in tomorrow, those of us that were left after the morning barrage, and she was so soft, so vulnerable. . . . I leaned toward Hetty and we kissed as her arms snaked around my neck, long and deeply and well we kissed, and then she murmured, "Bed me, Saltire, bed me now," and another great wave of pain swept over me, fetching great beads of sweat out on my brow as I staggered from her embrace to my feet, feeling my stomach begin to rise like an enormous balloon, and dashed desperately for the bathroom, gurgling.

The series of wild whoops and spine-shattering rumblings which ensued left me pale, perspiring, exhausted and dead cold sober, leaning on my arms over the john. At length, I succeeded in pushing myself erect, washed my face and brushed my teeth, and returned to the living room, badly shaken. The gin, vermouth, brandy and champagne had produced a nuclear explosion the like of which I had never previously experienced, and never wish to again. But I will not dwell on the details.

Hetty had gone.

The FM station was transmitting "The Star-Spangled Banner."

It was time to go to bed. I thought of Hetty's words, just before the upheaval, and I thought of Brooke. "Bless you," I said simply, and patted my stomach.

☞ *16* I'M not certain that a wrathful conscience, swinging a baseball bat and mouthing oaths, wouldn't have been easier to live with than a battered self-esteem. Had I, to employ her expression, bedded Hetty, it would have been no more than a mere physical exercise, with no emotional involvement and, consequently, no really grievous moral breach of my obligation to Brooke, I told myself the next morning. Hetty might, as a result, think of me as something of a bounder, but nonetheless a virile bounder. As matters stood, how could she help but regard me as other than a buffoon? N. Saltire, demon lover, says, "It's Fletcher's Castoria for me, every time."

It was not only Hetty's opinion of me which merited pondering, but there was her own situation as well; when a girl has urgently suggested that you take her to bed, and you don't, for one reason or another, there is bound to be a degree of unease between you thereafter. It was not a question of a woman scorned, for, as noted, scorning was far from my mind when my digestive system backfired. But doubtless Hetty would be expecting me to take her up on her offer when next the opportunity provided. At which time she would doubtless burst into laughter. Or would she?

The question was: did I want another opportunity?

To be frank about it, yes. That is, the glandular Saltire did. But the moral Saltire felt otherwise. Hetty must have been aware of the relationship between Brooke and me; we'd made no effort to conceal our fondness for one another. So that if the glandular Saltire took charge, Hetty would always have the quiet satisfaction of knowing that she had but to flick her finger and I had come running, Brooke forgotten. Certainly I'd given her no reason to think otherwise.

It must not happen again, I told myself firmly.

I wondered what I was going to say when and if Hetty arrived to do some more work on the letters. A manly apology was in order, with no mention of the bed bit, as though, in my abdominal agony, I hadn't heard her. That was the ticket, by George!

Of course, I would not allow another incident like the previous evening's to take place, but . . . did Hetty, I meditated, try out all the new boys in town? Was she an incipient nymphomaniac? Or an all-out good-time girl? And if such were the case, what was I really proving by denying myself the dark satanic pleasures of her lust? Would I not, in fact, be doing the poor child a service? Might she not otherwise seek out evil companions?

The telephone rang and I managed to cram the glandular Saltire back into the mind's dungeon. It was Hetty.

"How're you feeling?" she asked brightly.

"I'm going to live," I replied, matching her tone. "About last evening . . ." I began my manly apology.

"I thoroughly enjoyed it, Saltire darling. But I thought you might sooner be alone afterward. You sounded dreadfully ill."

"I am sorry. It's never quite hit me like that."

"Forget it. We'll do it again sometime. Cook supper, that is, not be sick. The reason I called is to say that I can't come over this morning. I've got to get back to Greensboro."

"Nothing wrong, is there?"

"No. But Pierre thought it was about time to let my father in on the happy tidings. He was home when I got in last night. And by the way, he wants you to call him at his office later this morning. Deep down, I think he's really thrilled by old Marius. Take care of yourself, Saltire. I'll see you around."

I spent the next couple of hours carefully retyping the letters we had deciphered and putting them into proper chronological order, adding notes here and there to tie them together and to point out the relationship between the information they contained and consequent developments of the war. It made an impressive dossier, and one which, I felt, would convince any reasonable historian of the validity of our findings.

At ten o'clock, I phoned Pierre and we discussed our plans for unveiling the Confederacy's master spy. He agreed to my suggestion that we try for the following Friday, which gave me a week in which to work up a formal statement, secure the services of some eminent personage to act as our spokesman and get out the invitations to the press and other dignitaries.

"Who've you got in mind to be spokesman?" Pierre wanted to know.

"Henry Clay Drummond," I replied promptly. "You know him?"

"The name rings a faint bell, but that's all."

"He's a history professor, head of the department, I think, at Chapel Hill and, according to *Who's Who*, a very large wheel in the groves of Academe. I wrote to him a couple of days ago for an appointment for tomorrow afternoon and asked him to let me know if it wasn't convenient. He hasn't, so I guess he's expecting me. Is that okay with you?"

"Fine and dandy. As a matter of fact, it ties in very nicely with an idea I've had. Provided Cousin Teddy agrees, I don't see why the letters shouldn't be housed at the university library where they might be some use to somebody."

"That ought to sew Drummond up. Can I tell him?"

"Go ahead. We'll present Teddy with a *fait accompli*, and I don't think he'll try to back out of it."

We hung up and I went to work putting the finishing touches on the dossier. Then I phoned Brooke downtown, and suggested that we drive to Chapel Hill that same afternoon, spend the night at a hotel, and do some sight-seeing the following morning before my date with Drummond.

"Do you think I ought to take so much time off from the job?" she asked anxiously.

"It'll do us both good to get away. I hear tell it's a right pretty town."

"It is. You'll love it."

"Let's figure on leaving around lunchtime; maybe we can find someplace to eat along the way."

"I admire your optimism," Brooke said, "and I'm dead game."

We set out upon the fifty-odd-mile drive to Chapel Hill at the time specified, and finally decided to hazard the cuisine of an establishment which rejoiced in the name of The Sanitary Dixie Dining Room (Genuine North Carolina Hickory-Smoked Ham Our Specialty) in the hamlet of Woodbine. If we were in luck, Brooke said, we were in for a treat.

Happily, we were in luck, and I was introduced to red-eye gravy, a native delicacy with the improbable capacity of making hominy grits palatable.

"How come you haven't gone dashing off to see your folks?" I asked Brooke over our coffee.

"Oh, they don't live in North Carolina anymore. I thought I'd told you, Bent. They moved down to Florida a couple of years ago when my father retired."

"What did your dad do? Before he retired, that is."

"Tobacco. He and my Uncle John had a small exporting firm. They sold out to one of the big outfits and the two of them took off for Florida with their wives like kids getting out of school for the summer vacation."

"What is this fatal attraction I seem to have for tobacco heiresses?" I asked.

"Forget your wild dreams, Bentley Saltire. The Hastingses aren't in the same league with the Mindlebergs by a long shot. If it's money you're after, stick with Miss Henrietta, my lad."

"Who needs it? We'll live on love."

"That's my boy. Shall we be off?"

We drove the remaining distance to Chapel Hill, which came as a pleasant surprise—a misplaced New England village, with broad, tree-shaded streets and an air of vast, easy relaxation. At Brooke's suggestion, I drove directly to the big inn adjacent to the University of North Carolina campus where the ever-efficient Miss Brownhill had reserved rooms for us, and we checked in.

Afterward, we took a leisurely stroll down the main drag, window-shopping, and stopped for coffee at a little restaurant which specialized unexpectedly in Viennese confectionery, of all things, before going on to inspect the campus, holding hands like a couple of sophomores.

"You went here, didn't you?" I asked Brooke, who shook her head.

"Not to Chapel Hill, but the Women's College over in Greensboro. We used to drive over for football games and dances, though, so it's almost like home territory."

"It's a lovely place."

"Where'd you go, Bent?"

"Penn State. Funny thing, though; I have absolutely no feelings about the place. Maybe because it's simply too big. And I always had the feeling that the liberal arts were merely attached for rations and quarters, but that's probably true of most state colleges. Engineering-wise, we were very big, on the other hand. But I just can't get sentimental over the alma mater dear and those golden college years. I'm probably missing something."

"I don't really see you as the reunion type," Brooke said, grinning. Her expression grew wistful. "But weren't they nice years, though, when all the questions had answers and the world was your very own oyster?"

"With you, the world is still my oyster, Miss H."

"Thank you kindly, sir," she said. "That was a very sweet thing to say."

We had dinner at an astonishingly good steak house just outside of town, the management of which, unlike most, maintained a good selection of wines, and later stopped by a *studentenkeller* downtown, full of noise, smoke, and beery song, which was pretty good fun. "Except," as I told Brooke, "that I feel ancient as hell." Brooke, however, was enjoying herself thoroughly: the student-waiter who served us had asked if she were over twenty-one and demanded to inspect her driver's license in proof.

"That's the second nicest question I've been asked recently," she declared.

"And what was the first, pray?"

"Why, Mr. Saltire, I do declare! What a short memory you have."

"Ah, yes, but *I* didn't get an answer."

"You did so get an answer."

"Of sorts," I sulked. "This is the longest month I've ever lived through, dammit."

"Would you be happier if I wore your fraternity pin?"

"If I had one. God knows what ever happened to mine."

"You gave it to some girl. Don't try to kid me, Bentley Saltire."

"Cross my heart and hope to die. It just got lost somewhere along the line. I haven't even thought about it for years."

We ordered a second pitcher of beer, and, when we had finished it, walked back across the campus to the inn.

"So this is where they keep all the moonlight and magnolias," I said as we neared our lodging for the night. "Potent stuff, by God."

"If you're going to kiss me good night, you'd better do it here," Brooke murmured. "Somehow, I don't think the management would approve if you kissed me in the lobby."

"The management has an evil mind, but I grasp your reasoning," I replied, and we kissed. Ardently.

"Oy!" said a strange voice in a tone of brisk authority. "Break it up, you two."

I disengaged myself to ascertain the source of this rudery. It was a campus cop, looking stern. "I beg your pardon," I begged.

"Not on campus, Mister. You know that," the cop said. Brooke giggled.

"I do? Oh. Sure. Sorry, officer."

The cop glanced at his watch by the light of his torch and then looked reproachfully at Brooke. "And you've only got five minutes to get back to your dorm, Miss, unless you've got a twelve o'clock permission."

"Yes, sir," Brooke returned promptly, and the cop moved off, his duty discharged, the dignity of the campus upheld. Brooke and I went back to the inn, feeling like a couple of teen-agers and disturbing the night clerk's tranquillity with our cheery laughter.

Next morning after breakfast we drove the few miles to look at the mock-Oxonian grandeurs of Duke University, and returned in time for my appointment with Dr. Henry Clay Drummond, who turned out to be a giant of a man, built along the general lines of a Highland caber-heaver, with a great thatch of white hair and a properly skeptical historian's grin, when I finally located him at his office in one of the academic buildings. But, as I had hoped, the dossier slowly erased the grin as he read it carefully through.

"Well, I'll be damned," he said gently when he had finished with it. "I've never run across anything quite like *this* before. I take it there is absolutely no question as to the authenticity of the letters, no doubt of their provenance."

"None whatsoever."

"Speaking frankly, Saltire, I'll tell you now that these letters could confirm something I've suspected for years and never been able to prove, that is to say, the operation of a highly skilled intelligence service in behalf of the Confederacy. Not the amateurs like Belle Boyd and Rose Greenhow, but professionals. There's simply no other explanation for some of the Confederate military and diplomatic successes."

"Then you think this could be important?"

"Good heavens, yes. You're aware that, so far as we know, old Judah Benjamin destroyed all of the records of the Confederate intelligence branch, so our sources are almost nonexistent. It could be that these letters will give us the answer to questions we've always considered to be hopeless. That's how important I think they are."

Drummond hemmed and hawed a bit when I sprang my proposition that he act as our spokesman at the forthcoming press conference, but came around handsomely when told that the Mindleberg Papers were to be presented to the university library for safekeeping and posterity.

Then the old boy sprang *his* surprise. Would there be any objection to his taking a few days off from his lecture schedule and coming to Textilia to assist in deciphering the remaining Mindleberg letters? In this way, he could thoroughly acquaint himself with the letters' content and, from his own far-ranging knowledge of the Civil War period, assist in connecting them with subsequent events.

It was more than I had dared to expect, and I assured him heartily that his help would be more than welcome.

"Don't give it a thought, Mr. Saltire. Bear in mind that, professionally, being in on the ground floor of a discovery like this is a privilege not many historians enjoy. I'll drive over tomorrow after I've seen to my schedule, and I'd be grateful if you could line me up a hotel room."

Brooke and I drove back to Textilia well pleased with the results of our expedition. But not before I had conducted a small transaction with the manager of the Chapel Hill branch of the E. G. Hodgett Company, of Brattleboro, Vermont, manufacturers of college jewelry, who seemed unable to understand why I couldn't wait for my shiny new fraternity pin to be properly engraved.

"Wear it in good health," I told Brooke, pinning it onto the lapel of her tweed suit. And kissed her.

☞ *17* *THE DAYS* before the press conference were spent in arrangements and getting out telegrams of invitation to the various news-papers and press associations we hoped would attend, as well as to the historians who specialized in the Civil War period. I had no idea there were so many of them until Brooke handed me the list she had worked up with an assist from the historical society's redoubtable Miss Liddie.

What I did not anticipate was the tremendous response we got. Practically everybody wired back to advise that a representative would be present, in the case of the papers and wire services, and a surprising number of the historians also promised to turn up. Until now, I had thought of Marius Mindleberg as more or less of a regional story, of interest to Textilians and North Carolinians generally, but it was becoming swiftly apparent that the discovery of a Confederate spy had aroused far more than a regional curiosity. Actually, my telegrams hadn't come right out and said anything about Marius's clandestine career, but merely that Dr. H. C. Drummond, of the University of North Carolina, on behalf of Pierre and T. R. Mindleberg, would make an announcement of considerable historical importance in connection with a hitherto unknown phase of Confederate intelligence operations.

I began to wonder whether the boardroom would be large enough to accommodate everybody, and decided not to switch the conference site to the auditorium provided for sales meetings. Better to risk a crowded room than the appearance of a poor attendance, in case some of the press boys changed their minds and didn't show.

Drummond had arrived, as promised, and was happily at work deciphering and annotating away like a mad thing. I had installed him in my office and recalled Miss Jermyn from her researches at the historical society to lend him a hand. By the end of his second day with the letters, the old boy was declaring that Marius Mindleberg might well rank in importance with James Bulloch, the Confederacy's chief agent in England.

Of Hetty, happily for my peace of mind, I heard naught.

When the appointed Friday morning arrived, the boardroom filled early with the television newsreel technicians, who proceeded to clutter up the place beyond belief with their floodlights, tripods, cables and other necessary impedimenta. All three network news services were represented, I was gratified to observe.

"How do you explain the size of this turnout, Nick?" Pierre asked, stopping by the door of the boardroom to peer in at the bustle. I had stationed myself there to greet and sort out the incoming press from the dignitaries.

"Probably they figure that when the Mindlebergs have something they think warrants a press conference, it'll be worth listening to," I replied. Pierre nodded thoughtfully and continued to watch. I greeted a tall, stooped character who identified himself as an official of some sort with the Civil War Centennial Commission, and directed him to the rows of chairs we had reserved for his ilk.

"What sort of a surprise are you people springing here, Saltire?" boomed John R. Ploughman genially as he arrived a few seconds later. "Turned down a fishing trip to Hatteras to be here, so I hope it's worthwhile." Rebel Jack moved along to join the Centennial Commission's observer, and I checked in the Associated Press and a man from the *Time* Atlanta bureau.

"Quite a show, Bent," Hetty's voice spoke behind me, and I turned to find her accompanied by a tall, stout, gray-haired man who could only be Theodore Roosevelt Mindleberg. " 'Lo, Pierre," she added brightly.

"Glad to know you, Saltire," said T. R., giving me a thin smile as Hetty introduced us. "I gather from my daughter that we Mindlebergs have reason to be grateful to you."

"Hardly that, really."

"I believe you've heard from my old friend, Will Cecil," T. R. went on, dodging more nimbly than I would have expected in one of his bulk as a television technician heaved yet another chunk of camera gear through the doorway.

"Dr. Cecil? As a matter of fact, yes."

"What's all this about?" Pierre inquired, intrigued.

"Mr. Saltire is receiving consideration as Claiborne's new writer-in-residence," his cousin informed him gravely. Pierre's eyebrows arched, and he fingered his chin with thumb and forefinger as he digested this intelligence.

"Hmmm," he murmured. "You hadn't mentioned it, Nick."

"Nothing to mention," I said. "I don't know too much about it, so far."

"Hmmm," Pierre mused again, giving his cousin a thoughtful look. "Well, what do you know?" He appeared to dismiss the subject. "We'll be in my office, Nick. Call us when you're all set to roll." So saying, he led Hetty and her father down the thickly carpeted corridor of the executive suite.

By ten o'clock, the boardroom was packed solidly, and the air conditioning was struggling mightily to keep the smoke cleared. The air was loud with the profane yells of the television newsreel boys telling one another to get the hell out of the way for God's sake, and the still cameramen, weaving and dodging as they sought positions, added their yelps to the uproar. I left Syd Cheek at the door to check in any latecomers and went to fetch Drummond from my office, where I called Pierre and told him the show was ready to hit the road. Then, carrying the tin trunk, I returned to the boardroom with the professor.

Drummond took his position at the head of the big directors' table, putting the trunk on the table before him. Flanking him were Pierre, T. R., and Hetty, and we waited while the still photographers got their group shots. Then we waited some more while the newsreel boys got in their preliminary licks, paying most of their attention to the glamorous Henrietta, who appeared to be enjoying the whole bit to the hilt.

"She's quite a girl," Brooke, who was standing beside me at the door, where I had resumed my station, murmured. There was no cattiness in her tone, but rather, honest admiration. I looked down at her.

"That makes two of you then," I said quietly. She looked at me, her eyes serious.

"Please don't fall for her, Bent."

"Never," I told her, and meant it. "Never," I repeated.

There was a hush as Drummond pushed himself to his massive height and surveyed the room.

His speech was the more impressive for its brevity and simplicity. He traced the discovery of the letters, their decipherment and the import of what they contained.

"In sum, then, ladies and gentlemen," he concluded, "we now know that Colonel Marius Mindleberg was the Confederacy's chief intelligence agent in Union territory. There is every reason to believe that he was largely responsible for the New York Draft Riots, and superintended the unsuccessful attempt to burn the city, as well as the planning of the famed raid on St. Albans.

"But perhaps it is not too much to say that the man's true greatness lies in the fact that he never betrayed his trust, and died in exile, his lips sealed to the last, considered a traitor to his own land. Only his father knew how well he had done his duty. With one word, he might have ended his days a hero at home. For Colonel Marius Mindleberg, sworn to silence, that word remained forever unspoken."

There was a brief, awed hush as Drummond sat down, and a faint, small voice from somewhere in the back of my head cried plaintively, "Why?" Why hadn't Marius spilled the beans when there was no longer any point in keeping quiet? When the government to which he had sworn his oath no longer existed?

Then the questions began like a volley of musketry. The AP wanted to know more about the Vigenère Cipher; UPI was interested in more biographical details, and the man from *Time*, for reasons of his own, wondered if Marius had ever visited Binghamton, New York, in the course of his operations. *Newsweek*'s reporter wanted to know where the letters would be kept, and I rejoiced at Pierre's decision when Drummond made the beaming announcement.

"Mr. Nicholas Saltire, who is the man responsible for the discovery and decipherment of the letters," Drummond concluded graciously, "has prepared a detailed statement incorporating all of the information presented this morning, and copies of these will be available for you as you leave."

With which the conference broke up as individual newsmen converged on the group at the head of the table and myself for further questions. I found myself cornered by the Charlotte *Observer* and the *Greensboro Daily News* and a plump, bespectacled little man, smoking a frayed cigar, who looked vaguely familiar.

"Who'd ever think of a Jewish James Bond?" he asked of no one in particular. "It's delightful."

"Sounds like something you dreamed up, Harry," the *Observer* remarked, and then we were joined by a newcomer, a youthfully middle-aged, tweedy type, complete with pepper-and-salt moustache, black-framed glasses and silver-banded briar pipe, probably polished alongside his nose. I hadn't noticed him when he arrived, but my interrogators seemed to know him, for they greeted him courteously but with a kind of reserve, as if he were a publisher.

"Mr. Saltire?" the newcomer inquired. "I'm Carleton Oglebay." His tone indicated that I should recognize the name immediately, but I didn't. Instead, I told him I was glad to know him and he gave me a tolerant smile. And proceeded to rock me back to my heels. "I look forward to working with you," he said. I looked blank.

"Working with me? Of course, I'll be glad to answer any questions I can, Mr. Oglebay—" I said, and quit, not knowing where to take it from there. The three newspapermen, sensing that this might be a sticky situation, drifted tactfully away as Oblebay appeared to realize that I hadn't the foggiest idea what he was talking about. He looked mildly embarrassed.

"I imagine everybody's been so busy getting this morning set up that nobody's had the chance to mention it. I'm doing the authorized biography."

"The authorized biography?" I asked stupidly. "Whose?"

"Old Marius," Oglebay replied casually around his pipe stem.

"I see you two have met," said Theodore Roosevelt Mindleberg from astern. "You know Mr. Oglebay's work, of course, Mr. Saltire?" He came alongside.

"Not as well as I should, I'm afraid."

"Mr. Oglebay is one our state's finest writers. His biography of General Joe Johnston won last year's Pulitzer Prize in its field," T. R. explained pompously. "At my urging, he has consented to apply his great talents to a similar study of my granduncle." Oglebay smiled modestly and blew out a jet of blue smoke in appreciation.

"Oh," I said numbly.

"I'm sure you'll give him your fullest cooperation," T. R. went on, eyeing me in a fashion which said plainly that I would, or suffer the consequences, possibly including keelhauling.

"I'm sure he will," Oglebay put in, as if I weren't there.

Suddenly the import of what they were talking about hit me with a sickening thud, right at the base of the skull. Or, perhaps more aptly, like a slap on the chops. In moments such as these, my self-control takes a terrible beating; my heart starts to pound and I have great difficulty in speaking steadily. A couple of seconds and I'm all right again, but for those couple of seconds I just stand there, white-faced.

These jokers were calmly stealing my discovery.

☆ *143* ☆

Was Pierre in on this deal? I couldn't believe it.

"Sure," I finally managed to say. "If you'll excuse me, I've got to find Miss Hastings."

"I'll drop by your office later, Saltire," Oglebay promised, his manner amiable, and I left without waiting for T. R. to dismiss me from The Presence.

Brooke was talking with a girl-type reporter in the corridor outside the boardroom.

"Excuse me, please, but could you spare me a second," I interrupted, manners aside. Brooke looked at me, startled and then concerned as she saw my expression. She apologized to the girl-type reporter and followed me down the hallway.

"What on earth's the matter, Bent? You look as mad as a wet hen," Brooke said when we were out of earshot.

"I've just been shafted, I think," I told her grimly. "I've got to talk to you. Let's get the hell out of here and have some lunch. No, wait a minute. I've got to talk to Pierre first. Wait for me here, please."

"If I'm not here, I'll be in the office," Brooke promised. I took off in the direction of Pierre's office. His secretary told me, to my surprise, that he was waiting for me, and waved me brightly on into the Great Man's private offices, where I found him with his feet up on his desk, elbows on his chest, chin resting on his knuckles, expression wry.

"I know," he said before I could open my mouth. "Oglebay. Teddy sprang him on me just before the conference, and for your information, Nick, I told my fat cousin I thought it was a stinking lousy thing to pull. Unfortunately, there's not a damned thing to be done about it. Old Marius was Teddy's granduncle as well as mine, and the papers are public property now." He swung his feet down from the desk top and sat back in his chair. "Simmer down, Nick. This thing isn't over with yet.

"What's more you're still in charge here. I have an idea that this morning's gabfest was only the beginning, and that when this story hits print all manner of curious things are likely to happen. In fact, they already have. You know that madman who calls himself Rebel Jack Plowshare?"

"Ploughman," I corrected automatically.

"Whatever the hell it is. He barged in here a few minutes ago insisting that I address something called a Civil War Round Table, an organization of which I have been, up to now, happily ignorant. I said my schedule wouldn't permit—which was a lie, of course, but shows some pretty neat footwork on my part, I think—and allowed as how you'd be happy to stand in for me."

"Great," I said, scowling. Pierre grinned.

"I knew I could count on you, my boy. Plowshare will be in touch with you."

"Just one thing. Did your cousin give you any idea before this morning that he was planning to muscle in on Marius?"

Pierre shook his head firmly. "No. Not in so many words, that is. But if you'll recall, he dropped us both a hint."

"Hint?"

"The sop, Nick. The unexplained sop, to soothe your ruffled vanity. You may not be famous enough in Teddy's book to be entrusted with Marius's biography, but you'll settle down and be a good little writer-in-residence, and make no nasty trouble for anybody, won't you?" Pierre's smile was grim.

"It started off as a bribe," I told him. "In any event, the hell with it."

I left Pierre to find Brooke and take her out to lunch, where I poured out my tiny sorrows on her slender shoulder.

"The point is," Brooke observed calmly when I had finished, "will you take this writer-in-residence thing if they make you an offer?" Her eyes were solemn.

"No," I declared. Brooke smiled.

"That's my Bent," she said.

☞ *18* AS Pierre had predicted, all hell broke loose when Dixie discovered her brand-new hero. It would take a tome to chronicle the aberrations which ensued. Space, pace and grace demand that this narrative restrain itself to but a few of the highlights of the larger lunacy. Thus . . .

The North Carolina Legislature, which was in session at the time, immediately and unanimously declared November 22, the anniversary of Marius Mindleberg's birth, a state holiday, and their action was duly proclaimed by the Governor.

The North Carolina delegation to the Congress of the United States proposed that the Postmaster General issue a commemorative stamp in tribute to "The South's Unknown Defender." *Time's* ever-alert Washington Bureau noted, without comment, that the senior Senator from North Carolina occupied the chair of the committee charged with examining the Post Office Department's annual appropriation. As well as others. Never slow to take a hint, the U. S. Army Engineer Corps announced that the chief earthwork of the Hixahattamoy Flood Control Project would henceforth be known as Mindleberg Dam, behind which would eventually back up Lake Marius to provide Dancey County with water sports and fishing.

The town of Walnut Level, in western North Carolina, elected to change its name to Mariusville, and in larger communities throughout the state, Fourth Streets and Seventh Avenues became, overnight, Mindleberg Roads, and Marius Boulevards.

The Mayor and City Council of Textilia, in conjunction with the Textilia Association of Commerce, announced the organization of Historic Textilia, a nonprofit corporation, the primary function of which would be the annual production of a historical drama depicting the career of the gallant Marius. It was hoped that the services of DeWitt Snaveley, the writer of several other enormously successful pageants produced elsewhere in the state, would be available, and that the drama could be written, cast and put in readiness in time for a November 22 opening.

Mr. Snaveley said he was honored, and felt fully up to the job. "We will write it as we rehearse," he told the Textilia *True Democrat.* "Working with a skilled director, I'm sure we can bring it off. In fact, I've already got my title—*Lee's Other Eyes.*"

Dr. Hugh Pontefract, head of the Department of Speech and Drama at Carolina Wesleyan University, volunteered his experience, gained from such notably successful Snaveley works as *Honey on the Mountain* and *Gunfire at Guilford,* as the producer-director. "I plan," he advised the *Greensboro Daily News* in an exclusive interview, "to start casting as soon as Witt can give me a rough draft of the first scenes."

Life threw a platoon-strength task force into Textilia to work up the Mindleberg Story in Depth.

The *Saturday Review* reported that Carleton Oglebay was dickering with an eminent New York producer for a dramatization of his as-yet-unwritten biography, and that the motion-picture rights were but a matter of days from settlement.

The United Daughters of the Confederacy disclosed plans to hang a portrait of Marius in the Confederate White House, in Richmond, provided one could be located.

Theodore Roosevelt Mindleberg announced the establishment of the Marius Mindleberg Fund, to be administered by the president of Claiborne College and disbursed to qualified scholars for studies of Confederate history.

And, for once, Pierre failed to riposte.

"How come?" I asked Syd Cheek during one hectic lunch period during the midst of all this.

☆ *147* ☆

"I frankly can't figure it, Nick," Syd replied, his tone puzzled. "It's not like the Old Man, but when I mentioned it to him all he said was that he thought everybody was going overboard on the subject. 'After all,' he said, 'the Confederacy still lost the war, didn't it?' I dunno, Nick, but sometimes I think that finding that Marius wasn't a son of a bitch took something out of Pierre; you know what I mean?"

Where was I while all the foregoing bombs were bursting in air? Right in the rockets' red glare, that's where. When I wasn't digging up obscure data for *Life*'s crew, I was making arrangements for Carleton Oglebay's office space, and when I wasn't on the phone answerinug DeWitt Snaveley's endless, long-distance queries, I was at my desk, wondering why the hell I should be saddled with the same questions from Dr. Pontefract.

"Dammit, Saltire, this is a casting situation," Pontefract would keep saying. "I've got to know whether I need a tall man or a medium-tall. Can't you give me anything on how the old bastard looked, for God's sake?"

"Try Carleton Oglebay," I kept telling him, not without a certain bitterness. "He's the big expert on the subject."

"Dammit, Saltire, you've got to keep these people off my back," Oglebay kept protesting. "It seems to me you ought to be handling these routine queries." He had moved into the apartment directly above mine in the Mindleberg Arms, and I kept hearing him stomping around his room late into the night, wooing the muse with hard marching.

Every now and then, Brooke and I managed to snatch a couple of quiet moments alone, but not nearly as many as I could have wished. Her life was being hideously complicated by a tall, moose-faced woman who had been commissioned by *American Heritage* to write an article on old Solomon Mindleberg, the hero's father.

During the period under survey, I saw Hetty only once. She was having dinner at the Country Club with Carleton Oglebay.

My bleakest moment came with that God-awful meeting of the Textilia Civil War Round Table. This dismal rite was celebrated in the Palm Room of the Golden Glow Cafeteria, which meant that there wasn't even the feeble consolation of beer.

As speaker of the evening, I was seated at the head of the table, to the right of Rebel Jack Ploughman, and to my right was an equally maniacal type who identified himself as Dr. Cornflower (That's correct. Cornflower. I looked it up in the phone book.) and who turned out to know everything there was to know about Confederate artillery practice, a subject almost totally lacking in fascination for me and, I venture to assume, for anybody without a brass Napoleon around the house. Cornflower had one, as a matter of fact, and told me, his loony's open face beaming fatuously, that he and a group of his chums were accustomed to spend their weekends in, so help me, Confederate uniforms, firing the damned thing.

"We fire beer cans, usin' black powder," he told me in a corn-pone drawl as we waited for Rebel Jack to start things going. "Filled with cement, of course."

"Of course," I agreed. What else?

"We're members of the North-South Gunnery League, and summers the boys and I travel all over the country, shootin' in tournaments and such. Like to have you come out to the farm some Sunday and join us for a few rounds. Afterward, we always have a few rounds of somethin' else. Get it?" He dug me smartly in the ribs, chuckling.

Before I could toss back a suitably witty rejoinder, Rebel Jack got into the act with a merry ho-ho-ho. "Don't get yourself involved with Doc, there. Too much work. What you want is our map study group, Saltire."

"Sounds like grand fun," I declared, appalled.

Rebel Jack glanced at his watch, heaved himself to his feet, and we were off. First we stood and pledged allegiance to the United States, wunnashun innavizzable, and then we all fifty-odd

☆ *149* ☆

of us sang one stanza each of "America" and "God Bless America."
That put us right with the Federal authorities and the American
Legion. After that, we pledged allegiance to the Confederate
States of America and sang the whole of "Dixie." We remained
standing while a reverend divine among our numbers pronounced
an invocation, and finally we sat down to our fruit cup, pot roast
of beef and two veg., apple pie à la mode and coffee. During the
course of this Lucullan repast, Rebel Jack invited members who
had brought guests to introduce them, but I could pay little attention to these unfortunates since Cornflower was beating my
ear with tales of the cannoneers.

The ice cream finished, Rebel Jack opened the meeting for
reports and, these delivered, announced that State Senator Julian
Barker, from High Point, would be the speaker at the next
monthly meeting.

"Julian Barker probably knows more about Confederate horse-
procurement policy than any man alive," Cornflower informed me
in a rumbling whisper. "I could listen to him talk for hours." I
looked at him, trying to ascertain if he were jesting. He wasn't.

Then it was my turn, and Rebel Jack gave me a joshing introduction incorporating many a thigh-slapper at my Yankee background, following which I arose and gave the gang a brief run-
down on the discovery of the Mindleberg letters. The fact that
one and all appeared to hang upon my every word I deemed no
compliment: these were, after all, men prepared to sit still for a
lecture on Confederate horse-procurement policy. In any event,
they gave me a great big hand when I sat down.

Another clergyman closed us down with a benediction, and, as
the meeting broke up, a gratifying number of those present approached the head table to tell me how much they had enjoyed
my address and what a fine thing I had done for Textilia. I com-
ported myself with what I trust was a becoming modesty.

I had just got rid of Dr. Alexander Renshaw Cates, who pressed
a leaflet entitled *The Cross, the Kremlin and You* into my hand,

when Dave King drew nigh, bearing in tow one unknown to me. "He's one of them," Dr. Cates hissed as he withdrew.

"Nick," Dave said, "I'd like to have you meet Dr. P. T. Wattersby, who's here as my guest."

"Delighted to meet you, Mr. Saltire," said Wattersby in an unexpectedly reedy voice. He was a large, paunchy, rumpled-looking man with the complexion of a gefüllte fish, watery blue eyes peering from behind gold-framed spectacles, and a fringe of nondescript hair, the longest strands of which were laid with great precision across the dome of his softly gleaming skull. His smile disclosed a sad, yellow expanse of false teeth. "I believe," he continued, giving me an arch look, "that we share a common interest, sir."

"We do?" I asked, not very politely, I'm afraid, but the idea of sharing a common interest with P. T. Wattersby had taken me somewhat aback.

"An interest in Colonel Marius Mindleberg, that is."

"Oh! Yes. I see what you mean."

"Seems Dr. Wattersby's a stranger in Textilia," Dave King put in. "He arrived only this afternoon and stopped by my office to find out where you could be located, Nick. I told him you were speaking here tonight and suggested he come along with me to meet you."

"Mr. King has been more than kind," Wattersby declared. "More than kind. Actually, Mr. Saltire, I'm hoping you will be able to spare me some time at your office. I have some material concerning Colonel Mindleberg I'm certain you will wish to see. Indeed, my purpose in traveling here to Textilia, rather than writing to you, is to permit you to inspect the material personally and evaluate its importance for yourself."

"Why certainly, Doctor. How about tomorrow morning?" I suggested, wondering what the hell he might have concerning Marius, and why I had to have it shown, rather than described to me.

"Excellent, sir, excellent. Would ten be too early? No? Then ten it is, sir, ten it is. And now I must be getting along back to my hotel for my syrup of figs. I sincerely trust you are not a sufferer from dyspepsia, Mr. Saltire. It has afflicted me for the past ten years." Wattersby grinned hopelessly and turned to make his adieus to King before lumbering off behind his paunch.

"I'm afraid I've stuck you with another oddball, Nick," King said, his expression apologetic. "Sorry, friend."

"What's one oddball more or less? Come on over to the Micah Dancey and I'll buy you a beer."

"I've got a better idea. Let's go over to the Merchants and Planters. I've got some Jack Daniels in my locker."

I made my manners to Rebel Jack, and then Dave and I took off for Textilia's sole gentlemen's club. Syd Cheek had earlier asked me if I wanted a guest membership, and I had declined with thanks, feeling that the country club was sufficient to my needs. But when King and I were finally seated in a couple of deep leather chairs in a cheerfully lighted, paneled bar, I began to regret my earlier decision.

We exchanged a few rude comments on the Civil War Round Table and good old Rebel Jack, and King twitted me for having stirred up a hornet's nest. "The whole town has gone Marius-crazy," he complained. "I hope the rest of the state comes to see this damn pageant, because there won't be any audience left in Textilia; everybody's in the cast. That nut, Pontefract, even tried to haul me into the thing as director of publicity."

"That figures."

"Thanks, but no thanks. How's Oglebay coming along with his book, by the way?"

"Damned if I know. All right, I guess."

"That was a raw deal, Nick. If I were you, I'd be mad as hell at the Mindlebergs."

"Not Pierre. Pierre's a good egg in my book. But his Cousin Theodore is something else again."

"And Hetty?" King stared innocently into his glass.

"What about Hetty?" I lobbed back.

"Just don't get caught in the machinery, that's all," he said inscrutably. I looked at him quizzically but he did not enlarge on the subject, and we left it at that.

☞ *19*   THE next morning's mail brought me a long, ringing letter from Walter Gregory, who hailed me as the greatest thing since sliced bread for my achievements in Textilia, and announced that Bannastre Masters himself had telephoned from his home to direct that my salary be suitably increased at once. In the mad whirl of the past weeks, I'd almost forgotten that I was working for Masters except, of course, for the paychecks that arrived every other week. I had come more and more to think of Pierre Mindleberg as the boss-man.

Brooke, too, had shared in the Masters munificence, as she informed me happily upon entering my office. "Now my conscience will stop hurting me about that tweed suit I bought last week at Montefiore's. In fact, I might even buy another."

"Let's drive over to Chapel Hill again this week and celebrate," I suggested. "I liked that town."

"It's a deal." Brooke's expression grew serious. "Bent?"

"Yes?"

"What's the situation with us? I mean, so far this history of the mills and the Civil War—is it still on the agenda, or is Pierre planning to drop it in favor of Oglebay's biography?"

"Nobody's told me to quit, so I guess we keep on with it until we hear otherwise. It does seem just a teensy bit futile though, I must admit."

Brooke nodded unhappily. "Old Marius has certainly fouled things up." Little did she wot.

Ten o'clock arrived and with it Dr. P. T. Wattersby. He looked even seedier in the morning's clear light, exuding a faint aura of perspiration, cigars and failure. Placing an elderly leather briefcase, a seam of which had parted, on the floor by his chair, he extracted his wallet and produced his card, handing it across the desk to me. It identified him as P. T. Wattersby, Ph.D., professor of American history at Indiana Midwestern Junior College, Gary, Indiana.

I asked him if he had enjoyed an easeful night, and his naturally mournful expression cracked into a melancholy smile.

"I felt so much better after throwing up," he declared. "Then a refreshing glass of citrate of magnesia and my rest was undisturbed, I am happy to say. I wonder if I might trouble you for a glass of water from your carafe."

"By all means." I poured him a glass. He took it, and removed a small, flat tin box from his vest pocket, out of which he daintily plucked two egg-shaped brown capsules and popped them into his mouth, following them with a swallow of water.

"Ah," he sighed. "There we are. They ease the gas wonderfully, these little fellows do." He surveyed his pillbox fondly, and suddenly belched. "See what I mean?"

I was wondering what the next step in the morning therapy might be when Wattersby reached down and picked up his frayed briefcase and began fumbing with its straps.

The case opened, he sat back and gazed at me thoughtfully for a couple of seconds before speaking, meanwhile managing to stifle a second, lesser eructation. "I am not a well man, Mr. Saltire," he announced sadly. "There is nothing seriously amiss, you understand, but of late years I have found my strength insufficient to the demands made upon the head of a collegiate department. Unfortunately, my mandatory retirement is still some years distant."

Now what was all this leading up to?

"I have, in consequence," Wattersby forged ahead, "given no little thought to the need for an extended leave or, on the other hand, some means of supplementing the reduced pension I would receive should I retire before the mandatory date."

A touch, for Pete's sake? Couldn't be.

"As a historian," Wattersby continued, "it not unnaturally occurred to me that I might well devote what little leisure my schedule permits me to the writing of a book in my field of endeavor. To enjoy a large sale, such a book, it seemed to me, must throw fresh light upon a fresh subject, and BRRRREKKKKK!" I leaped involuntarily as at the sound of a thunderclap. Those little brown capsules were certainly doing a grand job somewhere inside Wattersby's noble paunch. "I beg pardon, Mr. Saltire, but I was about to say that I gave the subject much consideration. I observed the enormous success enjoyed by such authors as Bruce Catton, for example, and noted the vast and growing public interest in the Civil War. Here, I concluded, was the area in which I could best achieve my aims, but, alas, an area of which almost every conceivable aspect has already been exhaustively examined. Except—" Wattersby paused dramatically. "Can you guess, Mr. Saltire?" I shook my head, but I had an inkling. My visitor lowered his mortician's voice. "Espionage," he said.

"I see," I said, playing it close to the chest.

"More specifically," Wattersby took up his tale again, "espionage as practiced by the Union. I began, therefore, to study the operations of Pinkerton and Baker. Pinkerton, of course, you will have heard of, but La Fayette C. Baker has been a largely neglected figure. Here, I determined, was my man, and I began the serious collection of data and documents associated with him and his work as the first chief of the United States Secret Service.

"Happily, fortune smiled upon my labors, and my quest led me in time to a Miss Emily Hoover, of Hooversburg, Maryland, a collateral descendant of General Baker. For reasons with which I am unacquainted, a great mass of the general's papers had come down to Miss Hoover, and, as she is an elderly lady in somewhat precarious financial circumstances, she was persuaded to permit me to purchase them."

"I hope she didn't try to hold you up," I said, more for something to say than anything. Wattersby gave me another of his licensed embalmer's smiles.

"We were both well satisfied with the transaction," he said smoothly. "In my own case, the money invested represented most of my meager savings, but I feel it was well worth it.

"Taking the papers to my home for examination, I was able to fill in a great many gaps in my admittedly limited knowledge of Baker and his operation, and I was, as a result, exceedingly interested in your own remarkable discoveries here in Textilia."

"The Mindleberg letters would help you understand Baker's opposition, is that it?" I asked.

Wattersby pursed his lips and looked judicious and sly at the same time. "Opposition, Mr. Saltire? Hmmmm. Now we arrive at a most interesting point." He fumbled in his briefcase again and drew from it a time-yellowed envelope. "I think it might help if you were to examine this letter," he added, handing it to me. I saw that it was addressed to General Baker, The War Department, Washington, D.C. There was no mistaking the handwriting on the envelope. Feeling curiously detached, I removed the letter inside. It was in code, but not, I recognized, the Vigenère Cipher.

"The letter is in what is known as 'Route Cipher,' " Wattersby explained. "It was the cipher most generally employed by the Union Army."

"And old Marius was actually conning the head of the Union Secret Service? That's marvelous!"

Wattersby's expression became that of a patient man dealing with a backward child. "Mr. Saltire," he said solemnly, "Marius Mindleberg was not, uh, 'conning' General Baker."

"Then what the hell . . . ?"

"Mr. Saltire, there is not the slightest doubt in the world that Marius Mindleberg was a double agent in the employ of the United States Government, and the proof is here in my briefcase." Wattersby sat back in his chair, beaming.

"Holy cow," I said slowly, reverting to the language of my infancy in my dumfounderment. "Jesus H. Christ," I added, getting along a few decades.

"I can sympathize with your bewilderment, Mr. Saltire, indeed I can," Wattersby assured me. "It does come as something of a shock, doesn't it?" I nodded, wordless.

It took Wattersby less than half an hour to make his ironclad case, substantiating every statement with a relevant document, some of which were in cipher, others in the clear.

Marius Mindleberg had, in truth, been intellectually and morally opposed to the Civil War from its inception and had accordingly made his arrangements, even before the events at Fort Sumter, to serve the Union by appearing as a loyal Confederate. It was agreed that he should feed the Confederate authorities just sufficient authentic information to confirm their trust in him by supplying them with a number of tactical, as opposed to strategic victories. And the deception had worked perfectly. Only one person besides Marius and Baker had ever known of it; old Solomon Mindleberg, like his son, a secret Unionist. Wattersby produced a number of reports from Marius to Baker incorporating information supplied by the old man, relative to Southern industrial output and supply shortages.

There was no question about it, Wattersby's evidence was conclusive. It also explained why Marius had never come home. As well as the curious name old Sol had given his home. I could imagine his ironic enjoyment in calling it after a two-faced god. But that was neither here nor there. What *was* here was a very sticky situation.

"This is going to raise a good deal of hell," I told Wattersby at the conclusion of his presentation.

"I'm afraid it will," he said, nodding gravely, and his pale eyes focused on a point somewhere behind my right shoulder. "But need it, Mr. Saltire, need it?" He sighed like the wind in the eaves.

"I don't see how it can do anything else," I replied. Wattersby shifted heavily in his chair and sighed again.

"Writing a book, Mr. Saltire, is no easy task for one in my physical condition—the long hours at the typewriter and the concomitant pains in the lower back muscles, the correction of several drafts, the preparation of an index. Indeed, there are times when I ask myself whether the game is worth the candle. Why not let this cup pass, as it were, and make my findings available to someone younger and readier to assume the burden?"

"And what do you tell yourself?" I asked, a trifle tartly. Let the man come to his point, whatever it was.

"At best, Mr. Saltire, I could hope to earn, oh, say as much as twelve thousand dollars, assuming a successful sale from the current popularity of works concerning the Civil War. But I would be a drained man, sir, an exhausted man. What good would such a sum do me then? None, sir. Why not accept a lesser sum now and thus be free to enjoy it, if you follow me?"

So here it came, at last.

"You mean, sell your set of Mindleberg letters?"

"Exactly, Mr. Saltire, exactly. I commend your perspicacity. My wants are simple, and my physician recommends at least a year's leave of absence. Ten thousand dollars would supply my every need."

"And if you can't sell the letters?"

"In that event, Mr. Saltire, I will have no other choice but to go ahead with my book, painful as that prospect is, not only from the selfish standpoint of my own physical and mental exertions you understand, but as well from consideration for the Mindleberg family."

I followed him all right. The book would probably take him a minimum of six months to write, by which time Oglebay's "authorized" biography would already be in print, celebrating Marius as Dixie's knight in cloak and dagger. And then there would be hell to pay. Oglebay, the Mindlebergs, Textilia, everyone connected with the present whoop-de-do would be made to look like absolute fools. Or rather, worse fools than all of us now looked.

Clearly, the truth would have to come out at once, before we went any further. It would be painful, but not nearly so painful as it would be later on, and Wattersby knew it. He had us neatly over a barrel. We couldn't afford to wait while he exploded his bomb at his leisure, and we had to have proof that Marius actually had been a double agent. Who would believe us without proof? More likely, they'd clap us all into the nearest laughing academy, if they didn't lynch us beforehand.

"You understand, of course, that the Mindlebergs would require complete authentication of these letters," I said sternly. "Assuming that they ·agree with your estimate of their importance."

"I had naturally anticipated the requirement," the professor said, extracting a sheaf of papers from his briefcase. "I have here a letter from Colonel T. W. Folsom, formerly assistant chief consultant on cryptanalysis to the Department of Defense, attesting the accuracy of the decipherment of the letters, and, of course, notarized statements from Miss Hoover, extracts of birth records, and so on. And there is the letter in clear text from General Baker to Marius Mindleberg, written after the war to thank him for his services, and endorsed as a true copy by the general himself. Sufficient, I trust you will agree, to establish provenance."

"May I show these to Mr. Mindleberg?"

"I would prefer to retain the originals, but I have a complete set of photostats which you are most welcome to.'"

"How soon must you have a decision?" I asked, getting down to brass tacks. Wattersby pursed his lips and knitted his brow.

"My finances are limited, Mr. Saltire, and I cannot extend my stay here beyond four days at the most. Surely that should afford ample time to reach a decision. I'm staying at the Commercial House."

"I'll be in touch," I promised.

I saw the professor out of my office with a mixture of revulsion and sympathy. The poor old bastard was capping off his dim career with a shabby attempt at blackmail, and for a measly ten thousand bucks when he might have hit for fifty and probably gotten away with it.

Right now, the essential action was to bring things to a screeching halt until we got them sorted out. I glanced through the set of photostats Wattersby had left with me and reached for my phone to call Pierre's office but it rang instead. My caller was Pierre's secretary, asking me to come by at my earliest convenience. "You've got a visitor," she concluded archly.

"I've already had one too many," I told her grimly and set out to take the bad tidings to the Great Man. A couple of thousand years ago I would have been ceremonially slain for my pains. It was a small consolation.

☞ *20* MY second visitor of that thrill-packed morning turned out to be Walter Gregory, looking debonair as ever and grinning mightily as I entered Pierre's office.

"Just flew in fifteen minutes ago, Nick," he explained jovially. "After I put that letter in the mail, I decided I just had to see for myself what sort of crazy miracle you people are pulling off down here. I tell you, Nick, this is the damnedest show I've ever heard of, and the whole outfit is damned proud of you. And that comes straight from Bann Masters, too." Walter wrung my hand vigorously as he led me leaden-footed into the room. "I promised you nothing but the best, didn't I, Pierre?" he asked the Great Man, who nodded, giving me one of his wry smiles.

Gregory finally observed that my expression was inappropriate to the occasion. "What's the problem, Nick. Hangover? Sit down and tell us all about it, boy." He winked merrily at me.

I sagged into one of Pierre's armchairs. "Gentlemen," I said wearily, "the egg is about to hit the fan. We are in the soup up to here."

"Soup? What soup?" Gregory asked, bewildered, his tone nettled.

"It's like this," I began and then, as briefly and coherently as I was able, outlined my interview with Professor P. T. Wattersby, and showed them the photostats.

"Great God in the foothills," said Walter Gregory, in the tones of Napoleon discovering an empty Moscow, at the conclusion of my horror tale. Not surprisingly, Pierre was chuckling with delight.

"Marvelous," he declared. "Oh, marvelous, Nick. My God, wait until Teddy learns about this!" His eyes went wide suddenly and he stopped chuckling. "How soon can you get your hands on these new papers, Nick? We've got to get into print fast with this thing."

"You're not serious, Pierre," Gregory blurted, aghast. "You can't possibly be serious about letting this out."

"What are you talking about, Walter? Of course I'm serious. We've got to put a stop to this damn foolishness over Marius before it goes any further," Pierre snapped decisively. "It's gone far enough already."

"But . . . my God!" Gregory's voice was an agonized wail. "Have you thought of the consequences? Surely you must see that it would be a disaster to let this get out. I'm talking about Mindleberg Mills now, Pierre, and the effect it might—what the hell am I saying?—the effect it *will* have on corporate public relations? If you do this thing, you'll be making fools out of Textilia and the whole state of North Carolina. They'll never forgive you, Pierre. Never." Gregory was striding around the room, waving his arms to emphasize his points.

"I'd sooner they looked like fools than liars," Pierre argued. "Dammit, Walter, you can't sit on the truth."

"There's more involved here, Pierre, a whole hell of a lot more. What about all the money the city's putting into this? What about the tourist business it'll pull in, not only this year, but next year and the year after that. Now *you* tell *me* who the hell would travel two miles to see a pageant about a traitor, assuming anybody would be crazy enough to put one on."

"It depends what you mean by traitor," Pierre said, chilling slightly, but Gregory was too wrought up to observe the effect of his breach of diplomacy.

"All right, then, what about your family? What about your cousin in Greensboro? What's this thing going to do to them," Walter asked angrily. "You owe them *some* consideration."

"You're really in dead earnest, aren't you, Walter?" Pierre murmured, his face thoughtful.

"Never more so in my life. I tell you, Pierre, the thing to do is buy these letters and bury them so deep they'll never be found again. From what Nick says, this joker Wattersby won't talk, and even if he should, what could he prove without the original letters themselves?"

"What do you think, Nick?" Pierre asked me abruptly.

"Me?" I replied, startled. "Well, I'm no public relations expert like Walter here, but it seems to me that sooner or later we're going to have to face the truth about Marius, and I'd say the sooner the better." I wasn't especially enjoying being in the middle of this one.

"You're goddamn right you're no public relations man, Nick," Gregory said savagely, giving me an angry glare. "You stick to your last and I'll stick to mine, boy." I was taken aback by the fury of his manner, and Pierre apparently decided it was time to reach a decision before fisticuffs broke out.

"Well," he said slowly, running a hand through his iron-gray crew cut, "let's look at it this way: we lay out a fair amount of cash money for professional public relations advice from Bann Masters, and it would seem sort of damn stupid to pay for it and not take it into consideration. I do see Walter's point, and I agree that to blow the Marius thing now would play hell with Textilia's plans, and he's right when he says we have a certain responsibility to the community.

"Take Joe Simons, for instance, Nick," Pierre went on, turning to me. "He's going to change the name of his hotel from the Cotton Queen to the Marius Mindleberg. He's ordered new china and silverware and linens with the new name, and he's planning a big celebration to coincide with the opening of the pageant. What's going to happen to Joe if we debunk Marius? It's one of the things we've got to think about, as Walter points out. The main thing is, we buy Wattersby's letters, today, if possible."

"It's the only sensible thing to do," Gregory agreed. "Nick, can you get on the phone and line it up?"

"I'll give you my personal check," Pierre said.

"Better make it in cash, Pierre," Gregory suggested.

Pierre nodded and spoke briefly into the intercom on his desk, meanwhile shoving his telephone toward me. I couldn't help grinning at the incredulous note in his secretary's voice when I asked her to get me Professor Wattersby at the Commercial House; very likely it was the first time the top man of Mindleberg Mills had ever called the city's seediest hostelry.

Wattersby finally came on the line and agreed to meet me in his room within the hour. He sounded much gratified, and I hung up as Pierre's secretary, looking even more baffled, came into the office with a packet of bills which she handed to her employer. He, in turn, handed them to me, and waited to speak until she'd gone.

"Ten thousand dollars, Nick. You know, this Wattersby doesn't seem too greedy, does he? I'd have asked for at least twice as much."

I gathered up the sheaf of photostats I'd laid out on Pierre's desk and stuffed the packet of bills in my coat pocket as I left on my errand, feeling vaguely criminal. Additionally, I felt badly let down by Pierre's agreement with Walter Gregory. Certainly I could understand his position, vis-à-vis Textilia, but what we were conniving at was, at best, morally dubious, and in Pierre's case, completely out of character. On the other hand, it was his baby, not mine.

Wattersby admitted me to his room, uttering greetings. It was a depressing little room with a medicinal aroma, doubtless accounted for by the array of phials and pillboxes spread out on the top of the bureau. I got right to the point.

"I'm delighted that the sum proposed is satisfactory," the professor declared happily. He thumped his briefcase on the lumpy-looking bed, and pulled a bulging, expandable file from it. "The complete Baker-Mindleberg correspondence," he added, "covering the entire period of Major Mindleberg's service—I should explain that he held the lesser rank with the Union Army—to the United States. Decipherments accompany all of the coded papers, needless to say. I trust my labors will be put to some good use, Mr. Saltire."

"Rest assured," I lied. "I take it," I went on, sounding like Sherlock Holmes, "you'll be leaving Textilia, now that our transaction has been concluded, Dr. Wattersby?"

P.T. nodded briskly. "I arranged for my reservation immediately after your call. I shall be leaving on the four o'clock plane for Pittsburgh and Chicago."

Then, with Wattersby looking on, I inspected the contents of the file and ascertained them to be as advertised, after which I handed him the packet of bills. He looked startled at the sight of the cash.

"I would have preferred a check," he muttered worriedly. "I hesitate to carry such a large sum on a long trip."

"Mr. Mindleberg felt you might want cash, in case you were worried that he might stop payment," I replied, shooting him a significant leer which he caught guiltily.

"Ah, yes, of course. I see. Most considerate. Naturally you will want a receipt, Mr. Saltire?" Wattersby seated himself at the room's shaky writing desk, uncapped a large, old-fashioned fountain pen, the barrel of which was covered with silver filigree, and wrote out the receipt on hotel stationery. "And now, sir," he continued, handing it to me, "will you join me in a drink. To seal the bargain, as it were."

I had no urge to spend anymore time than was absolutely necessary with the professor in such dismal surroundings (or any others, for that matter) and attempted to decline, but the old boy was insistent, and there seemed no point in making a Federal case out of it, so I agreed. Wattersby hauled a bottle of inexpensive bourbon from a bureau drawer and poured us each a couple of fingers of the stuff.

"Your very good health, sir," he toasted. I raised my glass in return.

"Cheers."

Wattersby took a large gulp, looked momentarily as if he were going to be sick on the floor, and then smiled contentedly. "I find a glass of whiskey an excellent stimulant to the digestive juices," he declared, and then looked at me thoughtfully for a couple of seconds. "Mr. Saltire, you have played the game with me, sir, and I appreciate your fair dealings. There is something I feel you should know.

The nerve ends started to tingle. The old bastard was about to let fly his curve ball and tell me that there were still more of the Baker-Mindleberg papers and that another ten-thousand-dollar bill was in the cards. "Such as?" I asked guardedly.

"During my own researches, I became aware that mine was not the only interest in the undercover operations of General Baker. A few inquiries among my professional colleagues disclosed that a young historian by the name of LeRoy C. Smelzer is now engaged in preparing his doctoral thesis on the subject of the general. He is, I believe, a candidate for the degree at Temple University in Philadelphia, and while I have no reason to suppose that he has any knowledge of the letters now in your possession, it is not impossible that he may discover others of a similar nature. General Baker was a stickler for detailed reports from his agents, and Marius Mindleberg may have supplemented these letters with others of which we remain unaware."

It took a couple of seconds to digest this information.

"So that if Mr. Mindleberg should by any chance decide that the immediate publication of these letters wouldn't be in the family's best interests, this Smelzer might just go ahead and blow the gaff by accident, is that it?" I asked. Wattersby nodded gravely.

"There is that possibility, Mr. Saltire. A faint one, but we cannot deny its existence." His smile, while more melancholy than ever, was ever so faintly tinged with triumph.

"Thanks for your frankness, Professor," I said, rising. "I don't see that there's much we can do about it, though."

"Except to hope that all turns out for the best, Mr. Saltire."

I took my file and myself back to the Mindleberg Tower and Pierre's office, pondering the significance of LeRoy C. Smelzer and his labors in the City of Brotherly Love.

Not to mince words, I was inwardly shaken by the greedy fashion in which Pierre took possession of Wattersby's file and stuffed it into his safe. Earlier, he had seemed enchanted with the possibility that Marius might have been a rogue, and now that the old boy had been proven one, by Confederate standards at least, Pierre seemed to be doing his best to hush the whole thing up. Was he, after all, only another Theodore Roosevelt Mindleberg in a crew cut? The conclusion seemed inescapable.

"Whew!" Walter Gregory whistled when the safe door swung shut. "A few more of these situations and I may really develop an ulcer. Nick, I hate to think what could have happened if old Wattersby hadn't come to you. Suppose he'd opened up to your boy, Dave King. Aye-yi-yi! What a field day the papers would be having."

"I could almost wish he had," I said stubbornly. Gregory looked shocked, and Pierre glanced at me speculatively.

"Don't forget that King has community responsibilities, too, Nick," Pierre said, his manner bland. "He might well have done what Walter recommends: sit on the story rather than blow Textilia's plans to kingdom come."

"I doubt it," I argued. "He's a good newspaperman."

"There is also the angle that Mindleberg Mills owns a majority interest in the True Democrat Publishing Company," Pierre observed coolly, looking me straight in the eye. "King would have that in mind, too, you know."

"You'd bring pressure?" I demanded.

"Let's just say that I could." Pierre gave me an amiable smile

. . . Captain Putnam rebuking Tom, the fun-loving Rover brother.

"Well, anyhow, the issue is settled, and the best thing to do is forget about it," Walter Gregory put in smoothly. "You say Wattersby is leaving this afternoon, Nick?"

"He's got the four o'clock plane out."

"Might be an idea if you drove him out to the airport, just to make sure he gets aboard," Gregory suggested.

"We don't want to look as if we're ready to lock him up if he doesn't skip town. But I'll drive out myself and check him aboard, if you're that concerned," I replied.

"I am," Gregory said flatly. "The sooner he's back in Indiana, the happier I'll rest."

Returning to my office, I dropped in to ask Brooke to drive along with me to the airport. We would have to leave right away, I told her, and I'd explain what we were up to on the way out.

"You look grim, Bent," she said as I steered the Ford up the ramp from the garage beneath the Mindleberg Tower. "Something wrong?"

"That would depend on your definition of what's right," I replied as we eased out into the traffic and I headed west on Elm toward the airport. As we drove, I told Brooke about Wattersby, the letters and the deal in which I had just served as Pierre's agent. She looked more and more thoughtful as I filled in the details.

"Somehow I didn't think Pierre would operate like that," she said when I had finished. "In Walter Gregory's case, it's perfectly natural, but Pierre . . . I don't know . . . I'm disappointed. The question is, what are you going to do about it, Bent?"

"Do? Me? I'm damned if I know. In fact, I'm not even sure there's anything I can or should do. After all, I *am* working for Pierre, and I guess he rates a certain amount of loyalty. You got any ideas?"

"I agree about the loyalty part, but there's a limit to it. I don't think it ought to include dishonesty," Brooke said, looking at me firmly.

"You think hushing up Marius Mindleberg's Yankee connections is really dishonest, Brooke? Really and truly? What the hell difference does it make, when you come right down to it? Textilia has itself a hero to celebrate and everybody's happy. What possible good could it do to blow the whole thing to smithereens? You tell me."

We were on the outskirts of the city by now, and I let the Ford's six tiny cylinders begin to sing their song of power. Brooke hadn't answered my question. "Well?" I asked.

"I just think that whether it's good or bad for Textilia doesn't enter into it," Brooke said slowly, gazing straight ahead. "It's a question of the truth. Either you're for it, or you aren't, or you don't care, which is worse."

"You're certainly being a great help, I must say."

"We endeavor to oblige," Brooke replied, favoring me with a bright smile which was not, however, reflected in her eyes.

The airport hove into view, and I swung off the highway onto the vast parking lot by the terminal buildings. We had, I reckoned, about half an hour before plane time, and I suggested we have a beer in the terminal's restaurant. Accordingly, we found a booth which afforded a good field of observation on the lobby entrance through which P. T. Wattersby would shortly make his appearance from the airport limousine. I inspected the menu idly after I'd ordered.

"See what I mean?" I asked, giving it to Brooke. Attached to the cover was a message from the management: "Coming soon," it said. "Your friendly Sky-Rover Lounge, serving the finest food in Textilia, will have its face lifted to become 'The Confederate Spy's Lair.' We beg your indulgence during the period required for renovation and redecoration."

"Piedmont Air Lines Flight Number Fifty, for Charlotte, Spartanburg and Columbia," the public address system announced. "Now loading at Gate Number Two. Eastern Air Lines Flight Four-eighty now arriving at Gate Number One from Atlanta, for Roanoke, Charleston and Pittsburgh." That would be Wattersby's flight, and the airport limousine should be arriving momentarily.

Our waitress arrived with our beer, and I poured Brooke's for her. We clinked glasses. "Stop looking so solemn," I told her.

"Sorry, darling. I didn't mean to brood. Shouldn't your professor be getting here?"

"Speak of the devil," I said as the limousine eased up to the terminal entrance and began disgorging its cargo. P. T. Wattersby was the third man out, and I watched as he checked in at the Eastern Air Lines desk and then moved off toward the ramp leading to the gate where his plane would load, his round shoulders sagging under the weight of his luggage. Not the sort one would choose to pal around with during every leisure moment, I reflected, but not too bad a type, all things considered. As Pierre had observed, he wasn't greedy, and that's saying a lot for anybody these days. I wished him luck and a year's surcease from flatulence, and then phoned Gregory to confirm his departure.

The Atlanta passengers were filing into the lobby now to await their baggage and I was astonished—why, I don't really know—to see Hetty Mindleberg among their number. And then I spotted Carleton Oglebay, waiting attendance upon her and wearing an expression which can only, if tiredly, be described as one of spaniel-like devotion. Miss Mindleberg, on the other hand, had the look of the cat that swallowed the canary.

"Well, well," Brooke murmured, eyebrows arching as she, too, caught sight of Hetty and her escort. "That's interesting. But hardly surprising."

"Mee-ow," I mocked.

"What Hetty wants, Hetty seems to get."

"Not necessarily."

Brooke looked me straight in the eye. "Doesn't she, Bent?"

"No," I said, firmly and finally. "She does not."

☞ *21*　WE finished our beer and then drove back toward town, passing a freshly papered billboard advertising "Lee's Other Eyes—A Powerful Drama of the War Between the States, Presented by Historica Textilia, Inc."

"I wonder who they've got in mind to play Marius," I pondered aloud as we drove into the city limits. "It ought to be a neat little casting problem, with nobody having any idea of what the old boy looked like." Which was a fact. So far, nobody had been able to turn up even a dim tintype of Marius, which wasn't too surprising. Espionage agents do not like too many photographs of themselves floating around, or so I gather from the spy novels.

"I still see him as Sir Laurence Olivier," Brooke said. "And that reminds me: the eminent Dr. Pontefract came by the office this morning while you were in with Pierre and Walter, and asked us to come watch the rehearsal for the first act this evening in the high-school auditorium."

"Do we have to? I was thinking maybe we could keep right on going over to Chapel Hill and have dinner at that steak place."

"I think we really ought to look in on the rehearsal. After all, Bent, we ought to have some idea of what's going on."

"Why?" I asked bitterly. "It seems to go on whether we know about it or not."

"Nevertheless I think we should go," Brooke argued firmly. "I'll cook us some dinner at my place, if you'll stop somewhere to pick up groceries, and we can go on to the rehearsal later."

"Now that puts an entirely different light on the matter," I returned gallantly, and headed the Ford toward the nearest supermarket.

It's odd how shoving a shopping cart along behind a girl becomes such an intimate experience in domesticity. I have a theory, which probably won't stand too much scrutiny, that it also tells you a great deal about the particular girl you happen to be shoving a shopping cart along behind. Brooke shopped decisively and intelligently, with no dawdling, and when we stopped to have one of the free cups of coffee dispensed by the management I told her that I admired her style. She grinned with pleasure.

"But I'm glad you've never seen me shopping for a dress," she said.

Dinner was a study in contrast. Where Hetty Mindleberg had insisted on doing her stuff solo, to demonstrate her casual mastery of the art, Brooke was all for my getting into the act, with the result that I ended up preparing one of my few culinary accomplishments, a limp lettuce salad, which involves the outer leaves of the lettuce, crumbled bacon, a bit of its dripping, and an egg slopped over the whole business. The end product, while not wildly attractive in appearance, is delicious.

"Pennsylvania Dutch," I told Brooke when she complimented me on the stuff. "We Dutchmen never waste a thing, and this is a good way of using up the leaves you'd throw away otherwise. Same way with scrapple; you use all the bits and pieces."

"Saltire doesn't sound like a Dutch name," Brooke said.

"It isn't. But in a town like Dexter, names don't mean what they sound like. My mother's maiden name was Schmidt, which will give you the idea. Someday, when we're married and I think you're psychologically ready for it, I'll tell you all about ponhaws and schnitz-und-knepp."

"Are they relatives of yours?" Brooke asked dubiously.

"Only by marriage," I explained, unwilling to shatter such child-like innocence. "We won't have to meet them socially."

Dinner over, we cleared away the dishes and had a cigarette

over our coffee. Brooke apologized for not having a liqueur on hand.

"Who needs it?" I asked, stretching hugely.

"What made you decide to leave Dexter, Bent?" Brooke asked, taking a sip of her coffee.

"The usual reasons. Broader horizons, that sort of thing."

Brooke nodded understandingly, and from there we got into one of those conversations about what makes people want to write and so on, during which I unloaded all manner of sophomoric wisdom, seasoned with a good deal of self-pity.

"My trouble is, I'm a lightweight," I concluded. "I can't even take myself seriously, so why should anybody else, and I can't think of any reason why you should have to put up with my tale of woe."

"You listened to mine," Brooke replied gently. "And Bent—I happen to think you're not a lightweight, not as a person. I take you very seriously indeed, Nicholas Saltire."

"But not seriously enough to marry me, Brooke?"

"That seriously, Bent," she answered quietly, her eyes steady on mine. "What does matter to me is that you take yourself seriously. As a person, that is." She held up her hand to silence my reply. "I know, I know—you say you can't. I think you do, deep down. When I know you do, I'll marry you in a flash."

"And when is that likely to be, pray tell? When I win a Pulitzer?"

"I'll know," Brooke said. "And it won't take a Pulitzer." She glanced at her watch. "Time to be on our way. Just let me put on some lipstick and I'll be right with you."

The auditorium of the Textilia Suburban Senior High School was a veritable hive of industry and bustle when we arrived and took a couple of seats well toward the rear, in the shadows under the balcony. Textilia treated its kids well, to judge from the size and fairly elaborate decor of the vast hall.

☆ 175 ☆

The curtains were opened to disclose the brightly lighted, bare stage, across which people kept dashing upon presumably vital errands, and in the pit the members of the Textilia Symphonic Association were busily tuning their instruments, producing the usual cacophony of melodic snatches and scales under the alert supervision of their conductor, Dr. Wilhelm Godbold. Seated in the left forward quarter of the orchestra were the massed choirs assembled to provide the requisite vocal background, being sternly lectured by their leader, the Rev. Dr. Jonas Hurkey, minister of music at the First Baptist Church. In the first two rows center sat the inevitable assortment of theatrical brass, among whom I recognized DeWitt Snaveley, and Dr. Pontefract, both wearing ascots, and a Miss Olga von Pankow, the professional directress of the Textilia Little Theater, wearing black velvet toreador pants and the tolerant smile of a real trouper who has been passed over for the top job. One and all had adopted postures of professional negligence, slumped well down in their seats.

Then Pontefract, clutching his script, got to his feet and, at his nod, the first trumpeter of the orchestra blew an ear-shattering "Attention!" The throbbings of his fellow instrumentalists and the general roar of talk quieted with commendable promptness; the stage cleared, and the producer-director climbed onto it, flashing a bright smile.

"All right, folks," he boomed heartily, "this is it; the first time we've all come together to run through the first act. Before we get started, I want to thank Dr. Godbold and Dr. Hurkey for the wonderful work they've done in getting our orchestral and choral groups so well along, and I want them to know that I know how tough a job they've had." There was a burst of applause from musicians and choristers, and the two conductors bowed formally in acknowledgment, smiling modestly.

"Now I want to make it clear," Pontefract resumed, "that no-body expects tonight's rehearsal to be anything but rough, and we'll all be making plenty of mistakes. We'd be crazy to hope for anything else. (Appreciative laughter) So don't worry if you miss a cue or forget a line; that's what I'm here for. And don't be surprised if Witt Snaveley changes a few lines here and there as we go along; they'll only be the first of many, if I know Witt. (More laughter and scattered applause)

"What we're aiming for here tonight is to start, just start, to pull the first act into shape. Now you've all been rehearsing separately; tonight's the night when we see how we all fit together, and by the time we're finished, I think everyone here is going to agree that we've got the makings of a truly great drama on our hands.

"One more thing. At the conclusion of tonight's rehearsal I'll have an announcement of great importance to you all, so please don't leave until you've heard it.

"All right, everybody, let's take our places and put the show on the road." (Loud, sustained applause)

Pontefract leaped gracefully down from the stage and moved backward up the right-hand aisle until he reached a spot from which he could command the situation. "Lights," he thundered as the applause died, with which the house lights dimmed and the curtains swept jerkily shut. The footlights came on.

"Overture, please," Pontefract called; Dr. Godbold raised his baton and the Textilia Symphony opened the ball, playing their conductor's very own composition, "Overture on Confederate Themes," which began with "Camptown Races" in a minor key, blended into a melody I have since had identified for me as "Lorena," incorporated scraps of "The Year of Jubilo" and "The Bonnie Blue Flag," and thundered to a triumphant conclusion with choir and orchestra belting out "Dixie" for all they were worth. The auditorium fell silent, and the footlights went off, leaving us in darkness.

"Textilia, North Carolina, Eighteen-Sixty," a solemn voice intoned lugubriously.

☆ *177* ☆

"Spot!" Pontefract thundered in the darkness. "Narrator's spot!" he repeated. Nothing happened. "Will somebody," he began to howl, and then fell silent as a beam of light wavered uncertainly across the stage and finally came on target to illuminate a tall young man in slacks and sport coat standing at one side of the apron. "Let's take it over again," Pontefract directed.

"Textilia, North Carolina, Eighteen-Sixty," the young man dutifully repeated, and leaned himself comfortably against the proscenium. "Seems like spring's a little early this year hereabouts," he continued, swinging into folksy style and letting his native accents take the upper hand.

"Thornton Wilder Snaveley," Brooke whispered irreverently. I shushed her.

"Mighty fine crop though," the narrator drawled on, "and plenty of work for everybody. Looks like a good year for Textilia, a real good year . . ." He fell silent as the choir took up a soft, Negro working song, and from the tympanist there came an ominous, low rumbling, signifying doom and war's alarums.

"Let's take off," I whispered to Brooke. She shook her head.

"Let's wait and see what Pontefract's big announcement says," she whispered back. "I'm curious."

At this point, the curtain parted halfway to reveal a kitchen table and a couple of chairs set stage center. A gray-haired man, presumably Solomon Mindleberg, sat in one of the chairs.

"Okay, I'll read Marius," Pontefract called. " 'You sent for me, Father?' "

"I wanted you to be the first to know that I'm going ahead with the new mill buildings, my boy," the man onstage said heavily.

"Hold it!" came the authoritative voice of DeWitt Snaveley, and the man onstage stopped and stared blindly over the footlights.

"I do that wrong?" he inquired querulously. "That's how it reads."

"No, that was fine. But let's change that 'my boy' to 'Marius,' and identify him for the audience right off the bat. Okay? Okay, Hugh, carry on."

"Got that, Dave?" Pontefract asked. "Right. Let's take it over the new way and go on from there."

The next hour and a half were just as tedious, but I couldn't help but be impressed by the earnest eagerness with which the assembled multitude took their work. A couple of thousand man-hours of work probably went into their preparations. And knowing what I knew, it was all a little pathetic.

Finally the curtain whooshed shut on the last of the first act's six scenes, in which Marius volunteered his services to Jefferson Davis, and the spotlight picked up the narrator once more, this time reading a simulated newspaper.

"Surely looks as if this man Lincoln is bound and determined to have himself a heap of trouble," the narrator declaimed, looking up from his nonexistent paper. "Yessir, says right here he's gone and called for seventy-five thousand volunteers. Sure hope old North Carolina can stay out of the fight that's a-coming." The tympani rolled solemnly for a few seconds behind a low rattle from the trap drums, and then there was silence.

"That's it!" Pontefract yelled happily, moving down the aisle toward the orchestra pit as the curtains reopened on a stage crowded with members of the cast and crew. Pontefract mounted the podium vacated by Dr. Godbold and held up his arms for silence. "That's all for tonight, folks, and you've done a great job, a really great job.

"Now I said earlier that I had an important announcement for you, and I do. I guess the same question has been bothering all of you, and I won't keep you guessing. You've all been wondering who's going to play the role of Marius Mindleberg, and I know you all realize how important it is to the success of all our efforts that we get the right man.

"Well, ladies and gentlemen, I think we've *got* the right man!" Pontefract paused to let the murmur of surprise die. "But before

I introduce him to you, let me give you a few facts about him. He's had a very successful professional career in the legitimate theater on and off Broadway, but most of you will probably recognize him best from the many roles he has portrayed for television as a featured actor. He has just completed his appearances with the national company of the New York hit, *No Cup Runneth Honey*, and I think we're lucky in signing him up before some other producer got to him. (Chuckles of approval)

"I wish I could say that he is a product of my own department at Carolina Wesleyan. Ladies and gentlemen, he's flown into town only late this evening and he's very tired, which is why I didn't ask him to read his sides, but here he is, our star, Mr. Paul Kenyon!"

Brooke gasped, her hand gripping mine fiercely, her face drained white, as the auditorium resounded to a great burst of applause and a tall, lean, black-haired young man arose from the midst of the group I had noted earlier, seated in the first rows. I couldn't see his face until he joined Pontefract on the podium, but then I was enabled to observe that he was indeed a damned handsome fellow, with a Barrymore profile and a glossy wave that swept up and back from a widow's peak. Small wonder that Brooke had fallen for him. He was wearing a dark suit of very conservative cut, and a white shirt with the highest-rise collar I'd ever beheld. One of the legion of mass-production Cary Grants who help cancel out all of the mass-production Marlon Brandos infesting the theater.

"Please, Bent, get me out of here," Brooke said tautly. "I can't see him face to face." She started to rise but I restrained her as Kenyon bowed mock-formally, and bared his teeth in a boyish smile to show that he was just a regular guy even though he was the star.

"Hold it," I whispered. "We'll stand out like a sore thumb if we move now. Wait 'till he gets himself caught up in the mob." Brooke subsided. I could feel the tension in her arm, and she was breathing unevenly. Kenyon said a few words I couldn't hear and then was surrounded by the cast and others involved in the production as Pontefract introduced them, giving Brooke and me the opportunity to slip quietly out of the place. I got us into the Ford and took, off, and, once we were several blocks away, lit a cigarette and handed it to Brooke, who was staring straight ahead. She was in tears. Not snuffling, no hysterical sobbing, though. Brooke even wept well.

"Does he still have that much of an effect on you?" I asked, my own voice a trifle unsteady because I was afraid of what her answer might, even now, be. Brooke took a deep, shuddering puff of her cigarette.

"I despise him. The tears are just emotion, that's all," she said, exhaling. "Oh, Bent, of all the lousy things to have happen. What am I going to do? I won't stay here, I can't; I don't even want to be in the same state."

"Now look," I soothed, "let's not panic. You won't have to have anything to do with him. There's no law that says you have to see him, and Textilia's a big enough town that you probably won't even bump into him by accident."

"You don't know Paul Kenyon, Bent. He's sure I'm still wildly in love with him, and, if he finds out I'm in the city, his vanity won't rest until he's seen me."

"Over my dead body," I replied grimly. "And what about the boys? He'll probably find some local chum for fun and games."

"He's too smart to risk it, Bent. New York is something else again, but not in a place the size of Textilia," Brooke said bitterly.

"What we both need is a drink," I declared, in the decisive fashion of the late General George Patton ordering a tank attack. And here I made a grievous error of judgment, for instead of heading toward home, I turned toward the country club, feeling vaguely that Brooke's morale needed the pleasantly relaxed atmosphere and excellent service provided by the lounge.

Brooke disappeared toward the ladies' room to repair her

☆ *181* ☆

makeup, and I ordered a couple of bourbons, doubled and on the rocks, to be brought to us after I had located a secluded corner. She returned as our waiter, the same one who had first served me there, proved he had not lost his old speed and zest, and within minutes we were considerably calmer, tensions eased by our giant dollops from the jug of Virginia Gentleman in my locker. Brooke promised she would do nothing rash, like taking the 6 A.M. mail and express back to Washington. I advanced, not much liking it, the suggestion that maybe we owed it to Pontefract to alert him to Kenyon's bent for boys, but we agreed that to do so would be extremely dirty pool. It was entirely possible that he had given up such obscure pleasures, in which case we would be doing him a grave injustice, much as he deserved it.

"The main thing," I declared, "is to keep calm and look at this thing sensibly." And was about to say more when there was a burst of murmuring beyond the entrance to the cocktail lounge, followed by the appearance of a brightly chattering group of people, in the center of which walked Paul Kenyon and Miss Henrietta Mindleberg, on the fringe of which, looking like a man chewing a crust of Carborundum, stalked Carleton Oglebay, jaw muscles twitching dangerously. I cursed my stupidity in not having anticipated this development as the group gathered by the bar amid many a cheery cry announcing locker numbers and orders. Brooke shrank deep into her chair, her expression hunted.

Why the hell couldn't this bunch have adjourned to the home of one of the several big wheels of the Textilia Little Theater who were assisting Pontefract in his labors, damn their eyes?

I couldn't hitch my chair around without attracting attention, so I twisted and leaned forward, presenting my back and shielding Brooke as best I could from the gaze of the people at the bar.

"Steady, darling," I said, hoping for the best.

It was too much to hope for.

"Why, it's Saltire. And Brooke!" I heard Hetty say. "Paul do come over and meet these two." I took a deep breath and stood up to face them as they advanced. Kenyon looked jolted for just the fraction of a second and then smiled whimsically, after the manner of Robert Montgomery. I didn't take the hand he held out, but simply nodded. Kenyon's eyes flickered, but the smile was there to stay while Hetty performed the introductions.

"Hello, Brooke," he said amiably. "Small world."

"Hello, Paul," Brooke said, managing a little, lost smile. I felt myself going tight all over.

"You two know each other?" Hetty asked, looking honestly startled: at least, she hadn't engineered this confrontation.

"Oh, very well indeed, don't we, Brooke?"

Brooke said, "A long time ago."

"We used to make beautiful music together," Kenyon went on, speaking to Hetty. He turned back to Brooke. "Surprised you're not in the show, pet." And back to Hetty, as my breathing started to get jerky. "Brooke's quite an actress, you know." And to me. "She used to model professionally, as a matter of fact." The smile was vicious now, and mocking.

"Isn't that marvelous," Hetty declared while I fought to steady my breathing and get control of my voice, which would otherwise come out as a harsh croak.

"Yes, isn't it?" Kenyon agreed, and I got control.

"I think we'd better be going now," I said to Brooke. "I'm sure Hetty will excuse us."

"Not so soon," Kenyon said reproachfully. "Just when the party's starting."

"Now," I said. Brooke got to her feet, but Kenyon didn't move. He was blocking our line of retreat. "If you don't mind," I added.

"Oh, but I think I do mind. Brooke and I have so much to talk about after all this time."

"I think you'd better move, friend," I said, and Hetty got the message.

"Come along, Paul, for God's sake," she urged, panicking, as the group at the bar realized that something was going on and shut up to stare at us, their grins frozen and expectant.

"Please, Bent," Brooke said, her voice an agonized whisper.

Kenyon didn't move. He stood there, trim and dangerous and probably in much better physical shape than I was, and smiled lazily past me at Brooke. The situation was rapidly becoming ridiculous. I could either sit down like an oaf or do something.

Some submerged grain of common sense told me not to try tangling with Kenyon: quite apart from the ghastly scene, and even if I managed to win the brawl—which seemed doubtful— Kenyon could charge me with assault and battery and then sue me blind for damaging his facade. Instead, I reached out, grabbed his lapels and hauled him against me, and then, before he could demonstrate that he, too, knew some judo, I gave him my right knee, not too hard, where it would do the most good, and let him go. He turned chalk-white, his eyes glazed in anguish, and he sat down heavily in one of the chairs grouped around us, his mouth opening and closing silently.

"My apologies, Hetty," I said. She simply stared at me.

Nobody said good night as we walked past the numbed group at the bar, Brooke on my arm, her small, firm jaw tilted high, but trembling.

☞ *22* *BROOKE* and I sat in my apartment drinking strong, black coffee and not saying much. There was no point in moaning over the miserable luck which had led Pontefract to select Kenyon from hundreds of equally capable actors. It might have helped if Pontefract had given us some hint in advance of his selection, instead of springing Kenyon on us as a giant surprise package; we could have braced ourselves for the shock. But he hadn't, and what was done was done.

I doubted whether any repercussions would ensue from the incident at the country club—Kenyon was hardly in a position to explain why a total stranger should have thought it necessary to knee him—and found myself not particularly caring if they did. Curiously, I felt a kind of serenity. Maybe, I suggested to Brooke, we might both be better off out of it, despite my lack of definite prospects for the future. Sooner or later, LeRoy C. Smelzer, or somebody like him, would bring the whole shaky edifice built on the myth of Marius, the Confederate spy, crashing down like one of those plaster-of-Paris temples they put up for the Hollywood Samsons. Which would be rough on Pierre, but no more than he was asking for.

"And when that happens," I concluded, "I don't want to be among the victims."

Brooke gave me a long, thoughtful look. "What about the victims who don't know the temple's made of plaster of Paris?" she asked finally. "Dave King, for instance. The *True Democrat*'s going to look pretty silly when the roof caves in. And all those people in Snaveley's pageant, working like slaves."

☆ *185* ☆

"Not pageant, 'historical drama,' please," I replied with an attempt at levity which went over not at all. "Sorry, Brooke," I added contritely, "but it's just that I can't feel it's my responsibility any longer. I did my damnedest to make Pierre see reason, and he chose to see it Walter Gregory's way. So maybe Gregory's right."

"Maybe?" Brooke's smile was tired, and I felt a great wave of sympathy and love sweep over me; she'd had a rough evening. "I'm done in," she announced. "Not even this coffee can keep me awake. It must be nearly two."

"Two-fifteen on the nose," I told her after a look at my watch. "What, besides the possibility of getting fired for l'affaire Kenyon, looks big on the schedule tomorrow?"

"Oh, Lord," Brooke sighed. "I'm sorry, Bent; I meant to say something, but so much has happened. I've known about it for a week, and I think Miss Whatsername has it on your desk calendar or at least I told her to make a note of it, and—"

"To the point, girl," I admonished her sternly.

"It's a general meeting of the Historica Textilia bunch. In the sales auditorium. I think the idea is to present Paul as the star of the pageant, and the Governor's supposed to be there, and maybe Senator Purdy, if he can get away from Washington, and the local Congressman—"

"Manchester," I supplied helpfully.

"Manchester, that's right," Brooke went on. "Supposed to start at eleven o'clock and finish in time for lunch. Anyhow, we're expected to be on hand."

I remembered now that Dr. Pontefract had been making noises about some sort of wingding, but I'd been too busy with my own problems to pay much attention. "There's no need for you to show up," I said. "As long as one of us is on hand to show the flag, nobody's going to gripe. Why don't you sleep in tomorrow morning, and I'll go?"

Brooke shook her head wearily. "Whither thou goest. And I've decided that I'm not going to let Paul Kenyon think he's got me scared. Sleep tight, Bent. I'm off." She stood up from the sofa where we'd been sitting and lifted her arms high over her head in a lazy stretch. "It looks," she murmured sleepily, "as if our temple is getting bigger and bigger, doesn't it?"

I walked her down the hallway to her apartment, got a small-girl good-night kiss, and then returned to my own quarters. With the amount of black coffee I'd shipped, I didn't expect to sleep, and instead poured myself a long, not-too-powerful highball, got out of my clothes and into a bathrobe and sat down to ponder. Hanging up my coat, I saw that I had forgotten to turn over Wattersby's photostats to Pierre along with the rest of the professor's file. They were still stuffed in my breast pocket, and I made a mental note to return them in the morning. If I returned them at all.

Clearly, Brooke was leaving the decision up to me.

Textilia was fast asleep now, except for the mills, where the work never seemed to cease, and I found myself wondering whether the thousands of millworkers gave a tinker's damn about Textilia's Civil War Centennial plans. What difference would those plans make to Bonnie Jean Clodfelter, for instance, save for a potential increase in her clientele from among the visiting tourists? As a total realist, Bonnie Jean would appreciate that aspect, but that aspect alone; for the rest, she would regard it as so much nonsense. And so, probably, did the majority of the city's working people. What happened or didn't happen a hundred years ago didn't matter in the least, so long as the mills kept on rolling and the pay envelopes kept on coming in every week. Yet Walter Gregory had raved about community relations.

What community relations did he have in mind? How the local Rotary Club and the Daughters of the Confederacy would react? Whether the Association of Commerce and the membership of the Mindleberg Hills Country Club would approve? What the hell possible difference could it make to Mindleberg Mills, Inc., how a relatively tiny segment of Textilia's population regarded its corporate image?

As for the rest of the state, in the long run everybody, including the Governor, would be a lot less angry with Pierre if he told them now that Marius was by way of being a bogus hero, rather than after things had gone too far. Not that they hadn't gone almost too far already.

What, finally, was this whole Civil War Centennial hysteria all about? Wasn't it really, as Pierre had put it, a sentimental orgy celebrating a hideous war that never should have happened? A war that hadn't succeeded in settling most of the major issues over which it was fought, that left both sides as hypocritical as ever? What high comedy even the concept of a centennial celebration must be to the Negroes.

Big goddamn deal. This was what everybody was commemorating in ten thousand flatulent speeches, and God knows how many scores of half-baked pageants, with the local National Guard Company refighting the Battle of Smashed Privy, complete with blank ammunition and ice-cold Coca-Cola on the sidelines.

Let us now praise the red-necks of the world and that for which they so bravely fought and laid down their lives—the inalienable human right to hate the next guy. Let us hymn the gentlemen butchers who led them, and drown out the screams of the harddiers; spread magnolia blossoms over the stinking dead.

Who needed it?

No wonder Lincoln wept a lot.

And I wondered what old Marius would have made of this whole idiotic flummery, and especially the giant circus about to be unveiled in his honor. Probably he would have briefly enjoyed the sheer magnificence of the fraud, and then puked. The old boy had seen the war for what it was, had really believed in the ideal that Lincoln wept for, and sacrificed everything most men want

for his belief, and now, a century later, he was about to be can-
onized as a Confederate saint for trying to destroy it.

Marius deserved better than that.

Which left me. And I had an idea that on the way I resolved
my decision would depend Brooke's decision about me. She hadn't
tried to influence me, but this was, for her, a test: she had to be
sure she wasn't getting a second dishonest husband.

But where, in this instance, did honesty lie? Wouldn't it be a
betrayal of Pierre's trust if I were to blow the whistle on Marius?

Don't dodge the issue, Saltire. Could be, I told myself uneasily,
with almost a feeling of astonishment, that issue-dodging has been
your trouble for too long. You've been rolling with the punches,
and going along the easy way, not fighting City Hall and chicken-
ing out when things got sticky. Maybe, subconsciously, I'd wanted
to get sick instead of going to bed with Hetty Mindleberg because
it took the decision out of my hands. It occurred to me that the
last real honest-to-God decision I'd made was in combat in Korea,
damn near ten years before. That particular decision had cost
two nice guys, but it was the only one I could have made or we
might have lost a dozen nice guys, me included. It was time I
got back into practice. I reached for my telephone, feeling suddenly relaxed.

"I want," I told the operator who finally answered, "to place
a person-to-person call to New York. That's right, New York City.
To Mr. James MacAulester, and I don't have his home phone, but
you can probably get it through his office: they're open all night.
The Associated Press. I don't have that number either; sorry." The
electronic empire of the Bell System began flexing its muscles for
me in great style, and I took advantage of the time to light myself
a cigarette.

This decision-making was easier than I remembered. And the
way I planned it, Dave King wouldn't be put on a spot, nor would
there be any chance that the power of the Mindlebergs could be
employed to kill the story I proposed to relate to my ancient pal,

Jim MacAulester, himself something of a power among the mightier chiefs of the AP.

Some ten minutes later the fearful deed was done, and young Joshua collapsed onto his sofa without bothering to knock it down into its bed version and without donning night clothing. D-day was dawning and he was too pooped to care.

I was awakened some four hours later by the at first gentle and then outraged buzzing of my alarm clock to find the lights still burning and the room filled with the stale fragrance of tobacco smoke and cold coffee. My mouth tasted as if it had recently been resurfaced with mocha-flavored asphalt, but the head was clear and the eye bright. I advanced briskly upon the bathroom and opened the proceedings with a zesty blast of purest Listerine. For some obscure reason, I felt it imperative to give myself an extra-close shave and was unwrapping a fresh blade when I recognized the sensation—the condemned would also eat a hearty breakfast before receiving the chaplain. I followed the shave with a long and vigorous shower to the tune of "Danny Deever" (". . . in the mo-ho-hor-ning . . ."), and then attired myself in fresh linens and fine raiment, after which I brewed up the morning jolt of fresh coffee and carefully boiled a couple of eggs, savoring to the full these simple domestic tasks. I consumed breakfast in the living room, with all the windows open to admit the cleansing breezes.

Fully restored and nourished, I telephoned Brooke and told her what I'd done. There was an alarming silence at the end of my saga. "Wait right there," she commanded firmly after a few seconds. Moments later she was at my door, looking concerned.

"Anything wrong?" I asked, observing the gravity of her expression as she gazed about the establishment and then inspected me.

"It doesn't look as if you had yourself a solitary drunken evening after I left," she remarked thoughtfully. "Your pupils aren't tiny, or wide, or whatever they get when you take dope."

"I was stone-cold sober and I haven't taken morphine since I was a child. It was me, Father, me and my little hatchet."

"In that case, you may give me my ring," Brooke said, and grinned. "A fraternity pin really isn't official, is it?"

"Ring?" I asked stupidly. "Ring?" And then the import of her statement sloshed the back of the skull. "Ohh! You mean 'ring,'" I gargled. Brooke laughed aloud. "Ring," I said again, dully. I didn't have a ring to give her. Somehow I'd figured in my bone-headed fashion that there'd be plenty of time to see to these details. Or that Brooke and I, chortling happily and holding hot little hands, would lean over some jeweler's counter while she picked out the diamond of her heart's desire . . . a *Saturday Evening Post* cover by Norman Rockwell.

"I'll settle for the one you're wearing," Brooke said softly.

I looked at my right hand and the battered old ring I'd worn so long that I'd forgotten about it. Once it had borne the seal of the Infantry School at Fort Benning, where I'd somehow managed to get through the Officer Candidate School and bought the ring at the Main Post Exchange in an excess of sentiment. Now it was just a chunk of some sort of blue stone, cracked across the middle, set into a smooth circlet of gold from which the carving had long since been worn away. It was one hell of an engagement ring for a girl like Brooke.

I took it off and slipped it over the third finger of her left hand, and it slid crookedly all the way down to the knuckle. At which point, I filled up.

"Why, Bentley Saltire, I declare you're all dewy-eyed," Brooke said, leaning back in my arms when I stopped kissing her. Her eyes were misty, too, and shining.

"Just call me 'Sloppy,'" I advised, the voice cracking like old varnish, and kissed her again. "I'll buy you a proper ring this afternoon, and we'll find out how long it takes to get married in this state and after that . . . well, after that, we can start figuring out where we go from there."

"Maybe we'll be staying on here."

"You jest, Missy. After I see Pierre this morning, I plan to start packing."

"Now who's getting panicky?"

"I am. Now you run along down to the office in the car. I've got to wait for Jim MacAulester to call me back, and I'll be down as soon as I've talked to him. And remember, you don't know a thing, darling. This is strictly my baby." I gave her the keys to the Ford. "I'll grab a cab."

"Luck, my love," Brooke whispered, and away she marched. I saw that she had clenched her left hand to keep that sad excuse for an engagement ring from slipping off. From here on in, I decided, I would be making a lot of decisions. They paid off.

MacAulester's call came through about half an hour later.

"For a man who got me out of bed at four o'clock this morning," he declared bitterly, "you sound awful goddamn bright-eyed and bushy-tailed."

"I got some sleep afterward," I told him.

"More than I can say. I've been up ever since. Chicago checked Wattersby out and—"

"I'll bet he loved that. Being called out of the sack at five A.M."

"Will you for Chrissakes shut up. Turns out that Philly also had a lead on this thing; some joker at Temple who—"

"LeRoy C. Smelzer?" I put it, the heart rejoicing.

"Like I say, will you— How the hell did you know?" Jim asked, sounding bewildered for the first time in our long friendship.

"You know my methods, Watson. So go ahead."

"So anyhow, we bulletined the story at seven, just an hour ago, and it'll be through with any luck at all in time for the early P.M.'s. I surer than hell hope you got a will, Bent."

"Why, pray, friend James?"

"Because," Jim replied cheerfully, "they're gonna kill you."

"And you shall have Daddy's gold watch. Mac, thanks."

"Forget it. Just send the watch. S'long, Bent."

We hung up, and I took a couple of deep breaths, feeling slightly Sydney Cartonish. It was time to face the music.

☞ 23 MY tumbrel ride downtown served only to sharpen the senses to the enormity of the petard whose fuse I'd lit. Our route took us past a blasted heath, around the edges of which were arising a series of long, low structures, soon, as an imposing billboard announced, to become The Rebel Agent Motor Hotel & Shopping Center. A block beyond, we turned down what had been Seventh Street and was now Marius Road, and looming ahead was a towering crane from which depended a gigantic electrical sign which had once emblazoned the Cotton Queen Hotel's name across the night skies. They were lowering it to make way for the new sign of the Hotel Marius Mindleberg. Now, to the right, came Bill & Charlie's Confederate Spy Used Cars, "Our Secret Is In Our Low, Low Prices!" We swung onto Elm, passing beneath a great canvas banner stretched across its width, "WELCOME TO TEXTILIA, HOME OF LEE'S OTHER EYES."

"Ol' town realleh jumpen'," my driver declared happily.

"Yeah," I said. "It sure is."

"Mah younges' daughteh's inna khwyah, en' mah oldes' is inna pageant," he went on. "Realleh gonna be somepen', whut Ah mean."

Had I, I wondered, misjudged the practical realism of Textilia's workers? My driver chuckled around the stump of cigar in his mouth, and expertly dodged a pothole.

"Yesseh," he said, "ol' Textahlyah's gonna make Shahlutt sit up and take notice, it sholeh to Gawd is gonna do jus' thet."

It was a thoughtful Nicholas B. Saltire who paid off his cab in front of the Mindleberg Tower and was carried aloft to his offices.

My plan had been to call Pierre's secretary and ask for an appointment with the Great Man the moment he entered his office, but from the expression on Brooke's face when I entered our suite I knew that the balloon had gone up.

"He wants to see you right away," Brooke said. Our Miss Brownhill was looking frightened, and our Miss Jermyn, who had ceased her labors at the historical society, was fingering her Golden Quarter emblem with unconcealed nervousness, doubtless envisioning the scene when it should be ripped from her thin bosom in a hollow square of her former fellows. "He knows," Brooke added unnecessarily. "The *Argus Record* called him to confirm the story."

The *Argus Record* was the *True Democrat's* afternoon sister.

"Stay here," I bade Brooke and strode manfully out of our offices down the long corridor toward the executive suite. I passed through the outer offices of the sanctum, and the three secretaries to Pierre's private secretary broke off their typing and stared at me coldly, so swiftly does news of doom and downfall spread in the business world. Syd Cheek was waiting for me just outside Pierre's private chambers, his plump face ashy, his moustache twitching. "Morning, Syd," I said cheerfully. He moaned.

"Oh, Jesus, Saltire," he croaked. "Jesus, Mary and Joseph." He peered at me through his rimless glasses, unconscious of the fact that Miss Herring, Pierre's private secretary, was doing her best to arch her eyebrows all the way up to her hairline, as if she were searching for flecks of foam at the lips. He grabbed me by the bicep more, it felt, for support than as guidance. "He wants us to come straight on in," Cheek went on, his voice steadying somewhat. "I've never seen him in this mood before, Saltire, never. He's got Walter Gregory in there with him." Syd appeared almost unwilling to accompany me into the Presence, so I moved toward the door, more or less dragging him along.

Pierre was sitting behind his desk, and the only adjective suitable to describe his expression is detached, idly toying with a silver pencil. Walter Gregory was standing at one of the tall windows, staring grimly out of it as though he were watching the erection of a gallows. He turned at our entrance, his throat working as he got the vocal chords under control.

"You . . . son . . . of . . . a . . . bitch," Gregory enunciated very slowly. "You . . . Goddamned . . . son of a bitch . . . you . . . are . . . fired. Out. Right now." Pierre shot him a quizzical glance, and went on toying with his pencil, saying nothing.

"I'd planned to tell you, Mr. Mindleberg," I said, ignoring Gregory. "I'm sorry you got the word before I could."

"Balls!" Gregory snapped. "Now, Buster, you get on that goddamn phone to the AP with a retraction, you understand? And make it fast." I stood still, and saw Gregory's fist clench. "By God, Saltire, you pick up that phone and call AP or I'll fix it so you'll never work anywhere, and that goes for the girl, too."

"Brooke had nothing whatsoever to do with this," I said, feeling that this interview had gone quite far enough, and that another few seconds would call for strenuous physical action. For the first time in memory, I didn't have to fight for calm because, somehow or another, I hadn't lost it. I was going to paste Gregory right in the mush if he used the term, "the girl," again in reference to Brooke.

"Horsecrap," Gregory snorted, and I moved toward him on mayhem intent. He drew back his right arm and we looked momentarily like those newspaper photographs of prizefighters posing at the weighing-in ceremonies. Syd Cheek gasped. "Come on, Saltire," Gregory begged softly. "Just give me the chance."

This was ridiculous. I dropped the John L. Sullivan pose. "The hell with it, Walter." And started toward the door.

"Nick!" Pierre barked. "Sit down. Sit down the two of you." This was Pierre's parade-ground voice, the sharp sound of a textile magnate giving a command. We sat down, glaring at each other. Pierre eyed us coldly. "Well?" he asked. "What about it, Nick?" I shrugged.

"I didn't want to see Textilia make a fool of itself. That's about the size of it," I said flatly. Pierre nodded, expressionless.

"Walter?" he asked. Gregory heaved a vast sigh.

"Well, the damage is done, Pierre, and I don't need to tell you that I accept full responsibility for whatever hell Saltire and the Hastings girl have raised with your public relations program. I hired them and they're my fault, and they're both fired as of right now."

"*My* public relations program, Walter?" Pierre asked mildly. "They haven't damaged *my* program in the least," he went on as Syd Cheek and I gaped and Gregory's face became what is so often called a study. "I will agree, on the other hand, that Saltire has raised a certain amount of hell with *your* program." Above his amiable smile, Pierre's eyes were icy.

"I'm afraid you've lost me, Pierre," Gregory muttered.

"Let me put it this way, then, Walter," Pierre said softly and patiently, like Mrs. Dinsmore explaining the birds and bees to little Elsie. "Mindleberg Mills has gotten along for more than a hundred years on the broad general theory that honesty is the best policy and, so far, it's paid off. We started labeling the contents of our materials long before they wrote the law. When we tell our unions we can't go along with a raise because we don't have the money, they know we're telling the truth because we've never lied to them. When we tell the state or a city that we can't take another tax boost unless we close this mill or the other, they know we're not trying to duck out of our honest share. It's taken a century to build that kind of integrity, and the first time we lie, Walter . . . the first time we lie to anybody about anything, all that will be shot to hell. Now are you with me?"

I heaved an enormous, internal sigh of relief. But Gregory wasn't going down without a fight.

"Nevertheless," he protested, "you agreed it would be smart to buy those letters from Wattersby. Dammit, Pierre, you went along with me then, and now you're telling me I'm all wet."

"I went along because I wanted to get my hands on them before Wattersby offered them to my Cousin Theodore, who *would* have burned them. And I would have been stuck once and for all with a lie I could never prove false."

"Who'd know? Tell me that, Pierre; who'd know?" Gregory persisted stubbornly. "If Saltire hadn't shot off his mouth?"

"I would," Pierre replied quietly. "You would. Nick and Brooke Hastings would. And Wattersby. There's five; five people who would know that I'm a liar. That's five too many. And sooner or later, Walter, somebody will dig out the truth about Marius."

"Somebody already—" I began.

"Shut up, Saltire," Gregory snapped. "That's not the problem," he went on to Pierre. "Until that unlikely event, Textilia's got its historical drama and something to be proud of; something more to thank the Mindlebergs for. Or I should say, *had.*"

"Did it, really. A phony hero? A spy for a rebellion?" Pierre's tone was harsh. "Maybe the Daughters of the Confederacy are proud of him. I'm a damned sight prouder of the man who stayed loyal to what he believed in, and in the long run, Walter, I have a hunch Textilia will feel the same way."

"If that's your thinking, why the hell didn't you say so?" Gregory asked bitterly. "Why didn't you break the goddamn story?"

"Oh, I would have, Walter, I would have, indeed. But to be perfectly frank, I was interested in seeing how you and Nick would handle the situation. To go on being frank, I think you both reacted honestly. But my point is, Walter, the old one about the forest and the trees. For the past half-dozen years, you've been concerned with our overall public relations program, and what it amounts to is that you couldn't see the trees for the forest. By the same token, Saltire didn't see the forest for the trees. And the biggest tree in our part of the forest is our integrity."

Gregory stood silent for long seconds before he spoke. "I'll ask Bann Masters to assign the account to a new man," he said quietly, and turned to me. "It seems I owe you an apology, Nick," he added, extending his hand. I took it, and peace was declared on that particular front.

"Forget the 'new man' stuff, Walter," Pierre said, relaxing. He glanced at his watch. "Right now, we've got to figure out just how we're going to break the news to all those people downstairs in the auditorium, and I'm wondering whether or not we ought to phone for the riot squad."

In the tension of the occasion, I had forgotten all about the general meeting of all of the scores of chairmen and subchairmen and committee members of Historica Textilia, Inc. Not to mention the Governor and Senator Purdy and Congressman Manchester, as well as all those connected with *Lee's Other Eyes*.

"Maybe I'd better go on down and see if any of them have seen the *Argus Record* story yet," Syd Cheek suggested hesitantly. "The first edition will be on the street any minute now."

"You do that, Syd," Pierre told him. "And see if the Governor's party has arrived yet. I ought to be on hand when they get in. The State Police are supposed to let me know when he hits the outskirts of town." Cheek left, looking unhappy, and I couldn't blame him. It was not a mission I would have enjoyed.

"Let me go to work on a statement," Walter Gregory said as the door closed behind Syd. "Nick, if I could use your office?" He grinned crookedly. "Be the first death warrant I ever wrote."

"It doesn't have to be," I said, as Gregory moved toward the door. He stopped and turned to stare at me. "Why a 'death warrant'?"

"What's your point, Nick?" Pierre asked swiftly.

"Look," I went on, "if we can get through to those people downstairs, why can't we make 'em understand that this whole thing is really a break?"

"Oh, for God's sake, Nick!" Gregory exploded.

"Wait, just wait a minute. Don't you see that now, instead of just a regional hero, they've got a kind of national hero, with a national attraction. The pageant could be rewritten without too much trouble. The Cotton Queen could keep its new name, if only for the Yankee tourists who'll come here. Nothing's really changed, if you stop to think about it. Marius can still be a North Carolina hero because he did what was best for the state in the long run, but now he's a Northern hero, too."

"Nick's right," Pierre said, and slapped the top of his desk.

"By God, I think he is," Gregory agreed. "If," he added grimly, "we can get through to those people." The telephone on Pierre's desk sounded off, and the Great Man answered it and listened intently, nodding several times, his expression grave.

"Right. Thanks, Syd," he said finally, hanging up. Now, more than ever, he looked like one of the mighty Hebrew captains about to order his chariots to charge and show no quarter. "They have the word downstairs," he told us, his tone flat. "Plus which there's been some sort of a foulup, and the Governor and Senator Purdy are already here, and apparently pretty steamed up." Pierre stood up behind his desk and settled his coat on his shoulders. "I don't think we'll have time to work up a formal statement, Walter." He grinned. "Well, gentlemen, it seems we have our work cut out for us. Shall we go?"

At which point, the door to the office crashed open to admit the rhinoceros-like charge of Theodore Roosevelt Mindleberg, scarlet of face, stertorous of breath, and followed at several paces by a white-cheeked Hetty, nostrils a-flare, and a frightened member of Pierre's secretarial staff. Teddy was clutching a crumpled copy of the *Argus Record*'s first edition.

"Libel, by God; libel, I say!" he thundered. "You've got to stop this, Pierre. We'll issue a denial and announce that we're suing for libel." He swung around, glaring, to me. "You, sir, are a liar, a liar and a swindler and a cheat." And to Gregory: "I hold you entirely responsible for this insanity; you *and* your firm. We'll sue you all, by God!"

"Shut up, Teddy!" Pierre rapped, moving calmly past his king-sized cousin toward the door. "The story's true, and I'm going downstairs now to confirm it. You can come along, if you'd care to listen. Meantime, shut up." He glanced at Gregory and me: "Coming, gentlemen?" We followed him.

"Pierre, wait!" Theodore Roosevelt boomed behind us. We kept going. "WAIT, I SAY!"

"You fool!" Hetty hissed at me as I passed her. I nodded politely and she added something else which chivalry forbids my reproducing here. Hetty was angry, and heedless of her manners.

Me, I was scared.

I RETAIN only a kaleidoscopic recollection of what followed our grimly silent descent in the paneled elegance of the private executive suite elevator to the sales auditorium on the street floor of the Mindleberg Tower. Even as we walked down the corridor leading to the backstage area, we could hear a kind of sullen roar not unlike that of a Roman multitude recently informed that today's circus was off. Only a few martyrs to be heaved to the lions, and then home to supper, I reflected uneasily.

We found Syd Cheek just inside the entrance to the wings, looking anxious. Brooke was with him, having presumably decided to come downstairs and see for herself how the land lay. Like Syd's, her expression was hardly reassuring. Several feet away stood a small group of men whom I assumed to be the Governor and Senator Purdy and their official parties. They were talking gravely together.

"I'm worried," Syd told Pierre quickly. "This thing's open to the public, you know, and normally something like this wouldn't have more than a couple of dozen outsiders on hand. Right now, it's packed, and still more coming. But what really scares me is a call I just had from the mills: Jim Stitze says he's had nearly five hundred people go sick this morning. And I'll bet most of them are right out there in that auditorium."

"Relax, Syd," Pierre said calmly. "They're good people. Now we'd better go make our manners to the Governor and Senator Purdy."

Brooke caught my arm. "Maybe you shouldn't go out there, Bent," she said hurriedly. "You don't know these mill hands when they get stirred up." I bethought me of Bonnie Jean Clodfelter, and winced.

"Duty," I replied, and followed Pierre.

"Brooke could be right, you know," Walter Gregory added as we approached the gubernatorial-senatorial party. His Excellency was tall and lean and wry, while the Distinguished Senior Senator was short, rotund and sceptical. Pierre performed the introductions as formally as if we were attending a state reception, and, in reply to the Governor's question, confirmed the *Argus Record*'s Associated Press dispatch.

"Gret Gahd," said the Governor, numbed. "Ah'd hoped against hope raht up ontil this vereh minute."

"Theh is just uh chance Ah could intruhdeuce uh res'lution revokin' yoh lett granduncle's Union Ahmeh commission posthumousleh," suggested Senator Purdy hopelessly. "Peeayeuh, Ah feel deepleh fuh yew an' yoh fahn famileh en this unhappeh an' distressin' situation. Not to mention the fahn people of Textahlyah en theah houh of sorrah." He laid a pudgy hand on Pierre's sleeve.

"Thank you, Senator. I appreciate your sympathy," Pierre replied solemnly. "Right now, I think it might be best if we went on out there and I made my statement."

And so we marched with slow and stately tread out from the wings to our chairs in front of the curtain to the strains of Dr. Godbold's "Overture on Confederate Themes," played right through to its thunderous finish while we all stood to attention. I had not realized that the planners of the general meeting of Historica Textilia, Inc., had included orchestra and massed choirs in their program, but there they were. Grouped in the central section of the orchestra were the group's several scores of officials, among whom I was able to pick out Miss Liddy, Mrs. Bredalbain, of the U.D.C., Rebel Jack Ploughman, Dr. Alexander Renshaw Cates, and, of course, Dave King, whose expression could only be termed inscrutable. Or perhaps apprehensive would be more apt an adjective. Looking beyond this responsible-appearing block of leading citizens, I began to understand the reason for Dave King's expression. The rows of seats in the rear and the whole of the balcony were packed with the plebs, shirt-sleeved and looking slightly embarrassed to find themselves in this place. Seated squarely in the center of the balcony's first row was my old pal, Brother Foley. The standing room at the rear of both balcony and orchestra was full.

Pandemonium broke loose as the overture ended; a wild roar in which were commingled Rebel yells, catcalls, boos, applause and foot-stomping, together with a frantic waving of small Confederate flags on the part of the plebs, some of whom also waved rolled copies of the *Argus-Record*.

The Hon. Maurice Funderburk, Mayor of Textilia and lineal descendant of the city's original founder, who was serving as the meeting's general chairman, stood behind the lectern in the center of the stage, perspiring freely, waiting for the commotion to subside to permit him to introduce the Governor and Senator. When it continued, he held his arms above his head and began pleading hoarsely into the microphone of the public-address system, praying silence. "Please, friends, let's have some order," he yelled. "Can't we have just a little order here?"

By now, all of the chairmen and subchairmen and committee members officially entitled to be present, who had sat down obediently at the conclusion of the music, were looking concerned. Things seemed to be getting slightly out of hand.

What the Mayor could not accomplish, the Governor did, after a few more seconds of observing the futility of the mayoral pleas. He unwound his lanky frame and moved at an easy shamble to stand beside His Honor, grinning amiably. Almost at once the uproar dwindled away to a few die-hard foot-stompers.

"Felluh Tahheels," the Governor boomed jovially, leaning over toward the microphone. "Ah know mah good frien's of Textahlyah will want to heah an' announcement of the gretes' empawtence fuh us all, an' Ah ask y'all to lissen an' pay attention to mah vereh good frien', Misteh Peeayeuh Mindlebuhg." The silence became complete. "Ah thank y'all," added the Governor, and ambled back to his chair, well pleased with his efforts.

With a courteous bow to the Governor and Senator Purdy, Pierre advanced to the lectern as Mayor Funderburk sat down and gazed serenely out over the auditorium, almost as if he were counting the house.

"My fellow citizens," he began quietly, and proceeded to apologize for interrupting the planned program of the meeting. Glancing into the wings from which we had just emerged, I saw yet another, anxious-looking group gathered: Pontefract, Snaveley and Paul Kenyon, apparently waiting to take their star-turns and slightly bewildered by Pierre's out-of-schedule appearance. And now, seemingly from somewhere out of the woodwork, appeared the photographers, loping along like so many Groucho Marxes in the cross aisle between the orchestra pit and the orchestra seats, to pause suddenly, crouch, aim and fire their flashguns at the speaker. A couple of radio newsmen, tape recorders slung over shoulders, extended their small hand microphones beseechingly toward the lectern.

"And now, ladies and gentlemen," Pierre continued, calmly ignoring the continual blinding flashes in his face, "I come to the reason for my being here . . ." With which, and without a minced word, he broke the bad news of Marius Mindleberg's true status, expressed regret that the discovery had come when so many preparations had been made, and his belief that his fellow citizens of Textilia and North Carolina would not have wanted, for honor's sake, the truth concealed.

"But, my friends, out of this seeming disaster to our plans, an even greater good may come, a really significant Civil War Centennial observance celebrating the reconciliation of our great nation," Pierre was saying, holding his audience by the sheer force of his personality, when that fat fool, Mrs. William Lacey Bredalbain, heaved herself to her feet with an assist from Rebel Jack Ploughman, who was seated next to her.

"Mister Mindleberg!" she said loudly, in the tones of one calling whole battalions of Confederate Daughters to "Present Arms." Pierre paused in mid-phrase, and for an instant his face wore the glacial look of a textile magnate interrupted during a private conference. Then he smiled politely: "Mrs. Bredalbain?"

"Is it not true, Mister Mindleberg, that these, ah, so-called documents, alleging to prove that Colonel Marius Mindleberg was a Yankee double agent, were, in fact, produced by a resident of Indiana, and is it not true that they were purchased for you by your agent, a resident of Connecticut?" Mrs. Bredalbain's mighty bosom heaved impressively with the effort of hurling her query.

"That is correct, ma'am, although I'm afraid I don't see what possible bearing the residence of—" Pierre said, to be cut off by the horse-cavalry voice of Rebel Jack Ploughman, suddenly on his feet beside *la* Bredalbain.

"Bearing, sir? Bearing! One Yankee fakes a set of lying, despicable papers, and sells 'em to another, and they split the take. There's your bearing, sir. And one of them two Yankees has the gall to sit right up there on that stage, grinning all over his fat face at the way he's pulled the wool over our eyes!"

What the hell?

Good God Almighty! What was Ploughman suggesting? There was no time to reflect, for Dr. Alexander Renshaw Cates was leaping into the act, his maniac's face working fearfully.

"A Yankee trick!" Dr. Cates screamed. "A Yankee Communist trick! Yes, and a Jew trick, too! A Jew Yankee Communist plot!"

"SMAHTE TH' ANTAH-KHRAST!" thundered Brother Foley, rising from his seat in the center of the balcony. "HEP EN' THAH!"

And the auditorium exploded. Too late I realized that I had entirely misjudged the temper of the mill workers. This must have been the way it was on that hot July morning when George

Pickett's ten thousand came boiling out of the woods along Seminary Ridge, on destruction bent, yelling. Down the aisles surged the assault platoons, miniature battle flags waving frantically, led by what appeared to be the most stalwart members of Mindleberg Mills Post of the American Legion, and, with a fine disregard for the courtesy due high officials, the reserve regiments in the balcony began bombarding the stage with rolled-up copies of the *Argus Record*. Over it all, I kept hearing Brother Foley's incredibly powerful roarings as he urged his host forward to do the Lord's vengeance.

"Let's get the hell out of here!" Walter Gregory yelled in my ear as we stood up, confused, with the Governor and Senator Purdy. From the corner of my eye I saw a tiny relief column, in the form of half-a-dozen burly North Carolina State Highway Patrolmen, moving swiftly into position to intercept the onflowing hordes. An *Argus Record* ricocheted from the side of my skull and caught Gregory on the jaw.

In the finest tradition of his calling, Dr. Godbold launched his gallant men into "The Star-Spangled Banner," hoping to calm the riot, but he reckoned without sectional feeling and heard himself betrayed as his entire brass section mutinied and blasted into a full-throated blaring of "Dixie."

It was time to go. Speech was no longer possible, so I grabbed Gregory's arm and headed for the wings, even as Pierre, the Governor and the Senator headed in the other direction, equally convinced that this was no time for logical argument. Just as I reached the temporary shelter of the wings, I saw our relief column overwhelmed where it stood, like Custer on the Little Big Horn. Gregory and I caromed off Pontefract, Snaveley and Kenyon and kept going, hoping that the corridor leading to the executive suite elevator was still in friendly hands. We found Brooke at the door, safe, thank God, and had just emerged into the corridor when all three of us were abruptly surrounded by four enormous state cops.

☆ *207* ☆

"C'mawn, y'all!" the largest of this quartet commanded brusquely. "We'ah gonna getchall outa heah fayust. Ah don' know how long thet doah at th' otheh end of the corriduh's gonna holt." Heavy thumpings from the door leading directly into the theater of war attested the necessity for haste.

Half-carried, half-shoved, half-dragged, we moved in a compact clump at considerable speed away from the thumpings. There was no time to wonder how Pierre and his party were faring, but it seemed unlikely that the attacking force would do any harm to their employer, Governor and Senior Senator. They were out for Yankee blood.

To my horror, the commander of our refugee band, who wore the stripes of a sergeant, led us past the executive suite elevator and the route to safety high above. "Ah can't resk y'all gettin' trapped up theah," he flung over his shoulder tersely, after the manner of John Wayne. "Folla me!"

As we clattered down a flight of bleak steel stairs toward the garage in the basement, I was seized with an abrupt and frightening suspicion that our sergeant was enjoying the drama of our situation tremendously; was possibly even now envisioning that sparkling morning when he should be called from the ranks of his fellows, drawn up at attention before their barracks, to receive from the commissioner the bronze medal for bravery above and beyond the call of duty. He didn't want our escape to end dully in the impregnable comfort of the executive suite.

In the echoing, shadowy, vaulted vastness of the garage, we were bundled into a plain black sedan, while one of our protectors dashed to press the electric switch which would open the steel doors. Our sergeant hunched over the steering wheel and started his engine with an ear-shattering roar, and we hurtled toward the garage entrance, catching our door opener on the way, and out onto the street behind the Mindleberg Tower. There wasn't a soul to obstruct our passage, but the sergeant drove as if we were being closely pursued by a long, black Mercédès-Benz.

"Getcho teah gas reddeh," he snapped tautly to the trooper who had opened the garage door and made it into our car by a flying leap. The two troopers jammed into the back seat with Brooke, Walter and myself were unable to move, so we were, at least, spared the hazard of an accidental discharge of tear gas.

We swerved madly around a corner onto South Dancey Street, and from somewhere beneath the hood there erupted the banshee scream of a siren as we shot around another corner and down a one-way street against traffic, of which, praise be, there was none except an ancient pickup truck which swerved out of our way and took down two parking meters before ramming the side of a building.

"Ain' nobuddeh can stop the sarge, an' thet's foh th' Gahd's truth," the trooper crushing my left hip observed admiringly above the siren's wail. "Seen him rush a nigguh outa Statesville one naht as pretteh as yew please, alla way to Rahlleh State Prison."

"Oh, Christ," Walter Gregory moaned.

Brooke giggled, and I suspected she might be on the edge of a slight attack of hysterics. "Is that where we're going?" she asked, as the siren died. As if to answer her query, the sergeant stamped down hard on his brakes and we shrieked to a neck-spraining halt which threw us all into a tangled heap against the back of the front seat.

"Inside! Fayust!" the sergeant yelped, leaping out of the car to stand behind it, a tear-gas gun cradled in his arms, ready for action. We untangled ourselves and tumbled onto the sidewalk, and I took Brooke's arm and propelled her along beside me up a flight of stairs and through a pair of plate-glass doors. The sergeant, having seen us safely inside, dashed to join us, accompanied by two of his associates, the third having taken over at the wheel. We were, I now saw, in the lobby of the Dancey County Office Building, which was an annex of the county courthouse.

"Take 'em upstayuhs to th' deetention room," our sergeant bade one of his companions. Then he flashed us a gallant grin. "Y'all be safe theah, frien's. We can hol' this buildin' foh as long as it takes the cap'n to get ree-enfohcements heah. Be'n a real pleasuah, he'ppin y'all."

We left him standing, legs braced wide apart, tear-gas gun still at the ready, facing the plate-glass doors and ready to die for the honor of his corps, and followed our guide up a flight of stairs and down a corridor toward a steel door with a small, barred window set into it. Our patrolman flung it wide, and waved us inside. "Y'all make yohseffs raht at home," he said cheerily, and swung the door shut behind us with a metallic clang. His face, smiling broadly, appeared briefly beyond the barred window and then vanished, to leave us alone.

Wooden benches ran around three sides of the room, which was painted the same, deadly men's-room green as the A.B.C. liquor dispensary, and lighted by a single, barred window. Here the posters cautioned of the dangers of veneral disease or warned that a $10 fine would be imposed on any person found spitting on the floor or defacing the furniture and walls. There was a plain wooden table in the center of the room, and beneath it a white enameled spittoon.

Brooke sat by me while Walter slumped down on the bench opposite us, clearly shaken to the core. "I'm getting too old for this sort of thing," he muttered, shaking his head as if to clear it.

I remembered something.

"What do you remember?" Brooke asked, as I lit her cigarette after advising her of memory's little feat. She exhaled a long, grateful burst of smoke.

"This was the afternoon I was supposed to look into our marriage license," I told her.

"Oh, God," Walter Gregory murmured.

The three of us fell silent, each thinking our own thoughts and neither spitting on the floor nor defacing walls and furniture.

Pierre Mindleberg got us out of durance vile about an hour later. Except for some minor damage, including a smashed bass violin, incurred during the initial charge of the American Legionnaires, the auditorium had suffered little, and, contrary to my last impression, the relief column had not been overwhelmed, Pierre told us. It had managed to re-form its ranks and retreat to the apron of the stage to cover the retreat of the Governor and Senator Purdy until the arrival of Textilia's municipal police in considerable force finally restored order. Passion spent, the mob had dispersed, ashamed of its performance, and the city was calm, save only for a group of juvenile toughs who were out ripping up the posters advertising *Lee's Other Eyes*.

"If that damfool cop had simply taken you up to my office," Pierre said apologetically as he surveyed our dismal surroundings, and grinned despite himself. "Walter, you look beat. Why don't all of us go on out to the house and have some lunch. I think we could all use it."

"You're sure it's safe out there?" Walter asked uneasily.

It was nearly five o'clock by the time we had finished a long and leisurely lunch at January Hill and Pierre had explained his plans to convince Historica Textilia, Inc., that in Marius Mindleberg it had a hero of national rather than merely regional stature. "I've already had a word with Snaveley," Pierre said, "and I gathered that he's quite prepared to do some extensive rewriting. But Pontefract's going to have to find himself another star: Kenyon—and, by the way, he struck me as something of a fairy, begging your pardon, Miss Hastings—seems to have gone off in a huff and apparently plans to take the next plane back to New York." He looked me straight in the eye. "I imagine that won't especially distress you, Nick." I gave him a sheepish grin. "Hetty told me," he added, smiling. "Curiously enough, it seems she has some shopping to do in New York. Wouldn't surprise me in the least if she weren't on the same plane with that Kenyon fellow."

Walter, who was Pierre's house guest, stayed behind as Brooke and I were driven off in the splendor of the Rolls-Royce for our return to the Mindleberg Arms. As we turned into the archway leading to the courtyard, I was stunned to see a gleaming State Highway Patrol cruiser parked squarely in the center of the cobblestones, and our sergeant of the morning leaning negligently against the hood, idly polishing a searchlight affixed to one fender.

"Now what the hell?" I inquired as the Rolls-Royce purred away, leaving Brooke and me confronted with our guardian.

"Govuhnuh's ohduhs, Misteh Saltyeah," the sergeant said happily. "Jus' foh t'naht we don' wanna take no chances, so me and Corprul Barefoot'll be outcheah 'til mawnin'. Y'all need hep, y'all jus' yell."

Brooke was laughing helplessly as I led her into the apartment lobby. "I think we need a drink," I told her firmly. She nodded.

"Just let me get something from my place and I'll be right there," she replied, and walked off quickly toward her quarters. I went to my own apartment and started the preparation of what I hoped would be one of the truly great martinis of our time, measuring with the precision of a Fermi building up the first chain reaction, and stirring just so, ever so gently so as not to bruise the imported herbs. We had, I told myself as I rubbed the glasses in some ice cubes to chill them properly, tumbled the temple and survived.

From the living room, I heard the sound of the door opening and closing and a small thump. "Be right with you," I called, and swiftly set about putting some cheese and crackers out on a plate. Then I put the whole business on a tray and moved into the living room.

Brooke was wearing the same greeny-gold velvet housecoat she had worn that first night aboard the Tintagel Castle, and was seated along the sofa, slippered feet resting gracefully on a cushion, that same gamine grin on her lovely face. An overnight bag stood by my desk, its lid unlatched. I simply stood there with my tray and goggled.

"With that great big hunk of a sergeant hanging around all night," Brooke said calmly, "I didn't want to have to traipse back and forth for my nighties. He might have been shocked."

A great burst of light illuminated the Saltire brain.

"But—" I said, Bent the Gent to the end, "we don't even have the license, darling."

"I'll take the thought for the deed," answered my Brooke.

And for the record, let it be stated here that my very first toast, after our very longest kiss, was to the brave men of the North Carolina State Highway Patrol.

☞ *25* *HAVING THROWN* its temper tantrum, Textilia sulked for a week, and there's no denying that, despite the new felicity for Brooke and myself, formally endorsed a couple of days later by the Reverend Jonathan Mott, rector of All Saints & Trinity Protestant Episcopal Church, in the privacy of his study, it was a fairly grim time.

But, as Pierre had predicted, Textilia finally got a-holt, with a tremendous assist from Dave King and the *True Democrat's* series of front-page editorials, as well as a barrage of national publicity, all of it friendly, all of it welcoming Marius Mindleberg to the ranks of the country's heroes. DeWitt Snaveley's rewritten historical drama, *The Loyal One*, is now scheduled for its first annual production next year, and Dr. Godbold has inserted passages from "Marching Through Georgia" into the score of his retitled "Overture of Reconciliation." The Hotel Marius Mindleberg will retain its new name, and the substitution of a single word, "Double," for "Rebel," saved the promoters of the new motel and shopping center all manner of embarrassment. The proposed commemorative stamp has since been given the support of the Sons of Union Veterans and will appear sometime later this year, as originally planned.

Only the Daughters of the Confederacy and Rebel Jack Ploughman remain inconsolable. Which is as it should be.

When Theodore Roosevelt Mindleberg finally realized that his ancestor was an even greater man than he had hoped, his massive rumblings ceased, and he went so far as to insist on paying Pierre half of the cost of the Wattersby papers. But Carleton

Oglebay, displaying a petulance I would not have supposed in one of his unquestioned eminence, announced that he would have nothing further to do with the biography of a "traitor to the cause." Actually, I suspect that his defection may have been due in large measure to his cavalier treatment at the hands of Miss Henrietta Mindleberg who, when last heard of, had extended her shopping trip to include Europe, where Kenyon had landed some kind of motion-picture contract. She will, Brooke and I are both quite certain, survive the experience without harm, being Hetty.

I am finishing this manuscript on the porch of the cottage Brooke and I are occupying here on Bermuda, thanks to Pierre Mindleberg, who also supplied the company plane which flew us down just a month ago when we wrapped up the company history, *Weavers for a War; the Mindleberg Mills, 1861–65,* by N. Bentley Saltire, with a foreword by Pierre Gustave Toutant Mindleberg.

"Now," he explained to Brooke and myself, "you two can understand why I take such a dim view of the late Rebellion. My mother, rest her soul, was a professional Confederate. Her idol was General Beauregard, and I've gone through life staggering under the weight of that name."

With Pierre's blessing, I'm working on my own, "unauthorized" biography of old Marius, and my agent, Sam Brewer, writes that the same outfit with which Oglebay was dickering is an almost sure thing for the motion-picture rights.

It's still too early in the game to be absolutely sure, but we think Brooke may be going to have a baby. N. Bentley Saltire, III.

Or Brooklet. I like that much better.

www.ingramcontent.com/pod-product-compliance
Lightning Source LLC
Chambersburg PA
CBHW030308200626
46816CB00002BA/813